Jennifer Greene

Praise for the
USA TODAY bestselling
author Jennifer Greene

Jennifer Greene sold her first novel when she had two babies in diapers. Since then, she's become the award-winning, bestselling author of more than seventy novels. She's known for her warm, natural characters and humor that comes from the heart. Reviewers call her love stories "unforgettable."

You can write Jennifer through her Web site at www.jennifergreene.com.

Lucky

JENNIFER GREENE

LUCKY

copyright © 2005 Alison Hart

isbn 0373880529

This edition published by arrangement with Harlequin Books S.A.

TheNextNovel.com

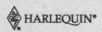 HARLEQUIN®

PRINTED IN U.S.A.

Foreword

This book is in no way a true story...except for
one part. Years ago, someone I love dearly had a baby born
with special problems—and who was misdiagnosed. The
original prognosis for that baby was so dire that it seemed
impossible to believe the baby had any kind of future. Yet
that prognosis was wrong.

The story nestled in my heart for years until I had to write
a book about it. It wasn't just the baby that captured my
heart. It was the crisis thrown at the parents. We all seem
to grow up, very sure what's right and wrong, very sure what
we'd do if we were tested. Yet life can throw us a curveball
that throws everything we believe right out the window.

I write romance because I truly believe that love has
power—I gave my heroine that massive "curveball" in this
story, because I think women can especially understand it.

Perhaps you've never had a problem remotely like the
situation in the story. But I'll bet you all grew up, aspiring
to be good women, striving to do the right thing, intending
to play by the rules. We're raised with an unspoken promise
that things will turn out fine as long as we're "good girls."
Only life doesn't always keep that promise.

It's so hard to break the rules and risk all the things that
make you safe. It's so hard to find yourself alone, bucking
the tide, when all you ever wanted was to be a good person
and stay out of trouble.

It's so hard to be more than you ever thought you could be.

This one's for you, ladies.

Jennifer Greene

For STEPHANIE

No, sweetheart, this isn't about you, because
I only write about pretend people. But I *did*
write it because I love you, and because
sometimes we all need someone to believe in us.

PROLOGUE

Damned if her hands weren't shaking.

Kasey sighed in exasperation. A year ago, she could never have imagined this moment—but then, a year ago, she'd believed she was the luckiest woman alive.

Thunder grumbled in the west as she hurried into the baby's dark bedroom. Tess was lying in her crib, gnawing on a teething ring, wearing nothing but a diaper. Michigan in August was often hot, but this intense, smothering heat just kept coming. Normally Tess would have long been asleep by now, but the looming storm must have wakened her.

Curtains billowed wildly in the hot, nervous wind. Clouds hurtled across the sky, bringing pitchforks of sterling-silver lightning and a hiss of ozone. When the first fat raindrops smacked against the windows, lights flickered on and off—not that Kasey cared. She wasn't worried whether the house lost power. She was worried whether she might.

She was born gutless. Pulling enough courage together to leave tonight was taking everything she had, everything she was—and she was still afraid that might not be enough.

"But you're up for a little adventure, aren't you, love bug?"

The baby kicked joyfully at the sound of her mother's voice.

"That's it. We're just going to be calm and quiet, okay?" Well, one of them was. The baby softly babbled as Kasey swiftly changed her diaper and threaded on a lightweight sleeper.

A short time before, she'd stashed suitcases in the back of the Volvo, but she couldn't leave quite yet. Quickly she packed a last bag with critical items—not diapers or clothes or money—but the things that mattered, like the jewel-colored mobile, the handmade quilt, and of course, the red velvet ball.

She juggled Tess and the bag, taking the back stairs, her heart slamming so hard she could hardly think. She grabbed rain gear on the way out. The garage was darker than a dungeon, yet Tess—who should have been tired enough to pull off a good, cranky tantrum—settled contentedly in her car seat. Kasey tossed in the rest of their debris and plunked down in the front.

It bit, taking the six-year-old Volvo. It wasn't a car she'd paid for. It wasn't a car she'd chosen. But compared to the new Mercedes and the sleek black Lotus and the Lexus SUV, it was the cheapest vehicle in the fleet, and God knew, the Volvo was built like a tanker.

A sturdy car wasn't going to do her much good if she couldn't get it moving, yet initially her fingers refused to cooperate. Yanking and snapping on the seat belt seemed to present an epic challenge. Then the key refused to fit in the lock. Finally she started the engine—which sounded like a sonic boom to her frantic ears—and then she almost forgot to push the garage door opener before backing out.

Her gaze kept shooting to the back door. Waiting for it to

open. Afraid it would open. No matter how well she'd planned, no matter what she'd said, she was still afraid something or someone would find a way to stop her from leaving, stop her from taking Tess.

In an ideal world, she'd have made contingency plans—but she hadn't been living in an ideal world for a long time now. She had no alternate plans, no contingency ideas.

This was it. Her one shot to tear apart her entire life in one fell swoop.

That thought was so monumentally intimidating that she considered having a full-scale nervous breakdown—but darn it, she didn't have time. Her hand coiled on the gearshift and jerked it in reverse. The instant the car cleared the driveway, she gunned the accelerator.

Rain slooshed down in torrents, blurring her vision of the house and neighborhood. For so long she'd thought of Grosse Pointe as her personal Camelot. It struck her with a flash of irony that it really had been. She was the one who'd goofed up the happy-ever-after ending. She'd not only failed to follow the fairy-tale script, she'd somehow turned into the wicked character in the story.

Kasey knew people believed that. For months, she'd believed herself at fault, too—but no more.

She leaned forward, fooling with knobs and buttons. The windshield wipers struggled valiantly to keep up with the rain, but the defroster was losing ground. Steam framed the edges of the windows, creating a surreal, smoky world where it seemed as if nothing existed but her and the baby.

Kasey spared a quick, protective glance at her daughter. In that tiny millisecond, her heart swelled damn near to bursting. She'd never imagined the fierce, warm, irrevocable bond between mother and child until she'd had Tess. Sometimes she thought that love was bigger than both of them.

It still struck her as amazing, what even a spineless wuss—such as herself—would do for her child. And for love.

Emotions clogged in her throat, welled there, jammed there. Even now, she knew she could turn back. It was hard, not to want to be safe. Hard, to believe she had what it took to take this road.

By the standards of another life—the life she'd been living a year ago—Kasey knew absolutely that others would judge her behavior as wrong. Dead wrong, morally and ethically wrong, wrong in every way a woman could define the word.

A sudden clap of thunder shook the sky. The storm was getting worse, lightning scissoring and slashing the sky over the lake. When Kasey turned on Lakeshore Drive, Lake St. Clair was to her left, the water black and wild and spitting foam. There were no boats on the lake, no cars on the road. No one else was anywhere in sight.

Sane people had the sense to stay home in storms this rough.

At the first traffic light, she whipped her head around again, but Tess didn't need checking on. The baby was wide awake and staring intently at the car windows, where streetlights reflected in the rain drooling down the glass.

The look in the baby's eyes warmed Kasey. It didn't suddenly miraculously make their situation all right—nothing could do that. But it was so easy to think of the storm as uncomfortable and unpleasant. Through the baby, Kasey saw the night diamonds, the magic in rain and light. Her vulnerable daughter had brought her miracles in every sense of the word.

Whatever frightening or traumatic things happened from here, she was simply going to have to find a way to cope with them.

The instant the traffic light turned green, she zoomed through the intersection. Quickly the lake disappeared behind them. The long sweeps of velvet lawns and elegant estates turned into ordinary streets. Lakeshore Drive changed its name when it got past the ritzy stuff. Kasey started sucking in great heaps of air at the same time.

The extra oxygen didn't particularly help. She still couldn't make her pulse stop zooming, her hands stop shaking. But it was odd. She didn't really mind being shook up to beat the band. At least those feelings were real. She didn't have to hide being anxious, being afraid—being who she was—anymore.

Love had the power to change a woman.

Kasey would never doubt that again.

The trick, of course, was for a woman to be able to tell the difference between life-transforming love and the kind of love that could destroy her.

She ran a yellow light. Then another. Courage started coming back in slow seeps. Of course, she was nervous and afraid. Who wouldn't be?

She knew where she was going now. It was just hard to stop the questions from spinning in her mind.

How could she possibly have come to this point?

How did a nice, quiet, decent woman who'd always played by the rules get herself into such a situation?

How had the dream of her life become such a soul-destroying nightmare?

But the answers, of course, couldn't be found in this night. The answers were steeped in the events over the past year. In fact, the whole story began almost a year ago to the day....

CHAPTER 1

"For God's sake, Kasey. No one's killing you. You're just having a baby!"

"Yeah, well, they told me all the pain would be in my head. None of it's in my head!"

"Yelling and swearing isn't going to help."

Well, actually, she thought it might. She should have known it would happen to her this way. Breaking her water at a party—right in front of people she wanted to respect her, people Graham respected. Still, knowing she was going to die within the next hour definitely helped. It was a little depressing, realizing that peoples' last memory of her would be with bloody water gushing down her legs in the middle of a dinner party. On the other hand, she'd be dead, so what was the point in worrying about it? For the same reason, there didn't seem much point not to howl her heart out when the next pain hit, either.

As far as she could tell, she wasn't likely to live through the next pain anyway.

"You wanted this baby," Graham reminded her.

"Oh, Graham, I do. I do."

"So try and get a grip. We'll be at the hospital in fifteen

minutes. Just stay here. I'll run upstairs and get your suitcase and some towels for the car...."

He was gone, leaving Kasey in the kitchen alone for those few minutes. She sank against the white tile counter as another contraction started to swell.

Something was wrong with her. It wasn't the stupid pain. They'd all lied about the pain—and she was going to stay alive long enough to kill the Lamaze instructor who promised that labor was simply work. It wasn't work. It was torture, cut and dried. Yet Kasey fiercely, desperately, wanted this baby, and had expected to feel joyous when the blasted labor process finally started.

Instead, she felt increasingly overcome by a strange, surreal sense of panic. Goofy thoughts kept pouncing in her mind. This wasn't her house. This wasn't her life. This wasn't really happening to her.

As the contraction finally ebbed, leaving her forehead flushed with sweat, she stared blankly around the high-tech kitchen. She realized perfectly well that anxiety was causing those foolish thoughts, yet the acres of stainless steel appliances and miles of white tile really *didn't* seem to be hers. She'd never have chosen a white floor for a kitchen. The doorway led to a dining room with ornate Grecian furniture that she'd never chosen, either. The dining room led into a great room with cream carpeting and cream furniture—Graham had chosen all that stuff before they'd married, wanting a neutral color like crème to set off the artwork on the walls. He was a collector.

But now, the more she looked around, the more she felt a building panic roaring in her ears. This whole last year, she'd basked in a feeling of BEING LUCKY so big, so rich, so magical that she just wanted to burst with it. She'd found a true prince in Graham, when at thirty-eight, she'd given up believing she'd find anyone at all. And living in Grosse Pointe was like living in her own private Camelot—which it was, it really was. It was just that this crazy panic was blindsiding her. Maybe it had all been a dream. She didn't live here. How could she possibly live here? She didn't DO elegant. Cripes, she didn't even LIKE elegant.

Not that she'd ever complained. Graham had said too many times that his ex-wife, Janelle, had been a nonstop complainer.

It wasn't as if she spent much time in the fancy-dancy parts of the house, besides. With the baby coming, the kitchen was the room that mattered, and all the high-tech appliances were a cook's dream. Still, the dishes were bone china. Heirlooms. Beautiful—but it was darn hard to imagine a baby in a high chair, drinking milk from a lead crystal glass and slopping up cereal from a 22-karat-gold-rimmed bowl onto that virgin-white tile floor.

Shut up, Kasey. Just shut your mind up. Another pain was coming. This one felt like lightning on the inside, as if something sharp and jagged was trying to rip her apart. Then came the twisting sensation, as if an elephant were swollen in her stomach and trying to squeeze through a space smaller than a spy hole.

She opened her mouth to scream her entire heart out, when Graham suddenly jogged into the room. "All right, I reached Dr. Armstrong. He'll meet us at the hospital. You holding up okay?"

Of course she wasn't okay. She couldn't conceivably be less okay. She was wrinkled, stained, shaky, and positively within minutes of death by agony. Graham, typically, looked ready to host a yacht club outing. Abruptly—and with all the grace of a walrus—she pushed away from the counter and aimed for the back door. "Which car are we taking?"

"The Beemer. Easiest to clean the leather seats if we have to. Although I brought towels."

For an instant she thought, *Come on, Graham, couldn't you think for one second about the baby instead of fussing over getting a stain in a car?* But even letting that thought surface shamed her.

Her attitude had sucked all day, when she knew perfectly well that Graham was unhappy about the coming baby. During their courtship, he'd been bluntly honest about wanting no children—he adored his nearly grown daughter, but that was the point. He'd done the fatherhood thing. At this life stretch he wanted Kasey, alone, a romantic relationship with just the two of them.

Maybe there was a time when Kasey fiercely wanted children, but even at thirty-eight, there were increased health risks with a pregnancy. More than that, she'd already settled into a life without kids—and she loved Graham and everything about her life with him, so it just wasn't that hard to go along with his choice.

Birth control hadn't failed them so much as life had. She'd tracked conception down to the week she'd had a bad flu and couldn't hold anything down—including her birth control pills. By the time she'd recovered, the fetus already had a grab-hold on life. If the problem had never happened, Kasey would undoubtedly have been happy as things were—but once she realized that she was pregnant...well, there was only one chance of a baby for her. This one.

She wanted this baby more than she wanted her own breath, even her own life. It was her one shot at motherhood. She just couldn't give it up.

And she totally understood that Graham wasn't happy about it—but there was no fixing that yet. Once the baby was born, she could work on him, make sure he never felt neglected, take care to shower him with love. Besides which, once the baby was born and Graham held the little one, Kasey felt certain the baby would win his heart. It'd all work out.

If she just didn't blow it in the meantime.

"I love you," she said in the car.

"I love you, too, hon." But immediately he fell silent, steering through the quiet night, his profile pale as chalk. Dribbles accumulated on the windshield. Not rain, just the promise of it. She heard a siren somewhere, the thunk of the occasional windshield wiper, and realized that she was doing better. The pains were easing up, not one galloping right after the other now.

Randolph Hospital loomed ahead. Graham pulled up to the emergency-room door where a sign read NO PARKING UNDER ANY CIRCUMSTANCES. The hospital looked more like an elegant estate than a medical facility, with security lights glowing on the landscaped grounds and garden sculptures.

Graham slammed out of the car. "I'll get a wheelchair or a gurney. I hate to leave you alone, Kasey, but I promise I'll be right back."

"I'll be fine."

But she wasn't fine. He'd barely disappeared inside before another lumpy gush of blood squeezed between her legs. How come no one ever said labor was a total gross out? Certainly not that nauseatingly cheerful Lamaze instructor. And then another pain sliced her in half, so sharp, so mean, that she couldn't catch her breath.

Pain was one thing. Being scared out of her mind was another. She fumbled for the door handle, thinking that she'd crawl inside the hospital if she had to—anything was better than dying here alone in the dark. She got the door open. Got both feet out. But then the cramping contraction took hold and owned her. She cried out—to hell with bravery and pride and adulthood and how much she wanted this baby. If she lived through this, and that was a big *IF*, she was never having sex again, and that was for damn sure.

The emergency-room doors swung open. She didn't actually notice the man until she heard the clip of boot steps jogging toward her, and suddenly he was there, hunkering down by the open curb.

"You need help?"

"No, no. Yes. I mean—my husband's coming. It's just that right now—" The pain was just like teeth that bit and ripped.

"What do you want me to do? Get you inside? Stay with you? What? I can carry you—"

"No. It's—no. Just stay. Please. I—" She wasn't really looking at him, wasn't really seeing him. Her whole world right then was about babies and labor and pain. Still, there was something about him that arrested her attention. Something in his face, his eyes.

Their whole conversation couldn't have taken two minutes. She only really saw him in a flash. Background light dusted his profile, sharpened his features. He was built tall and lanky, with dark eyes and hair, had to be in his early forties or so. His clothes were nondescript, the guy-uniform in Grosse Pointe of khakis and polo shirt, but his looked more worn-in than most. *He* looked more worn in than most. The thick, dark hair was walnut, mixed with a little cinnamon. The square chin had a cocky tilt, the shoulders an attitude—but it was his eyes that hooked her.

He had old eyes. Beautiful brown eyes. Eyes that held a lot of pain, had seen a lot of life. In the middle of the private hospital parking lot, mosquitoes pesking around her neck, panting out of the contraction, scared and hot…yet she felt a pull toward him. He exuded some kind of separateness, a loneliness.

She knew about loneliness.

Of course, that perception took all of a minisecond—and suddenly the emergency-room doors were clanging open again. The man glanced up, then back at her. "Damn. You're Graham Crandall's wife? And you're having your baby in *this* hospital?"

His question and tone confused her. She started to answer, but there was never a chance. Graham noticed the man, said something to him—called him "Jake"—but then he disappeared from her sight. The world descended on her. In typical take-charge fashion, Graham had brought out an entire entourage—a wheelchair, three people in different medical uniforms, Dr. Armstrong.

Graham was midstream in conversation with the doctor.

"I don't care what you have to do. She comes first. No exceptions, no discussion. You make sure she's all right and gets through this. And I want her to have something for the pain. Immediately."

"Mr. Crandall—Graham—first, I need to examine her, and then everything else will follow in due course. I swear that I've never yet lost a father—"

"I don't want to hear your goddamn reassuring patter, and forget trying to humor me. I want your promise that nothing is going to happen to my wife."

"Graham." Kasey had to swallow. She'd never seen her husband out of control. Graham didn't *do* out of control. And love suddenly swelled through her, putting the pain in perspective, reassuring her like nothing else could have. "I'm just having a baby. Really, I'm fine. The pain scared me. I didn't realize it was going to be this bad—"

"I'll take care of this, Kasey." Graham cut her off, and rounded on Dr. Armstrong again. "I don't care what it costs. I don't care how many people or what it takes—you don't let anything happen to my wife. You understand?"

The next few hours were a blur of hospital lights and hospital smells. The labor room was decorated to look like a living room, with a chintz couch and TV and even a small kitchenette. Dr. Armstrong did the initial exam. As always, he was patient and calm and as steadfast as a brick.

"But I can't be only three centimeters dilated! You have to be kidding! I thought I was in transition because of the amount of pain."

"I'm going to give you something to help you relax, Kasey."

"I don't want to relax! I want to get to ten centimeters and get this over with! And I want to be able to see the fetal monitor! Is our baby okay?"

"Your baby's just fine," Dr. Armstrong said reassuringly, but he hadn't even looked. What was the point of being all trussed up with the fetal monitor if no one was even going to look at it? "You can have ice chips. And your husband can rub your back. And you can watch TV or listen to music...."

She just wanted it over with. But at least, once they all left her alone with Graham, she thought she could get a better hold on her fears and emotions. Later—an hour, or two, who knew?—she remembered the man outside, and thought to ask Graham who he was.

"Name is Jake McGraw. Used to be from the neighborhood."

"I thought you called him by name, so I was pretty sure you knew him."

"Yeah, I knew him. He's Joe's son. You've heard of Joe, used to be one of GM's high-step attorneys. Money from generations back. Joe had a heart attack a while ago, put Jake back in the neighborhood now and then to help his father."

"So that's why he was at the hospital?" God. Another pain was coming on. How many did you get before you'd paid your dues? And now she knew you didn't die from the little ones, because there were lots, lots, *lots* bigger ones after that.

"I don't know why he was at the hospital. Forget him, Kasey. He's a loser. An alcoholic."

"Really?" For an instant she pictured those old, beautiful eyes again.

"Was part of a big fancy law firm, wife from the Pointe, fast lane all the way. Had a wild marriage, and I mean capital W wild. Gave one party that started out in GP and ended up in Palm Springs. They both played around, until some point when Jake went off the deep end. Or so they say. He's got a teenage son, Danny, lives with his ex-wife. Doesn't practice law anymore. You hearing me? He's bad news all the way. Lost everything. And deserved to."

"You never mentioned him before—"

"Why would I? And it beats me why we're talking about him now."

And then they weren't. She'd only asked the question in passing. The man wasn't on her mind. Nothing was, as the minutes wore on and the night deepened and darkened. Somewhere in the wing, a woman screamed. A door was immediately closed, sealing out the sound. The nurse came and went. Graham survived for a while—at least the first couple hours—but then he started pacing.

"Do you want some more ice chips, Kase? Are you cold? Warm? Want to watch any specific show on the tube?"

His solicitousness was endearing—except that every time a pain ripped through her, he paced again, like a panther who wanted to throw himself against the bars. Anything—but be trapped in here. "Graham, go out," she said finally.

"No way. I'm not leaving you."

"I know you're willing to stay. But this is hard…harder than I thought. And to be honest, I believe I'll handle the pain better if I'm alone. I've always been that way. Go on, you. Go get some coffee, or something to eat. Don't feel guilty, just go."

He kissed her, hard, on the forehead, squeezed her hand. But eventually she talked him into leaving.

She'd lied about wanting to be alone. The truth was, she desperately wanted Graham to be with her, yet he was obviously miserable, seeing her in pain. And for a while, for a long time, the fear completely left. Medical help was just a call away, and so was her husband, so it seemed easier to relax. She inhaled the silence. The peace. The feeling as if there was no one in the universe but her and the baby.

She cut all the lights but one, shut off the television. In between contractions, she rubbed her tummy, talking softly to her baby. This was about the two of them. No one else. "You're going to love your room. I bought you a teddy bear the size of a Santa, and the toy box is already filled. The wallpaper is balloons in jewel colors, and over your crib, I set up real jewels dangling from a mobile   amethyst, citrine, jade, pink quartz. When the sun comes, you won't believe what brilliant crystal patterns it makes on the wall. And there's a wonderful, big old rocker. You and I are going to rock and sing songs, and I'm never going to let you cry, never…."

An hour passed, then another. Suddenly a pain seared through her that was different from all the others.

Finally, she thought, the transition stage. All the books claimed this stage was the hardest—but it also meant that they were nearing the end. Soon enough she'd hold the real baby in her arms after all these months.

Another pain. Just like that one, only worse. More of the fire, more of the scalding feeling of being ripped apart. She hit the button for the nurse, then hit it again.

No one came.

Now she realized what a sissy she'd been before, because these contractions were completely different. And possibly that's why no one was coming now, because they thought she'd been crying wolf? Only Graham...where was he? Surely they wouldn't leave her much longer without someone checking on her?

This wasn't pain where she could scream or yell like before. This was pain so intense that it took all her concentration to just endure. This wasn't about whining how she could die; this was about believing for real that she may not survive this. Agony lanced through her, again and again, not ceasing, not letting up, not giving her a chance to catch her breath. Her body washed in sweat. Fear filled her mind like clouds in a stormy sky, pushing together, growling and thundering. She wanted her mom. She wanted Graham. She wanted someone, anyone. She pushed and pushed and pushed the call button, but she had no possible way to get up out of bed and seek help on her own, not by then.

Finally the door opened a crack. Then a nurse's voice. "Good God." Then...lights and bodies and motion and more pain. "There, Kasey, you're doing good—it's going to be all over very soon." By then she didn't care anymore—or, if she cared, she couldn't find the energy to respond.

They wheeled her into an unfamiliar room. Stuck her with needles. "Where's Graham?" she asked, but no one answered. Everyone was running, running. The baby seemed to be rushing, rushing. And the pain was there, but with that last hypodermic, the knife edges of pain blunted, and her mind started blurring.

Somewhere, though, she heard a woman's voice. One of the nurses'. Low, urgent. "Doctor, there's something—"

She tried to stir through the thick mental fuzz, recognizing that something was happening. Something alarming. She heard the doctor's sharp, "Be quiet." And then, "Get out of the way. Let me see."

"Is something wrong?" she whispered.

No one answered.

"Doctor, is something wrong with my baby?"

Still no one answered. But she felt another needle jab in her arm. And immediately came darkness.

Her dreams were all sweet, dark, peaceful. She remembered nothing until she heard the sound of a nurse's cheerful voice, and opened her eyes to a room full of sunshine. "Are we awake, Mrs. Crandall? I'm bringing your beautiful daughter. There you go, honey... I have on your chart that you want to nurse, so I'm going to help you get set up. Can we sit up?"

She pushed herself to a sitting position, listening to the nurse, taking in the pale-blue walls of the private room, the fresh sun pouring in the window, the washed-clean sky of a new day. All those sensory perceptions, though, came from a distance.

Once the bundle was placed in her arms, there was only her and her daughter.

OhGodOhGodOhGod. The pain and fear had all been real, but mattered no more now than spit in a wind.

The feel of her daughter was magic. Reverently she touched the pink cheek, the kiss-me-shaped little mouth, then slowly—so carefully!—unwrapped the blanket. She counted ten fingers, ten toes, one nose, no teeth. Without question, her daughter was the first truly perfect thing in the entire world. Love rolled over Kasey in waves, fierce, hot, compelling, bigger than any avalanche and tidal wave put together.

"She's all right? *Really* all right? I remember the doctor sounding worried in the delivery room. I was scared something was going wrong—"

The nurse glanced at the chart at the bottom of the bed, then quickly turned away. "She sure looks like a healthy little princess to me." Efficiently the nurse adjusted Kasey's nightgown, and finally coaxed Kasey to quit examining the baby long enough to see mom and daughter hooked up. "I'm going to give you two a few private minutes, but I'll check on you in a bit, okay?"

Kasey nodded vaguely. The nurse was nice—but not part of her world. Not then. She stroked and cuddled her miracle as the little one learned to nurse.

She and Graham had bickered about baby names for months. Boys' names had been tough enough, but girls had seemed impossible. Cut and dried, Graham wanted Therese Elizabeth Judith if the child was a girl. Kasey thought that sounded like a garbled mouthful…now, though, she found a solution to the problem in an instant. Graham could have whatever name he wanted on the birth certificate.

But her name was Tess.

Kasey knew. From the first touch, the first smell and texture and look…the name simply fit her. And it was hard to stop cherishing and marveling. The little one had blue eyes— unseeing but beautiful. Her skin had the translucence of pearl. The head was pretty darn bald, but there was a hint of rusty-blond fuzz. Little. Oh, she was so little.

Kasey thought, *I'd do anything for you*. And was amazed at the compelling swamp of instincts. How come no one had told her how fierce the emotion was? That mom-love was this powerful, this extraordinarily huge?

"Oh, Graham," she murmured as she caressed the little one's head. "Wait until you see how precious, how priceless your daughter is. She's worth anything. Everything. All…"

Kasey stopped talking on a sudden swallow. She looked up. Darn it—where *was* Graham?

Jake pulled his eight-year-old Honda Civic into the driveway on Holiday, touched the horn to announce his arrival, and then walked around and climbed into the passenger seat.

He saw the living room curtain stir, so Danny heard the car—but that was no guarantee his son would emerge from the house in the next millennium. Rolling down the window—it was hot enough to fry sweat—he reached in the back seat for his battered briefcase. Sweet, summery flowers scented the late afternoon, but the humidity was so thick it was near choking.

He glanced at the windows of his ex-wife's house again, then determinedly opened his work. The top three folders were labeled with the names of suburban Detroit hospitals— Beauregard, St. Francis and Randolph. All three hospitals had a history of superior care until recently, when they'd had a sudden rash of lawsuits, all related to rare medical problems affecting newborns.

Traditionally even the word *newborn* invoked a panic flight response in Jake—yeah, he'd had one. He still remembered the night Danny had been born fifteen years ago—and his keeling over on his nose. So babies weren't normally his favorite subject.

But he'd accidentally come across one of these mysterious lawsuits when he'd been researching a separate story for the newspaper, and then couldn't shake his curiosity. Every question led to another dropped ash—a lit ash—and no one else seemed aware there was an incendiary pile of embers in the forest.

In itself, the increase in lawsuits didn't necessarily mean beans, because everybody sued for everything today. People especially freaked when something happened to a baby— what parent didn't suffer a rage of pain when their kid didn't come out normal? Although Jake was no longer a practicing lawyer, he knew the system. Knew how lawsuits worked.

He'd already told himself not to get so stirred up. What looked like a Teton could still end up an anthill. But it smelled wrong, this sudden burst of lawsuits—and this sudden burst of serious health problems for babies, especially when the affected hospitals had longstanding excellent reputations.

Momentarily a woman's face pounced in his mind. Kasey. Graham Crandall's wife. Crandall was one of those starched-spine controlling types—a silver-tongued snob, Jake had always thought, the kind of guy who'd give you the shirt off his back—as long as you gave him a medal for doing it. There was no trouble between them, no bad history. Jake didn't care about him one way or another, even back in the years when he'd hung with the Grosse Pointe crowd.

But it had been a shock to meet Crandall's wife. Coming out of the hospital that night, he'd only seen a woman in labor—she was crying. Who wouldn't? About to give birth to a watermelon? Yet her face kept popping in his mind. The short, rusty-blond hair. The freckled nose and sunburned cheeks.

She wasn't elegant or beautiful or anything like the women Jake associated with Crandall. Instead, there was a radiance about her, a glow from the inside, a natural joyful spirit. The wide mouth was built for laughter; her eyes were bluer than sky.

Pretty ridiculous, to remember all those details of a woman he didn't know from Adam—and a woman who was married, besides. Jake figured he must have had that lightning-pull toward her for the obvious reason. It had momentarily scared him, to realize she was going into that hospital to have a baby—the same hospital where he'd been researching the lawsuits.

Now, though, he sighed impatiently and turned back to his papers. Kasey was none of his business. Hell, even these lawsuits weren't. For two years, he'd tried his best to just put one foot in front of the other, pay his bills, make it through each day, be grateful that the half-assed weekly paper had been willing to give him a job. Even the research on these hospitals he was doing on the q.t., his own time.

Jake had done an outstanding job of screwing up his life. Now he was trying to run from trouble at Olympic speed. He figured there was a limit to how many mistakes a guy could make before any hope of self-respect was obliterated for good.

The instant he heard the front door slam, he looked up, and immediately hurled his briefcase into the back seat.

Quick as a blink, he forgot all about lawsuits and strangers' babies. His focus lasered on the boy hiking toward the car. Just looking at Danny made him feel a sharp ache in his gut.

At fifteen, Danny had the look of the high school stud. The thick dark hair and broody dark eyes drew the girls—always had, always would. The broad shoulders and no-butt and long muscular legs added to the kid's good looks. The cut-offs hanging so low they hinted at what he was most proud of, the cocky posture, the I-own-the-world bad-boy swagger...oh yeah, the girls went for him.

Jake should know. He'd looked just like the kid at fifteen. But there were differences.

Last week Danny's hair had been straggly and shoulder-length; this week it had colored streaks. The kid's scowl was as old as a bad habit and his eyes were angry—all the time angry, it seemed. The swagger wasn't assumed for the sake of impressing the girls, but because Danny was ready to take on anyone who looked at him sideways.

Jake understood a lot about attitude. What knifed him in the gut, though, was knowing that his son's bad attitude was his fault.

The boy yanked open the driver's door and hurled his long skinny body in the driver's seat. "You're late."

Not only was Jake ten minutes early, but he'd been waiting. Still, he didn't comment. If Danny hadn't started the conversation with a challenge, Jake would probably have had a heart attack from shock. "You brought your permit? And you told your mom that you're going out with me?"

"Like I need to be treated like a five-year-old." Danny fussed with the key, the dials, then muttered, "If I had any choice—just so we both know where we stand—I'd rather be anywhere but here."

That about said it all. Danny wanted to drive so badly that he was even willing to spend time with his dad—and then, only because no one else wanted to practice-drive with him. Even his mother valued her life too much to take the risk.

"I suppose you're in a hurry." Danny used his favorite world-weary tone as he started the car.

"Nope. I've got as much time as you want—although I assume your mom wants you back by dinner."

"Yeah. Maybe. Can I go on the expressway today?"

Maybe Churchill thought there was nothing to fear but fear itself, but the image of Danny on a Detroit expressway at rush hour was enough to make bile rise up Jake's throat in abject terror. The kid had just gotten his practice license. The last time he'd tried to do something as basic as making a right turn, he'd climbed over a curb. "I think you probably need to get a little more comfortable with the stick shift before we take on the expressway."

"That's what you said last week." Danny shoved the stick in reverse, made the gear scream in pain, and then stalled out when he let up the clutch too fast. Red shot up his throat. "That wasn't my fault," he said furiously. "It's this old heap of a car. It's so old it doesn't respond to anything."

It was going to be one of their better times, Jake thought. Of course, as they aimed toward Lakeshore, the test questions began. *Can I play the radio. Can I drive by Julie Rossiter's house.* Can I this, can I that.

As far as Jake could tell, all the questions were designed to elicit a *no*, at which point Danny would instantly respond with a look of anger and disgust. Jake knew the game. He did his absolute best to say yes to any request that wasn't definably life-threatening. Sure, Danny could drive by the girl's house. Sure, he could play the radio—any station and at any volume he wanted. Jake encouraged him to drive exactly as he would be driving later, when he was alone, so he could see how distractions affected his concentration.

"Oh, yeah? Does that mean I can smoke while I drive?"

"No." Jake didn't elaborate, knowing how a lecture on smoking would be received. Besides, just then his right foot jammed on the imaginary brake and his pulse pumped adrenaline faster than a belching well. No, they hadn't hit that red Lincoln going through the intersection. No, scraping the tire against the curb wouldn't kill them. No, braking so fast they were both thrown forward didn't mean either of them was going to end up hospitalized.

"I'm going to be sixteen in another seven months," Danny said, as he turned on Vernier.

"I know." Jake resisted holding his hand over his heart. Suburban driving wasn't too bad, but Vernier eventually turned into Eight Mile. Eight Mile was a Real Road. The kind that tons of people actually used. Some of them might not realize how close they were to imminent death.

"So, any chance you might buy me a car?" Danny rushed on, "Mom'll never let me drive the Buick. It's uncool, anyway. But she's already warning me that I won't be able to use her car all the time. I really need wheels."

"I can't afford a car, Danny."

"You could. If you were still a lawyer. If we were still a family. If you weren't a drunk."

JENNIFER GREENE 33

There now. Every one of the accusations stung like a bullet, just as his son intended. Sometimes Jake wanted a minute with his son—just one damn minute—when Danny wasn't trying to wound him.

But of course he'd earned those accusations. And all he could do now was hope that time—good meaningful time together—could start to heal that old, bad history. "Getting you a car isn't just about having enough money to buy one."

"The hell it isn't."

"Danny, come on, you're a new driver. You know that you need more practice before you'll be safe—or feel safe—on the road. It's nuts to start out with a new car before you have some experience under your belt."

"You care about being safe on the road? You used to drive drunk."

"Yeah, I did. And I hope you never do. I hope you're way smarter than me."

"That wouldn't take much." Danny made a left on Mack, where approximately five thousand cars were speeding toward home. Horns blared when the Honda accidentally straddled two lanes. Jake reached for an antacid. Then Danny tried another jibe. "Mom's going out with some guys. Three of them, in fact."

"That's nice."

"I'll bet she's screwing at least one."

Jake understood that this comment was supposed to be another way to hurt him. Danny assumed that he still cared what Paula did. And even though Jake should have known better than to bite, he couldn't quite let this one go. "Don't use words like that about your mother."

"Oh, that's right. We're not supposed to tell the truth about anything. We just lie and pretend everything's okay, right? The way you lied about being an alcoholic. And about you and Mom staying together, that you were just going through a rough time but we'd all be fine."

Halfway through a yellow light, Danny gunned the engine and it stalled. The light turned red while they sat clogging the middle of the intersection. Sweat beaded on Jake's brow. He said, "Take it easy. The other drivers can see you, so there's no immediate danger. Just concentrate on getting the car started and going again."

On the inside, Jake marveled at the epiphany he kept getting from these practice driving sessions with Danny. You sure learned to value your life when it was constantly at risk.

Besides that—and in spite of Danny's sarcasm and surly scowls—Jake still felt the wonder of being with his son. It wasn't a given. Danny hadn't been willing to see him for most of the two years since the divorce—and God knew, that wouldn't have changed if Danny wasn't desperate to drive.

Jake realized he was riding a shaky fence. He fiercely wanted to make things right for his son, yet there seemed no parenting rule book for this deal. The kid was always egging him on, pushing him to lose his temper. What was the right dad-thing to do? Be tough? Or be understanding? Give him the tongue lashing he was begging for, or keep proving to the kid that he'd never vent temper on him?

Hard questions surfaced every time they were together. Jake didn't mind the kid beating up on him—hell, he had a lot to make up for. But just once in his life, he'd like some answers. Some *right* answers. He was already a pro at the other kind.

When Danny turned again, aiming down a side road toward Lakeshore, the boy suddenly muttered, "Julie's house is down here."

Abruptly the kid slowed to a five-mile-an-hour crawl—which was fine by Jake—until Danny made another left. Four homes down from Sacred Julie's house was the Crandall place. Jake spotted a BMW pulling into the driveway. Saw Graham Crandall climb out of the driver's seat. Saw the passenger door open.

And there was Kasey.

His pulse bucked like a stallion's in spring—just like it had the first time he'd seen her. The kick of hormones struck him as incontestable proof that a man had no brain below his waist…still, it made him want to laugh. The last time he remembered that kind of zesty hormonal kick, he'd been sixteen, driving Mary Lou Lowrey home from a movie, and 51% sure from the way she kissed him that she was going to let him take her bra off. Second base was hardly a home run, but sixteen-year-old boys were happy with crumbs. Even the promise of crumbs. At that age, the thrum of anticipation alone was more than worth living for.

Hormones were undeniably stupid, but damn. They made a guy feel busting-high alive and full of himself—a sensation Jake hadn't enjoyed in a blue moon and then some.

Temporarily his son diverted him from the view—primarily because he was doing something to torture both the gears and the brakes simultaneously. "Danny, what are you trying to do?"

Danny shot him an impatient look. "Parallel park, obviously."

"Ah." Perhaps it should have been obvious. They'd edged up the curb, down the curb, up on the stranger's grass, down on the grass, several times now. Ahead of them was a freshly-washed SUV, behind them a satin-black Audi. In principle there was an ample ten feet between the cars. "Try not to go quite so close—"

"Well, this is hard," Danny groused. "How the hell are you supposed to know where the back end of another car is if you can't see it?"

But he could see her. Kasey, climbing out of the passenger seat, holding a small pink blanket. She hit him exactly the same way she had before—as if he were suffering the dizzying, stupefying effect of a stupid pill.

The darn woman wasn't any prettier than she'd been the first time. No makeup. Her rusty-blond hair was wildly tousled. She was wearing some God-awful green print that overwhelmed her delicate features. But the details just didn't matter.

The sound of her laughter pealed down the street. She didn't laugh like a lady; she laughed as if her whole heart and belly were into it, joyful laughter, the kind of hopeless giggling that sucked in strangers passing by.

And the way she held the baby, it was damn obvious the kid was worth more than diamonds to her. As Graham crossed the car to her side, she climbed out, then surged up on tiptoe and kissed him. She looked up at him with a love so radiant and full that you'd think Graham was everything a woman ever dreamed of in a guy.

And there it was, Jake mused wryly. He got it, the reason he had such a hard time looking away from her. It was plain old jealousy.

He knew damn well no one had ever looked at him like that.

No one's fault for that but him. He'd grown up a spoiled rich kid, raised to be selfish, to feel entitled, to take whatever he wanted whenever he wanted it. God knew his parents only meant to love him, but that upbringing had still skewed his perspective. It had taken his losing everything for Jake to figure out what mattered. He'd run out of time. Either he got around to developing some character, or he was going to end up lost for good.

An alcoholic—at least an alcoholic who was serious about recovering—discovered certain things about life. There were things you couldn't do. Other people could. You couldn't. Life was as simple and mean as that. No one else had your exact list, but Jake knew what was written on the forbidden side of his sheet. Being attracted to a married woman—a very, very married woman—was as off-limits as it got.

He understood Kasey's tug on him. Something about her reminded him of what he once thought life could be—when he still believed in dreams, when he still believed in himself, when every moment of sunshine was a treasure. He understood—but he turned off the volume and the vision, promptly.

Danny had given up trying to parallel park. He took the first left turn, aiming back toward his mother's house. He didn't speed. His driving problems had never been about carelessness, but about having no natural sense for the stick shift and the car. The more impatient he got with himself, the more he tended to make mistakes. Jake tried to shut up. Time and experience were the answers, not carping. Besides, dads couldn't die from nerves, could they?

Danny accidentally hit the gas, pulling into Paula's driveway, tried to recover by slamming on the brakes, and then, of course, stalled. For the first time in almost two hours, the kid looked him straight in the eye.

"I suppose you don't have time to do this again on Thursday," he said disgustedly.

"I suppose I do."

It probably hurt the kid like a sore, but hope surged in those broody blue eyes. "Same time? Four o'clock?"

"I may be a little late."

"Yeah, so what's new? The question is whether you'll show at all, just because you say you will."

Jake said easily, "Damn right. You think I don't know how much I need to make up for, Sport, you're mistaken. And in the meantime, if you also want to take on a drive on Saturday or Sunday—there's less traffic early in the morning, so we could go for a longer trek."

"You mean get up early?" Danny's tone suggested that particular idea was as appealing as a snake bite.

"No sweat if you don't want to. I just know you're hot to get more driving hours in, and I can't get here during the work week until after four. Weekend mornings could give us more time."

Danny heaved out of the car. "I'll think about it."

"Okay." Jake got out, too, and crossed to the other side, conscious that his son hadn't used the word *Dad*, much less said anything as pleasant as "goodbye." This lesson, though, had been significantly more peaceful than the last one. Danny hadn't sworn at him. Hadn't hit anything.

"Hey." Danny stopped at the front door, key in the lock, turning back to offer one last belligerent look.

"Yeah?" Jake assumed the "hey" was meant as some kind of question.

"Thanks for taking me," Danny said stiffly, and then promptly disappeared in the house and slammed the door.

Well, hell. Jake was stunned speechless. The kid had actually thanked him? Maybe, just maybe, father and son did have a chance to mend their fences. Of course, earning the kid's respect was still an uphill battle.

CHAPTER 2

Kasey pulled into her mother's driveway, thankful she'd made it across town in record time. She had no time for a visit, not today, but she was too worried to postpone it.

Quickly she freed Tess from the car seat, then stole a few more moments to kiss her daughter's cheek, then her forehead, then her chin. "How do you like the day, snookums? Feel the breeze? See the leaves just starting to change color?"

Once she scooped up Tess, she grabbed the five tons of baby paraphernalia it took to travel with a six-week-old infant. Mentally she was already scolding herself. How could anything be wrong on a fabulous day like this? The afternoon sun was brilliant. The wind had the tickle of fall. And assuming she did need advice, her mom—much as she loved her—was not usually a source of reassurance. Still, for the kind of worries she'd been plagued with, her mother was the only person she could turn to.

"*Finally* you're here."

Kasey jumped at the sound of her mother's voice and whirled around. Ellen Markowitz clapped the screen door open and hustled down the porch steps, wiping her hands with a dish towel.

Kasey got the towel.

Grandma got the baby.

"I haven't seen you in two whole weeks!" Ellen crooned to the baby. "But look at how she's smothered you. Forty-seven blankets, and here it's almost sixty degrees. And you've grown so much in two weeks! She *knows* I don't like to drop by if Graham could be around. He's so busy and I don't want to be an interfering in-law, but you'd think my own daughter could find a minute to see me more often."

"Mom…" It was probably useless trying to get a word in, but Kasey made a first try.

"Oh, yes. You." Ellen turned around, smacked a fast kiss on her daughter's cheek. "Come in, we'll have tea—but we have to be quiet. Your dad's home. He hurt his ankle yesterday. Right now he's napping in the den and I'd just as soon not wake him up."

Kasey skipped a step. She loved her dad. But a sick Stan Markowitz was not a pretty sight. "Why didn't you tell me? I'd have called." She added quickly, "If you think the noise of the baby will bother him, would you rather I came back a different day?"

"Of course not. I want you right here, right now. We'll just be quiet. And now that I've got my hands on my darling, there's no way you're taking off with her this fast. Lord, Kasey. I swear that she's the most beautiful baby I've ever seen."

"You think?"

There. Her mom's praise for the baby immediately soothed Kasey like salve for a burn. She wanted to shake herself. She'd never been the high-strung type; she'd always easily gone with the flow and tended to be a hard-core life-lover.

It was just…Tess was her miracle baby. And she was a lot older than the usual first-time mom. Maybe her worries were crazy, but she just couldn't seem to feel confident in this new-mom job.

Everything about the working-class neighborhood was as familiar as an old slipper. The houses were older, all with front porches and huge shade trees, but the edges showed signs of financial struggling. A dead car sat in one backyard; the sidewalks had weedy cracks; the curtains sagged in Mr. Harwoljj's front window.

Inside her mom's house, it was too hot. Whether summer or winter, Ellen liked her house five degrees cozier than anyone else. This year, the living room walls were a dark aqua, the couch and carpet a neutral taupe. Ellen had read all about color coordinating. The curtains had a strip of aqua, the couch pillows were a taupe and aqua print; and the orange throw that everyone used to curl up with was banished to an upstairs closet because it didn't go with the current décor.

Kasey tiptoed behind her mother—and was hit with déjà vu. She remembered tiptoeing past the den when her dad had been sick before. In the narrow hall, the smell of Charlie perfume wafted from the bathroom, strong enough to bring on a sneeze. The kitchen was the long, skinny room at the back of the house—the only room that really mattered, because it was where the family had always eaten, fought, argued, and through thick and thin, come together.

"You're making the tea," Ellen ordered.

Like this needed saying? Kasey watched her mom shed Tess's blankets, coo and tickle and examine the baby. Ellen never changed. In an era when women didn't *do* middle age anymore, Ellen had embraced getting older as if she'd won a prize. She always looked tired, always reported a new ache. As a child, Kasey had no way to understand that martyrdom was a kind of comfort to her mother—even if it wasn't a healthy one.

"So…how are the hemorrhoids?"

Kasey blinked. "Somehow I thought we might start out with 'Hi, how are you,' before we got into the prying questions."

"You had a baby. You have hemorrhoids. One follows the other like night follows day, but all right, we won't talk about anything that isn't nice-nice. You always were a happy-go-lucky dreamer, wanting pies in the sky that could never be. I'd lost hope you'd ever marry. You were so lucky to find Graham."

"Mom." Kasey didn't have to struggle for patience. No matter what she'd done as a daughter, to Ellen, it was never enough. Sometimes her mother's belittling criticism hurt, but today was the opposite. If she could count on anyone in the universe to point out a problem or a fault, it was her mom. "I have to give a dinner party tonight, so I can't stay more than an hour, and there are some things I need to talk to you about—"

"So go on, make the tea and talk. But at least give me enough time to rock my baby."

The white rocker had been set up in the kitchen clearly for this visit. Kasey's gaze softened as she watched the two. She'd nursed Tess before coming over, so the baby was likely to be good for a couple more hours. Soft eyelashes lay on the baby's cheek like silken threads. There was a small tuft of blond hair on the top of her head now—not enough to put a bow—but enough to make her look like a miniature punk rocker.

"Kasey…" For one brief moment, her mother forgot to be critical. "She really is beautiful. Like a Gerber baby. Beyond beautiful. She takes my breath."

"Mine, too." Kasey knew where everything was. Tea was in the white cupboard over the stove, sugar in her great-grandma's porcelain bowl, and the half-and-half stored in the second shelf of the old fridge.

"All your friends from the neighborhood come to see her? Your friends from work? Everybody see how nice you're living in Grosse Pointe, the house and everything?"

"Well…they've all called." Kasey knew what her mom wanted to hear. That all her friends were envious—especially those from the old neighborhood. "Very few have stopped over, but it's a long drive. And I think they may be a little uncomfortable—"

"Well, of course they are. They're jealous of how lucky you are," Ellen said complacently.

Kasey didn't buy jealousy as the reason, but the truth was, she'd felt confused when her friends started severing contact. She'd never thought marrying someone of a "different class" would matter—not to real friends—yet the old habits of doing lunch and girl-shopping had disappeared. At first Kasey had been so busy preparing for the baby that it didn't matter, yet it was disconcerting to go from a gaggle of friends to such sudden isolation. That wasn't, though, what her mother wanted to hear. "Lots of people sent presents for the baby."

"I'm sure they did. Your Aunt Lorna send something good?"

"Yeah, something wonderful." Kasey couldn't remember what, but she wasn't about to get her Aunt Lorna in trouble. Finally, she had the tea steeped and poured and could sit down. She motioned to Tess. "Mom, do you think she looks fat enough?"

"You still breast-feeding her?"

"Yes."

"Well, then it's always hard to be sure she's getting enough milk. But for now, she couldn't look healthier. You should be giving her a supplemental bottle now and then, though, so if you get sick, she won't be so dependent on you. Is she sleeping all night?"

"No. But three nights ago, she went six hours." Six blissful, uninterrupted hours. Maybe that's why she'd been so oddly fearful and worried about the baby. Because too little sleep was making her batty.

Ellen adjusted the baby on her shoulder. "Bring me a cookie, Kase. The gingersnaps. Maybe you could try her with a little rice cereal. Like at dinner. See if that'll hold her, make her sleep longer at night."

"Mom…"

Ellen heard the start of the next question, and cocked her head impatiently when Kasey didn't immediately follow through. But it was as if the fear and worries of the last weeks were suddenly bubbling to the surface like trapped air in a giant ocean. She'd loved being a mom every second since the baby was born—even the tired, cranky parts. But she felt so constantly unsure. Nothing she'd done in her life had prepared her for this level of terror. And it was as if, finally being in her mom's kitchen, under her mom's critical scrutiny, Kasey could finally let the fear seep out that had been prowling in the closet of her heart for weeks now. "Does she seem…normal…to you?"

Ellen's jaw dropped. "You're worried Tess isn't normal? What are you, blind?"

"But she's so good."

"You're lucky beyond belief, yet you're complaining?"

"Not complaining. At all. It's just…" All the rest of her screwy worries came out in a gush. "She barely seems to cry. When she's awake, she just lays in my arms like an angel, or in the baby carrier, happy. I put her in one of the cribs, she's happy there. Wherever I put her, she doesn't seem to move."

"So where is the bad news in this? She's just a month old, you thought she would be doing cartwheels by now?"

There. She was finally able to laugh. "I guess I just thought she'd move around a little more. I was afraid I was doing something wrong."

"Well, of course you're doing things wrong. You know nothing. I don't care how old you are, you're still a new mother, and first-time mothers never know anything—that's why you've got women in the family to ask advice from. Like me. Oh, you darling, I hope you keep those beautiful blue eyes!" Ellen snoozled the baby's cheek, but then suddenly braced as they both heard a plaintive "ELLEN!" from the den.

"I'll go see what he wants," Kasey said immediately. As she hustled down the hall, she could hear Stan revving up the language, the kind of swearing that made her squirm when she was a kid—not because his temper was directed at her but because it was directed at her mother.

The instant she showed her face in the den, though, her dad's bark turned into an instant smile. "I didn't know you were here, sunshine! Come on, gimme a hug, I've missed you so much...." And then, "Damn it, your mother knows I can hardly walk with this ankle, and here I was calling and calling—"

Swiftly Kasey rushed to play peacemaker. "What can I do to help? Do you want a drink? A snack?"

"I need ice for my ankle. And a little nip. And the TV— I can't find the remote—"

"I'll fix it all, Dad, and in the meantime tell me all about what happened to your ankle."

Kasey charged around, well aware that the time was clicking away, that Tess would be hungry soon and she had a dinner party for sixteen to prepare for. Still, it wasn't that easy to escape the old daughter roles—placating her dad, and then hearing out her mother's stream of advice and criticism.

"You're pale, what is this, no makeup? You know how washed-out you look without foundation. It's a mistake too many new mothers make, Kasey, letting themselves go. Marriages don't survive by accident. They take work. And so do men."

Kasey washed the tea dishes, brought a fresh ice bag for her dad, changed Tess. Graham had gotten her parents a new television, the new couch in the living room, bought them a satellite dish. To Ellen and Stan both, he was a god.

"I still don't know what he saw in you," Ellen said frankly.

"Hey! Thanks a ton!"

"I wasn't trying to be cruel, Kasey. But you surely realize there's something odd in your relationship? I know you're wonderful because you're my daughter, but Graham was rich and smart and should easily have been able to pick a woman from his own circles. He had to see something in you that he couldn't get elsewhere. And that doesn't have to be bad—but it could be. No one is this lucky without having to pay a price. Don't blow it."

"Mom, I love him. We're happy. There's nothing to blow."

"So go home. Put on makeup. Make yourself pretty. Sexy. And do something with that hair." Both of them heard Stan yell for Ellen from the den, and Ellen got that worn-out look in her eyes again.

Kasey left with that "Don't blow it" still ringing in her ears. It took a full hour to drive home, primarily because I-94 turned into a gladiator den, and as if sensing her nerves, Tess started fussing.

Kasey murmured the instinctive mom there-there mantra, but Ellen's rantings were still smarting in her mind. She'd known for years why her mother carried such antiquated values about women. Her grandmother had been divorced and struggled, near desperation financially sometimes, to raise three daughters. Ellen had gone into her own marriage with a terror of divorce. She'd always catered to Stan, waiting on him, jumping for his every wish, running to avoid his anger.

Ellen had relentlessly raised Kasey to believe that accommodating and appeasing a man were critical keys to a woman's survival. Kasey got the shivers when she thought about following in her mother's footsteps—that was never, ever, how she wanted to live.

Yet she *did* try to please Graham. That wasn't being a doormat, was it? Didn't every woman want to please the man she loved? Give up things, cater, try to show her love in ways that made him happy?

Which reminded her of the dinner coming up tonight. As she turned off the expressway, she gnawed on a thumbnail. Technically the dinner was just a neighborhood gathering, yet she sensed it was important to Graham.

He wanted their life to return to normal, to start entertaining and doing business functions together the way they had before the baby. Life wouldn't end if this dinner didn't turn out perfectly, but Kasey still felt uneasy. Their marriage had changed the minute Tess was born. She'd sworn that she wouldn't let Graham feel neglected...but of course he did.

Tonight was a chance to make it up to him.

Kasey had been looking forward to the evening, yet that flash of uneasiness made her shiver again. She shook her head, laughing at herself loud enough to make Tess suddenly chortle from her infant seat. "Yeah, love bug, Mommy's just being silly, huh? Our whole world couldn't be better, and here I'm seeing shadows in the corners. How goofy can you get!"

At six-thirty the lobby of the weekly newspaper office was deserted. One lonely fluorescent light illuminated the hall, but the central office was as quiet as a tomb. During the day, phones and printers and faxes and people yelling made for a noisy bedlam. At this hour, the place looked like the aftermath of a riot, with wastebaskets overflowing with half-dead doughnut parts and reams of coffee cups, and the floor littered with paper and clips and everything else.

Jake sat at the far desk—his coat on, because he'd intended to leave some time ago. But he got studying a medical tome, and ended up concentrating so hard he never heard his boss approach his desk.

Barney couldn't walk or talk without an unlit cigar chomped between his teeth. Wearing boots, he was conceivably five-four and had to weigh a good 250. The chin was grizzly with whiskers by five o'clock; the breath invariably smelled of old coffee, and the narrow eyes had a born-mean glow. He was so ornery that he couldn't hire reporters fast enough to keep up with their quitting, and when he parked in front of Jake's desk, he clearly had his bristles up.

"What the hell is this? Six o'clock, and you already got your coat on? You got here when?"

"Six o'clock this morning," Jake answered.

"So. Twelve hours, and you think you can just go home. Knowing what I pay you for overtime?"

Barney hadn't paid overtime in his life. What he did pay for a functional eight hours made slave wages sound good. "I'm leaving in ten. My dad needs me to take him to a neighborhood dinner thing. Until my mother can go with him, I'm the self-elected volunteer."

"Like I asked you about your private life." Barney took out his half-bitten cigar, only to stick it in the other side of his mouth. "So when you gonna tell me what the hell you're working on so late these last weeks?"

"Nothing."

Barney purposefully blocked the egress to the door—not hard to do when your stomach took up an entire aisle. "It's something about kids. Babies. You got books and articles in here to the ceiling on medical crap. Somebody assign you a story I don't know about?"

"No." Jake marked the spot in the book he'd been reading, and carefully closed the tome.

"You *are* writing a story, aren't you?" It was difficult to evaluate Barney's expressions, but the sudden twist in his mouth was kin to a smile.

"I'm looking into an idea, but there's nothing to tell you until I'm sure I've got something."

That was all it took to make Barney start crowing. "Did I tell you you'd get into this job or what? Two years ago you walked in here with your hands shaking. Eyes looked like your best friend was a ghost."

"Come on, now. You know I've heard these compliments before."

"You told me you were a drunk. Couldn't promise me you'd last a week. I know you secretly thought you were gonna bite the bullet, now, didn't you, dimwit?"

Jake sighed. He refused to get embroiled in this conversation. Not again.

"But I told you you'd get your life back. And that you wouldn't be happy just pushing out legal articles from the back desk, either. I wasn't sure—hell, you were a lawyer, and who the hell can trust those dregs of the earth? But I still saw something in you. You picked up the writing bug, admit it."

"I wouldn't choose to write if it were the last profession on earth." And Jake wouldn't give Barney the satisfaction of hearing otherwise.

Barney ignored this, just squinched up his face so his eyes got smaller than beads. "So the story's about kids, babies. Abuse?"

"No."

"Not gang crap. I'm tired of that bullshit."

"No. It's about legal stuff. The stuff you hired me to look at."

"Ah. Some kind of lawsuit?"

Jake buttoned his jacket, stood up. Barney didn't budge. Jake sighed. "It's about an epidemic of malpractice lawsuits involving newborns in the last three years. All involving good hospitals, and not just good doctors, but the best doctors in the city. Which is why I got interested. It's a puzzle."

Barney got a feral gleam in his eye. He'd never made it to the top, never would, barely had the talent to keep a weekly newspaper together. But that didn't mean he didn't hunger for more. "What's wrong with the babies?"

Jake shook his head. "There's no point going into it until I'm sure I've got a story."

"God, you're annoying." Barney straightened up to his full five foot four. "All right, keep your story secret for now. But just so you know—if you quit me and go back to lawyering, I'll cut you in the street like a dead dog."

"I'm not going back to being a lawyer." Jake didn't have to swear it.

Barney nodded. "Of course not. Why would you go back to making a hundred, a hundred grand and a half every year, for a job that pays a little more than minimum wage? And have to give up a boss like me besides?"

"If I were only gay, we could be lovers," Jake assured him, which—thank God—was enough to send Barney cackling back to his office.

Still Jake lingered, knowing how much his dad wanted to attend this dinner, not wanting to be late…but really not wanting to go anywhere near the Crandalls.

Kasey was the problem. Jake had no intention of going near her, not in any personal way. Once he'd identified her as forbidden, that issue became easy. He'd shoot himself before going near a married woman—so that solved that.

But four days ago he'd come across another medical lawsuit stemming from the obstetrics department in Randolph Hospital. The hospital where she'd had her baby. Just weeks ago.

"Kasey, where are you?"

Hearing Graham's exasperated call, Kasey quickly patted the sleeping baby's rump one last time, checked that the baby monitor was on, and then closed the door to the nursery. In the master bedroom, Graham was fighting with his favorite burgundy and blue striped tie. The tie was winning. It always did. With a chuckle, she stepped under her husband's chin and took over.

"It's almost eight. Company's almost due. And then the tie got mean."

"I can see that," Kasey said. "Damn tie."

"That's what I *said*," Graham said, still sounding aggrieved, yet out of nowhere he suddenly handed her a small narrow box.

"What's this?"

"Just a little present. Finally, our lives are going back to normal as of tonight."

Kasey saw the familiar gleam of desire in Graham's eyes, and felt her heart sink. Graham knew she'd had her six-week checkup and the doctor had okayed sex again—and she'd always loved her husband's ardent lovemaking. It was just…she was so beat. Between the doctor appointment and the visit with her mom and night feedings, she was drooping on the inside, and the dinner party hadn't even started.

"Come on, love. Open the box."

She did—and found a heavy chain of diamonds. "Good heavens, Graham!"

"You like it?" Obviously pleased at her shocked expression, he stepped behind her and hooked the chain. In the bureau mirror she could see herself—wearing a black dress, to please him. Her fingers touched the stones at her neck. Truthfully, the setting was huge and heavy and didn't suit her—but how ungrateful could a woman be? They were diamonds.

"What an incredible surprise! I'm overwhelmed!"

"Good." He dropped a kiss on her neck, clearly approving the dress, her swept-up hair, his choice of jewels. "It's because you never ask, Kasey, that I love giving you things. And finally, tonight, I've got my wife back."

God knew, she hoped he'd feel that way. It was increasingly troubling to her that Graham still hadn't bonded with the baby and seemed to resent every minute Kasey spent with Tess. Tonight, though, she really hoped to turn that around.

When the doorbell rang, she went downstairs to greet the first guest. The Bartholomews arrived first, then the Fields and Mauriers. Although Kasey knew the neighborhood crowd now, her throat initially dried up as if she'd swallowed a cup of sand. There wasn't an ugly woman in the group— or anyone who had less than a bachelor's degree. Kasey always had the sensation that she didn't belong here, never had, never would. No matter how wonderful the women had been to her, they just weren't her brand of normal. They never got zits. Nobody's hair ever had a dark root or a split end. She couldn't imagine them suffering from gas, or a tampon leak, or even throwing up in an embarrassing situation.

Yet that first terrorizing reaction faded after a few minutes, as it often did.

She liked them. Really liked them. Kay and Mary Ellen ran their own businesses; Willa taught at U of D. Binky was too fast-lane for Kasey and always would be, but Karen—Bud Maurier's wife—had been a mentor and friend from the day she'd moved into the neighborhood. Besides. They all knew by now that she had hopeless taste in clothes, and she'd been frank about her blue-collar background. When she first married Graham, she'd just presumed that the Grosse Pointe neighborhood would be a nest of snobs, and she couldn't have been more wrong. Naturally there were a few elitists, but not many. From the beginning, they'd taken her in as if she were a fellow sister.

They did tonight, too. And she felt a little easier because she was dressed the way she was supposed to be—thanks to Graham. Bud Maurier gave her a kiss and made her laugh. She was flying around pretty high, still greeting guests. Only right after Jim and Chloe Cranston came the gentle, frail Joe McGraw—accompanied by his son, Jake.

Her heart oddly tripped when she shook Jake's hand and welcomed him. "I'm so glad you came," she said, as if he were any other guest, yet she found her hand clasping his for a second longer, her gaze oddly captivated by his.

He wasn't any other guest. She remembered him, from the night at the hospital, and he'd stopped to help her. Since then she'd heard more gossip about him from the neighborhood women, who'd slung stories about his wild years and drinking. It wasn't as if he'd dwelled in her mind—there'd been nothing in her mind for a month but her baby. But now, those deep, old, sexy eyes seemed to touch her. The tip of his smile. The way he was alone, even as he was helping his father join the gathering.

Of course, that odd moment passed, and then she was running nonstop. The pressure was on. She was determined to show Graham that she could easily put on a dinner the way she used to—that the baby wasn't going to inhibit them from resuming the social life he valued so much. She could have hired a baby-sitter for Tess and extra household help, but she'd always coped alone before.

Dinner was served at nine. The problem with making everything look effortless was that it took so much effort. Graham did like things just-so. The housekeeper, Gladys, had helped clean, but Kasey polished the sterling icers and water goblets herself, created centerpieces with cranberry candles and fresh flowers. She'd done the new baby potatoes in a clay pot, marinated the London broil with her own original sauce, made a twelve-egg sponge cake from scratch. Now she brought dishes, kissed guests, served the fresh shrimp, scooped the quiet ones into conversations, until finally, everyone was sitting down and digging in.

"Kasey, this is the most fabulous London broil I've ever had."

"Thanks." Trust Bud to relax her with a compliment, and Karen to add to it.

"You're going to give me the recipe for the sauce?"

She chuckled. "I've never had a recipe. I just made it up years ago, and then somehow it keeps evolving on its own."

"But it's always better," Graham said from across the table. "The way Kasey cooks, it's a miracle I'm not three hundred pounds."

"How's your daughter? Doing all right at school?" someone asked him.

"Laura's just fine—supposed to come home next weekend."

"Has she seen the baby yet?"

"No. She was just getting settled in at U of M, starting classes...."

Kasey kept checking the guests, making sure no one needed something. Yet every time she glanced at Jake, his gaze already seemed to be waiting for her, already studying her in a way that made her pulse rush. It wasn't a bad feeling. Just a little unnerving. Suddenly she was conscious of her flyaway hair and the pretentious black dress and how flushed her cheeks were from running.

"I can't imagine how you managed all this with a new baby," Karen said.

"Oh, Tess is no trouble, is she, Graham?" But when Kasey looked at her husband, he'd clearly been sucked into a conversation with Peter Felding. Cripes. Not Peter. The two men were friends, but Graham would definitely turn cranky if the two started arguing politics. She pushed back her chair. "If you'll all just relax a few minutes, I'll bring in dessert."

"Let me help, Kasey," Karen insisted.

"No, no, honest, it's no trouble. Everyone just put your feet up."

With a smile, Kasey pushed the swinging door into the kitchen. *Please let it keep going so well* went the mantra in her head.

And it *was* going good, she thought. If her head weren't pounding, the night would be almost perfect. And she did have to keep hustling. Fresh coffee had to be made—and not ordinary coffee, but fresh ground beans, with a pinch of salt and egg shells added to the ground for richness. Then the foot-tall sponge cake with the marshmallow frosting needed fresh cherries for a garnish. And then dessert dishes—where had she put the German china ones that were Graham's grandmother's?

She was just carving the sponge cake when a piece slid. It was right there. Sitting politely on the spatula, waiting to be transferred to the heirloom plate when, blast it, the slice of cake took off. Went flying through the air. Instinctively she grabbed for it. And caught it. Which meant that the marshmallow frosting and sponge cake were suddenly squished all over her hands—what didn't gush all over her black dress and the floor.

At that precise moment, the kitchen door opened.

"Uh-oh."

The masculine voice was filled with humor...Jake Mc-Graw, she saw, the instant she looked up with frantic eyes. "I couldn't imagine how you could do it all alone. Bring in coffee and dessert both. I was going to volunteer to help, but man, now that I've seen that cake...personally, I wouldn't be wasting anything that looks that terrific on company."

For some crazy reason, she found herself relaxing for the first time all day. "It's good," she said. "But not quite so good when eaten off a black dress."

"You got some on the fancy necklace, too."

"Oh no, oh no—"

"Let's see. Quit fussing. Nothing's that bad."

"They'll all be waiting for dessert—"

"They're all stuffed like pigs and having a good time shooting the breeze. Tip your head up." He grabbed a napkin and rubbed it on the necklace. Dipped the napkin in sink water, then rubbed the necklace a second time. He was standing so close she could see the cleft in his chin, smell his brand of soap, see his thick brown hair under the kitchen light, so dark and walnut-rich with that hint of cinnamon. Then he stepped back to take a critical look. "Well, it may still be sticky, but it doesn't look like a meringue necklace anymore. Turned back into diamonds." His eyes met hers, sexy and mysterious and darker than whiskey. "That necklace looks heavier than lead."

"It is. To be honest, I've never been much of the jewelry type." She added hastily, "Not that I don't love it. But the fear of losing it scares the wits out of me."

"Well, having to cut your fancy cake would generally scare the wits out of me. But I'm here, so you might as well put me to work. Besides, then you can blame it on me if anything else spills."

"I will, you know."

"You will what?"

"Blame any and all spills on you." How goofy was this? Teasing as if she'd known him for years. Yet he didn't seem like a stranger. He seemed…different. The way she'd always felt different, not one to easily fit in.

Maybe he had alcoholism and major mistakes in his personal closet, but Kasey couldn't see it to look at him. He was obviously a caring son—caring enough to chauffeur his dad to events that he didn't necessarily want to attend himself. And she loved the intelligence, the experience, the depth in his eyes. Yeah, she could see a trace of bad boy in his posture, in his lazy, lanky way of moving, in the kindling way he looked at a woman…but there was nothing to scare her from liking him.

The kindling potential nagged at her a bit, but not much. She was too old to pretend it wasn't there—too old to need to. She loved Graham. It was just nice to talk to someone who just seemed to like her….someone where she didn't feel as if she had to be ON all the time, striving to prove herself.

"Did you really come in here just to help me?" she asked Jake curiously.

"Yeah, basically. I kept thinking someone else was going to volunteer—because for damn sure, I'm not great shakes helping in a kitchen. But you've been running a hundred miles an hour alone, as far as I could see."

"It isn't really running. I like cooking—"

"Yeah. So your husband keeps saying. Anyway, I also thought you'd probably been warned against me. Right?"

Again, those shrewd dark eyes met hers, held hers. She had the sensation of a thirsty man taking a sip of a long, slow drink. "Right," she admitted.

"So I thought I'd better let you know—probably everything you heard was true. If my being in the kitchen with you could be a problem, just say the word and I'll leave."

"Hey, you just offered to help and already you're trying to get out of it? Fat chance." But she had to add more quietly, "Just for the record, though, I don't need anyone else's opinion to figure out who I want as a friend."

He started dealing pieces of cake to plates faster than a Las Vegas hustler, but he cocked his head toward the window. "Look out at the driveway."

She did, and saw the obvious crowd of cars belonging to all the guests.

"See the Beemers and Lexi and Mercedes and so on? And then do you see the eight-year-old Honda Civic?"

"Sure."

"Well, the Civic's mine."

"Ah. That's what you did wrong, huh? Have an old car?"

He sighed. "Obviously you haven't lived here long enough to understand the difference between the mortal sins and the venial ones. You can kill and cheat and steal and all, but if you live in Car Town, you care about your wheels or you're nobody."

"This is a revelation," she assured him.

Another sneaky, crooked grin, but it didn't last. "Yeah, well, I got another sin. A bigger one. I left Grosse Pointe a couple years ago after a nasty divorce—and I didn't try to come back. You can sin all you want here. But once you've cleaned up your act, you're supposed to come back to the life-style. Nobody'll forgive you for not wanting to be a Grosse Pointer again."

"Sheesh, no one ever mentioned these rules before. Wait a sec—"

She wagged a finger at him, then hustled a tray with the fresh coffee and demitasses into the dining room, telling the group that dessert was on its way. "Okay now," she said on returning. "You refused to come back to the lifestyle. Which means...?"

"Which means that I used to be a high-paid corporate lawyer. Not anymore. I took a job with a newspaper—not because I knew anything about newspaper work—but because
that was the only place that would hire me at the time.
Truthfully, the paper didn't want me either, but they had a
hole in their staff—they needed somebody who could wade
through legal jargon and convert it to something human be-
ings could understand. That's what I started out doing—for
which they were paying me pigeon feed."

"Yet you've stuck with it?"

"Yeah, in spite of the pigeon-feed wages." Jake shook his
head. "I'm not sure why. In the beginning, I was just happy
to be holding a job. I needed to prove myself. Prove that I
could stay sober. That I wouldn't fold. For a long time, that's
all I was looking for—something to do that didn't stress any
seams."

Kasey couldn't fathom why he was sharing all this personal
history, but she sensed he was determined to be honest—determined not to put himself in a good light, for that matter.
Whatever his motivation, she was interested. "It'd seem to
me that you've proven your share if you've stuck it out for
two years."

"Yeah. I didn't expect to like it. But I also thought the job
was going to be no challenge, no risk...and somewhere along
the way, it started to get interesting. The newspaper's owned
by a character named Barney Mendenhall. He's an overbear-
ing bully and a real tyrant."

"Something in your voice tells me he's a good friend."

"That's the problem. He is. He took a chance on me when
everyone else was fed up, which is a real hard thing to for-

give him for. And then the damn man kept telling me that writing stories would get in my blood, that one of these days I'd find a story I'd need to write, and then he'd own me, heart and soul."

Fascinated now, she started to ask another question. Only, damn, Jake had finished loading up another tray of desserts, so she had to quit talking and ferry it into the dining room. "Sponge cake," she announced to the group. "But in case anyone isn't fond of that, I'm bringing in a fruit bowl next."

She raced back into the kitchen. "So? Was your boss right? Have you found a story you can't let go of?"

He'd been working like hired help, putting stuff on plates and wiping up. But now he looked at her in a way that made her pulse still. A quiet look. The way a man looked at a woman when he was through with the bullshit. "Yeah, I have. I've been looking into some malpractice cases affecting some of the local hospitals. Kasey, I have to ask you something…"

"Sure. Shoot."

"Just tell me straight. Is your baby okay?"

"I beg your pardon?"

"Your baby. She's totally okay, right?"

Kasey felt as if all the air had suddenly been sucked out of her lungs. There was nothing in Jake's quiet, gentle eyes to cause such panic, yet it was there, slamming in her heartbeat, drying up her throat. It was as if he'd known how secretly she'd been worried about the baby. "Tess? Tess couldn't be more perfect. She's beautiful and healthy and the whole world keeps telling me how lucky I am. And, God, I couldn't love her more than my life. Why on earth are you asking? What made you—?"

When Jake first asked the question, she'd just opened the door to the dining room, carrying a tray with the fruit bowl and small bowls—but now she heard the baby's faint wail from upstairs.

She forgot Jake, forgot the question, forgot everything. The baby monitor was right next to Graham. It should have gone off if the baby had made any sound—but right then, the monitor wasn't the issue, simply Tess. The baby never cried unless there was something wrong. Kasey plunked the tray on the dining room table, gracelessly enough to make a clatter. She saw Graham shoot her a dark frown, but he probably hadn't heard the baby's cry. "Everyone help yourself to the desserts, okay? Don't wait—I just heard the princess, so I'm going to run upstairs and make sure she's okay. I'll be right back."

The instant she was out of sight, she shot upstairs to the baby's room. The jeweled nightlight illuminated the crib. Her heart didn't stop slamming until she scooped up the baby and snuggled her close. "Are you hungry, sweetheart? Wet?"

Yet the answer to Tess's distress was much simpler than that. A burp erupted from the rosebud lips, and that was it, the end of the fretful tears. Still, Kasey patted and rubbed and cuddled, unwilling to put the baby down, unwilling to leave her. She'd felt better after talking to her mother, but now Jake had aroused her worry level again. It was dumb. Just new-mother jitters. Anyone with a brain could see Tess was the most beautiful baby in the universe. There wasn't a single sign of illness.

What could her maternal instincts possibly be worth? She had no experience at all with newborns.

"You want to go back to sleep, dumpling? Or go join the party?"

The baby would have lain contentedly in the crib, but she also didn't look remotely sleepy, so Kasey voted to carry her downstairs. When she ambled into the dining room, she had to chuckle for the chorus of "Oh, you brought the darling!" and "Let's see her!"

Several minutes passed before she happened to glance up—and catch Graham looking rigid as stone and glaring at her.

"What's wrong?" she mouthed silently.

But then she realized that others might have noticed his tight mood—in fact, Jake was looking directly at Graham. This was obviously not an appropriate time to try and talk to him.

An hour and a half later, the company was gone, the lights turned off, and the door closed on the disaster in the kitchen. Kasey checked on the sleeping baby one last time before walking into the master bedroom.

Graham was already there, standing at the window. At a glance, Kasey could see his shoes were already neatly lined in the closet, his cuff links and tie on the bureau, his shirt already sent down the laundry chute. Sometimes she teased him that he was so anal he'd line up Campbell's soup cans by the label—but tonight that kind of joke didn't seem wise.

"The dinner went pretty well, don't you think?" she asked lightly. She slipped off her shoes and dress inside her walk-in closet.

"Fine." His voice was shorter than a bite.

"I couldn't love the necklace more, Graham. I thought

Karen was going to rip it off my neck. Everyone noticed. It was so generous of you."

He didn't respond.

She scooped on a nightgown, shooting him worried looks in the mirror as she carefully undid the necklace. Her fingers were unsteady. She'd never seen Graham in a temper, but she knew when he was unhappy with her. She hated confrontations, never seemed to know what to do, what to say.

From under the nightgown she peeled off her panties. When she caught her reflection in the mirror—the still baby-pudgy tummy, the wreath-sized circles under her eyes, the wild hair—she moved away from the mirror. Her stomach was starting to churn.

"Graham," she said carefully, "I know you're annoyed with me, but honestly, I don't know why—"

"I'll tell you why! Can't we have one night without the baby taking center stage!" His change clattered on the bureau. Then he stalked over to the bedside light and snapped it off.

In the darkness, Kasey frowned. This was about Tess? He was mad somehow about Tess? "I only brought her downstairs because she was crying—"

"And if you'd hired a nanny—the way I've urged you to, over and over—you wouldn't have had to interrupt the dinner party. For that matter, if we just had an in-house nanny, you wouldn't be so tired in the evenings, because of having to jump up every time the baby lets out the slightest cry."

Silently she slipped under the covers—as if being quiet might help make her more invisible. "I don't see how I was creating a problem or interrupting the dinner party. Everyone seemed delighted that I brought Tess down—"

"Well, of course they'd say that. It's not the point. The point is that both of us deserve free time—time to be with other adults, children not included or always interrupting. I want my *wife* back, Kasey."

"Oh, Graham. You have me." She understood now. Hadn't she warned herself about this a zillion times? He was jealous of the baby. The problem was in all the parenting books. Men wanted to be Number One in their mate's eyes.

"I want our life back the way it was. I want time with you where your mind isn't always on the baby."

"Oh, Graham…"

In the darkness, he grabbed her, tugging her close. Her instinct was not just to respond, but to respond with extra warmth and giving. And any other time, his urgent forcefulness would have ignited her own passion.

But tonight…they hadn't made love since the baby was born. And no matter what the doctor said, she remembered long painful hours of labor and was afraid that sex would hurt this first time. On top of that, she felt trembly and tense because of their argument. His mouth claimed hers roughly, possibly because he was still a little mad. It wasn't as if she were afraid. That thought was crazy. But…

She couldn't catch the mood.

His entry hurt. Really hurt. Exactly what she'd been afraid of. And although she knew Graham meant to come across as ardent and passionate, she couldn't shake the distressing, achy feeling that he was oblivious to anything but what he wanted. The more he pushed, the more she burned, until she couldn't help but cry out.

"That's it, darling. Take me. All of me."

She heard his words. And inside her head, she kept telling herself, all right, all right, this'll be over in a minute, and everything'll be different tomorrow. She understood better now, that he was having a difficult time relating to Tess and that their marriage needed more one-on-one time.

It was up to her to make this better. To make their marriage like it had been before.

She just had to try harder.

CHAPTER 3

Right in the middle of diaper changing, Kasey had to stop and blow a raspberry on the baby's tummy. "Oh, yeah, you liked that, didn't you? And here you're getting so fat that pretty soon you're going to be out of newborn diapers and into the next size. Although you do have the cutest butt since kingdom come, snookums."

Tess didn't laugh—maybe two and a half months old was a little too young for laughter yet? But she made a gurgling contented sound when Kasey finished with the sleeper snaps and picked her up. Snuggling the little one under her chin, Kasey strolled around the nursery, talking to the baby, trying to capture her attention—and just loving the precious smell and feel of her.

"See the purple jump on the wall, darlin'? See the diamonds dancing when the mobile goes around?"

She loved the nursery more than she loved any room in the house. The jewels that dangled from the mobile over the crib—amethyst, citrine, jade, pink quartz—caught the light. The late-afternoon October sun was watery, but still bright enough to create prisms and rainbows on the far wall. She lifted the baby's hand to touch the Santa-sized teddy bear in the corner, shook rattles and bells, touched the handmade purple-and-royal-blue quilt to the baby's cheek, bent down so the tiny toes could feel the fuzzy, fluffy blue rug, paused in front of the balloon-shaped mirror so Tess could realize how gorgeous she was.

Tess didn't cry or laugh or respond. She just seemed happy to look at her mama with those dark satin-blue eyes—until the eyelids started to droop. Kasey carried her over to the east window. Across the sweep of lawn, Lake St. Clair was rolling in silver-and-gray waves. Kids on their way home from school were bundled up in fall jackets. The gardener was raking huge piles of crusty leaves. Everywhere, there were signs of winter coming.

A red sports car suddenly zipped into the driveway. Kasey stilled. The blonde who stepped from the car had her dad's patrician bones and the same look of class and breeding—but there ended the similarities. Laura wore her jeans too tight, her leather jacket carelessly open, and she walked with a hip full of swagger.

The girl was breathtakingly lovely. Yet angry. Always, so angry.

Instinctively cuddling Tess closer, Kasey murmured, "You may have to be patient with your half sister, precious. I'm sure she's got a good heart, but sometimes she seems to hide it deeper than gold."

The baby snoozed in her arms, unconcerned. Typically, neither sirens nor stress nor storms bothered Tess. Even the major argument between her and Graham that morning hadn't bothered the baby, but now, just looking at her daughter's camellia-soft skin and exquisite face made anxiety roll in Kasey's stomach again.

"All you have to do is look at her to know she's all right," Graham had said this morning with bald exasperation. "I've been telling you the same thing for weeks now, Kasey. It's past time we hired a nanny. I don't want you so tired, and you're obsessed with her. She's fine. It's you. You need to quit nursing her, get a break from baby care."

The argument had become a too-familiar rerun. She fiercely wanted to give in, hated bucking Graham, felt guilty for the tension between them. She kept trying to go the longer mile, to show him love, to spoil and please him.

But the baby seemed to bring out a stubborn bone in Kasey. She just didn't want a nanny. Tess was her miracle baby, the child she thought she'd never have. She didn't want to miss a minute of mom-ing if she could help it. Graham just couldn't seem to feel a connection to Tess, where she felt that huge, engulfing tidal wave of love that kept growing. She only wished she could make Graham understand.

But her thoughts about Tess—and nannies—scattered faster than wind when she heard the front door slam downstairs. Swiftly she nestled the baby in the crib and then hustled downstairs. God knew why she was in such a hurry to face World War III, but hope seemed to spring eternal that she'd find a way to dent Laura's defenses this time.

Graham's daughter was standing in the front hall, slamming the door after her third trip to the car—where she now heaved another giant bundle of dirty laundry at the bottom of the stairs. She straightened when she spotted Kasey. Tugging off her leather jacket, she hurled it on the closest chair.

"I'm so glad you came home for the weekend," Kasey welcomed her. "I made spare ribs. Your dad said they were one of your favorites—"

"Used to be. I quit eating meat." Laura looked her over with the same critical appraisal she viewed a sales rack of cheap clothes. "I figured it was about time I got a look at the kid. Where is she?"

"I just put her down for her afternoon nap, but you can still go up and see her—"

Laura shrugged. "It'll wait. Where's my dad?"

"In the den. He just got a business call—"

"Like that's news. Jesus, Kasey, somebody needs to help you with some style. That color green makes you look like a washed-out pea. And God knows you were fat when you were pregnant, but now you're looking like a skeleton."

One of the comforting things about Laura, Kasey mused wryly, was always knowing exactly where she stood. Laura had made it clear from the get-go that her dad must have lost his mind to marry someone like Kasey. Still, she didn't snap back.

As relentlessly as Laura tried to hurt her, Kasey never saw real meanness. The girl's insults simply seemed a measure of how much she loved her own mother. Although Graham and Janelle had divorced long before Kasey came into the picture, Laura had apparently harbored hopes for years that her parents would get back together. Their marriage killed that hope, and damned if Laura planned to forgive her for it—at least in this century.

Besides which, Kasey couldn't defend the jab at her tastelessness. God knew, she never seemed to pick out the right clothes. She glanced down at her emerald-green tunic and slacks. "They seemed so pretty on the rack."

"They look like something Goodwill would reject."

"Does that mean you're volunteering to take me shopping?"

"You think I care what you wear?" With a flip of her long blond hair, Laura sashayed toward the den.

Kasey mentally tabulated the score. Laura, 531. Kasey, 0. By dinner, the whole house simmered with tension. Kasey had cooked all the dishes Graham had coached her were his daughter's favorites—ribs and a bacon-spinach salad, lemon meringue pie, homemade bread and fresh pasta.

Laura picked at her food as she waged war with her father.

"How's dorm life?" Graham asked her.

"Sucks. The food's inedible. If I didn't buy dinner most nights, I'd end up starving." She added, "I'm broke."

"You need more money, how are the grades?" Father-style, Graham made one question sound dependent on the other.

"I'm not overdrawn, if that's what you're worried about. Although I don't know why it'd make any difference. You've got plenty. Mom says you didn't pay her the last two months of alimony."

"Your mother knows well that I've never missed a payment."

"Well, it isn't enough for her to live on. She's got bills piled up all over the place." A stabbing glance at Kasey. "Of course, what would you two lovebirds care if Mom's struggling, right? And now you've got the kid. A new wife, a whole new family. I'm surprised I'm even allowed to visit anymore."

"I'm not going to tolerate that tone of voice from you, Laura." Graham slammed down his fork.

"Graham," Kasey said gently, and to Laura, "Whether you're fond of me or not, I don't want you ever doubting that you'll always be welcome here. It's your home, and you know how much your dad loves you—"

"I don't need your defending, Kasey," Graham snapped, then whipped back to his daughter. "And I want a straight answer out of you about your grades without all the attitude—"

Helplessly Kasey watched the tension mount. Laura was hurting. That wasn't really an excuse for her rotten attitude, but Kasey could see it. The anger in her posture. The hurt in her eyes. The confusion that made her flash out, lash out, with anything that successfully provoked her father.

Kasey took away dishes. Served pie. Checked the monitor twice in case she missed hearing Tess stir. Outside, once night fell, a wind picked up, slapping restless leaves against the windows, stirring the lake into a white froth. It was turning into a true Devil's Night, dark as tar, with thick clouds blocking any hint of star shine.

The voices kept rising in the dining room. Kasey tried not to feel unnerved. It was rare the two didn't fight like a snake and a mongoose, yet she had no doubts the two loved each other. She was the only one bothered by the yelling. Graham adored his daughter and Laura adored her dad. Kasey aimed for the laundry room, determined to get her mind on something else. Gladys, Graham's martinet of a housekeeper, did a super job with the house, but there were always baby clothes to fold and put away.

She dropped a bitsy orange sock and suddenly felt a memory-smile tugging the corners of her mouth. About a week ago, she'd taken Tess for a fast run to the grocer on the hill. She'd needed fresh baking powder. She'd found Jake McGraw in the store—he'd just taken his son practice driving, he'd said, and was getting a few things for his dinner on the way home. Only he'd reached for an orange, and the whole stack had started shifting toward him. He'd started grabbing and juggling, and suddenly he'd turned around to find her helplessly laughing.

The memory soothed and smoothed. It was just a moment of laughter, nothing more.

"I've never seen anyone go to war with oranges before," she'd said.

"You think *this* is war? Drive with my son. Now there's a test of courage... Is there actually a baby in there?" He'd motioned to the mound of pink cashmere blankets in her arms.

"There is." She shifted the blanket aside so he could get a peek.

He solemnly peered in. "What's wrong with her? She's being good. Not crying. I didn't think babies came in that model."

She'd laughed again. "I think I just got lucky. She really is an angel."

And then he'd looked at her, with those incredible dark eyes. "She's beautiful, Kasey. And she looks absolutely healthy and wonderful and just like her mama."

He hadn't meant the compliment, she thought. He'd just been trying to make up for scaring her the night of the dinner party. And it wasn't the compliment she remembered...it was the laughing. The letting loose of a true boisterous Mae West giggle, no stress, no tension.

It wasn't that Jake meant anything to her.

It just scratched her awareness, that it had been a long time since she'd felt like that kind of laughing.

She dropped another sock, and then, just as she was tossing a fresh wet load into the dryer, she heard Tess's thin cry on the baby monitor. Quickly she headed for the stairs.

Surprising her, Laura was already there, hovering on the first step. "So the brat's up, huh?" she said wearily, but somehow her gaze didn't have the usual jaded attitude.

"It sounds like it. You want to come meet her?"

"I guess I might as well. I suppose she cries all the time. I'll probably have to go back to school to get any sleep—*Oh,*" Laura said when she walked into the nursery and finally saw the baby. And then a quieter, "Oh. Oh, my God."

Kasey saw the starry eyes, the wonder. It was the first time Laura let down her fierce defenses and revealed the person she really was—a college-age girl who was trying hard not to be afraid of life, trying to be sophisticated about everything...but a new baby was her undoing. Heaven knew, Kasey could understand that, because Tess was her undoing, too. "Would you like to hold your sister?"

"Are you kidding? I'd drop her. And what's wrong? Why is she crying?"

"Because she's wet. She'll stop crying as soon as I change her, and when she's all warm and dry again, you're welcome to hold her."

"No. Really. You don't understand—I don't know anything about babies."

"What's to know? She's family. Your family. And she's going to love you so much. Trust me."

In a year, Laura hadn't softened, not even a little. Once she'd outright accused Kasey of seducing her father, calling her a gold-digging slut…which unfortunately had made Kasey laugh, aggravating Laura even more. But the insult was just so outlandish. Kasey couldn't imagine anyone believing she could play a femme fatale. She was too ordinary. Still, nothing she'd tried had won over Laura… so this sudden erosion took her breath.

Laura's eyes had turned softer than butter. She picked up Tess with infinite care and her strident voice lowered to a melted-chocolate whisper. "I thought babies were ugly. Red and wrinkled and stinky all the time."

"She started out pretty wrinkled looking," Kasey admitted, and slugged her hands into her pockets so she wouldn't be tempted to grab the baby. Blankets were slip-sliding, Laura grappling to find a secure hold—but Kasey understood the two sisters needed a shot at bonding.

"I had an abortion last year."

"What?" Kasey was positive she'd misheard. The naked confession had come from nowhere. Laura hadn't even glanced up.

"It was nothing. Mi—the guy—split on me the instant I told him I was late. What a jerk. It's not like I'd have wanted to marry him or anything like that, anyway. For God's sake, I was just starting school. What would I possibly have done with a baby?" Laura's head shot up, glared at Kasey with jewels in her eyes. "Don't you tell my dad."

"All right."

"It's nobody's business but mine. I was stupid to get involved with such a loser. I admit that. But I'm not ashamed of what I did. It was my problem. I took responsibility for it."

Kasey said nothing at all, just brought Laura a tissue from the holder by the crib. Head down, the girl blew her nose, sounding like a belligerent foghorn. It was all Kasey could do not to wrap her arms around her.

Laura, though, had likely never intended to share such a monumental confidence. The baby seemed to have shaken her timbers for those few moments...and was apparently still shaking her, because she was still willingly talking. "You really decorated this room wild. I love the giant Santa bear. All the bright colors and stuff. But I'll bet my dad had a stroke."

"Actually, your dad said I could do anything I wanted in here." Kasey wanted Laura to see her dad as generous. There was no point in mentioning how rarely he came in here.

Gingerly Laura carried the baby to the white rocker, snuggling Tess close, clearly trying not to move too fast or breathe too hard or do anything that could upset the little one. "Man. You're so soft. And you smell like baby powder. You know who I am? Laura? Your sister. You're actually my sister. Who'd ever believe this? That I'd ever have a sister?" To Kasey, without looking up, her voice low and gruff, "I thought...I was sure...I'd hate her."

"I was pretty sure you'd love her. It's me you've got the problem with, Laura. And I understand that you must be afraid that I'll take your place in your dad's heart, but all I can tell you is that will never happen. He loves you so much—"

"Come on, quit with the psychology crap. I know all that stuff. Reality is still that Dad loves you, that he's got a whole new life. And I've got my life, too. It's just... cripes, I don't even know why I give you so much grief all the time."

"Maybe I'd feel angry in your shoes, too."

"Kasey, sometimes when you're nice like this, I could just smack you." The baby stirred at Laura's sudden exasperated change in voice. Immediately Laura softened her tone. "I'm sorry, I'm sorry, baby. Don't get upset. Don't cry. Okay?"

Minutes passed. No sounds intruded from downstairs or outside or anywhere else. The baby just lay there in her sister's arms, seeming content with the world—and not at all surprised to find someone else who adored her. "Well," Laura whispered finally, "I guess I'd better put her down. This is pretty dumb, huh, just holding her? What are we supposed to do now, take her downstairs, put her back in bed, what—?" She glanced at Kasey and suddenly stilled. "Hey. What are you doing? Kasey, are you crying?"

"No. Of course not."

"You *are* crying. For Pete's sake. What's the matter?"

"Nothing. I just…" Truthfully, she hadn't recognized the sting in her eyes as tears until Laura had called her on it.

Kasey couldn't remember the last time she had cried. She was happy by nature, was deliriously happy about the baby. And no, of course, every single day wasn't perfect. There were times like this afternoon—when Laura had first walked in and was mean to her—when she thought nothing would work out. There'd been mornings when she could barely drag herself up because the baby'd kept her up at night. And there'd been occasions, like their dinner party, when Graham seemed completely different than the man she'd fallen in love with.

That seemed to be part of what she'd been holding in. For weeks now, their relationship hadn't been the same, no matter how hard she tried or how determinedly she put on a smile and tried to make their world right again.

"Kasey, for God's sake! Are you sick?" Laura, looking pet- rified now, hustled Tess to the crib and awkwardly laid her down, then whirled around. She didn't move any closer to Kasey, just looked rattled. "What's the matter? Tell me. Right now. God. Has my dad been mean to you? WHAT?"

"Nothing. Nothing that isn't stupid. I just…" Out it came. The other fear that she kept trying to bury, even though it had been shadowing her heart for weeks now. "I just can't seem to stop feeling scared that something isn't quite right with Tess."

"Like what? What do you think is wrong?"

Kasey couldn't imagine why she was spilling this to Laura, when she'd tried talking to family and Graham and friends, and everyone only smiled indulgently about how humor- ously overprotective new moms were.

"I'm sure it's in my head. I'm imagining something wrong because I haven't been around enough babies to know what's normal," she admitted wearily. "I already took her to the pe- diatrician for her first-month checkup. He told me to relax, told me I was doing just fine. Only darn it…Tess just seems impossibly good. She doesn't move or show any motivation to start moving. She doesn't seem to respond to anything. I mean, she's happy. I'm not worried she's in pain or sick or any- thing like that. But she's almost too good. I know that sounds crazy to worry about, but—"

Laura frowned. "What does my dad say?"

"I love your dad," Kasey answered.

"I didn't ask you that. I asked you what he said about my sister."

Her eyes started burning. Her throat clogged. Her head felt as if she'd had buckets of tears stored for months. "Your dad…is wonderful. I couldn't love him more. But on this…I think some men just don't relate well to babies. And your dad is so terribly busy—"

Again, Laura cut to the chase. "In other words, Dad won't listen when you try to talk to him."

"No. He's listened. He just…" Another choke.

"Quit it. I mean it now." Laura flipped back her hair impatiently. "The kid looks perfect to me, but what do I know? If you think there's something wrong, hell, you're the mom."

"But I—"

"Take her to a doctor." Laura's eyes narrowed. "If Dad's a problem, then just don't tell him. This is between you and the baby. Who cares if you're right or wrong? If you're that worried, just do it."

Kasey lifted a hand in a helpless gesture. "I can't go behind your dad's back."

"Why?"

Oh, God. The *why* was so obvious to Kasey. "Because he's my husband and I love him."

"Yeah? Well, if you two are so perfect, then how come you're crying and scared, and my dad isn't in here helping you? For that matter, I haven't even seen my dad touch Tess since I got here."

Because he didn't go near the baby. Unless Kasey actually manufactured a situation where he had to hold Tess. "Your dad's supportive. It's just not that simple."

"So explain."

Kasey didn't know how to answer. She felt as strung tight

as barbed wire, wishing she'd never started this conversation. She couldn't possibly explain—not to Graham's daughter— that her dad seemed to have no interest in his new daughter at all. And that the woman who was supposed to love him to bits—namely herself—couldn't seem to find a way to make him happy. Not lately. No matter what she did.

"Laura," she said quietly, "I know you've felt suspicious of me from the beginning. You think I fell for his money, not him. And you can't figure out what he sees in me—"

"Oh, for God's sake." Laura sighed heavily, looking very young and confident and nineteen-year-old sure of everything. "I know exactly what my dad sees in you. You look at him like he's the sun and the moon. You *treat* him like he's the sun and the moon."

Laura threw up her hands and then stomped—quietly enough—out of the nursery, as if she just couldn't tolerate being in the room with such stupidity even a second longer.

Kasey wasn't sure whether to laugh or cry. Obviously Graham's daughter had never been in love—no matter how close she'd been to that one boyfriend. Laura made it sound as if a woman showing appreciation to a man was subservience. She didn't get it. A woman naturally wanted to please the man she loved. Wanted to make him happy. Wanted to be the one he turned to in the lonely dark.

Still, it stabbed Kasey's nerves, scissor-sharp, that Graham's volatile daughter wasn't completely wrong.

She should be able to turn to her husband with a real problem, yet on the subject of Tess, they couldn't seem to talk the same language for love or money. In her heart, she knew it would be a betrayal if she went behind Graham's back to seek another medical opinion about Tess... yet she was becoming so worried that she just couldn't sit still and do nothing for much longer.

So what, for God's sake, was the right thing to do?

When you were carrying a baby, blankets, diaper bag, and a purse the size of a small airplane, it was hard to skulk around with any subtlety. Still, Kasey opened the lobby doors to Randolph Hospital wishing she could tiptoe.

A stranger volunteered to pick up Tess's fallen pink bootie. Then the baby's pink-and-white bonnet somehow fell, and a young candy striper crouched down to retrieve it. "Thank you, thank you," Kasey said repeatedly, wishing she could pull off an Alice-in-Wonderland and disappear down the nearest rabbit hole.

Good thing she'd never wanted to run for office, because she'd never make it as a politician. She couldn't seem to lie, couldn't do subtle, and guilt made her want to throw up. Technically, of course, she hadn't lied to Graham—she'd just never mentioned making this doctor appointment for Tess. But it was still deceiving him, and the mother-lode of guilt churning in her stomach knew it.

On the second floor, she turned quickly toward the Pediatrics wing—not where the hospital beds were, but the section where a handful of top-notch pediatricians maintained offices.

"Hi, Mrs. Crandall. It'll just be a few minutes." The receptionist cooed at Tess—but then, of course, gave Kasey 500 forms to fill out.

Twenty minutes later, she was stashed in one of Dr. Morran's examining rooms—a cubicle with pale-blue walls and pastel animals dancing across the wallpaper. By the time Kasey took off the baby's coat, her coat, and settled all the gear, a familiar aroma filled the miniscule space. Tess's cheeks puffed red from the effort of grunting.

Okay, so what was one more diaper in a day? Except that she wasn't home, so it was a federal project to get the premoistened wipes out, a new diaper put on and the old one disposed of—preferably without the entire hospital being asphyxiated.

After that project, the doctor still hadn't shown, so she wrapped Tess in a blanket and stood at the window. Outside, a gusty November wind was spitting snow…exactly like the day she'd met Graham.

Until that morning two years ago, Kasey had never been near the fancy twenty-seventh floor where Graham worked. When his executive assistant had an emergency operation, though, he'd needed help for a minimum of two weeks. A temp wouldn't do. Graham dealt with too much privileged information. He needed someone who'd already proven trustworthy in the company.

They'd unearthed her from beneath five pounds of payroll data. The cloistered accounting offices were buried on the twelfth floor, her office one of the farthest caves. When she'd been told to go to Graham Crandall's office, her first response was concern. She didn't know him, although she knew of him. He worked in the rarified PTB air, not a Vice President then, but still the same as a god.

She'd been with the car company for eight years—ever since her engagement to Hal had folded. She'd gone job searching because she couldn't keep working in the same place with Hal and his new lover. The change suited her. It had taken time for her to find her niche, but she'd settled in, entrenched—and done a darn good job, she kept telling herself nervously as she elevatored up to the sacred executive floors. She couldn't imagine why Graham wanted to see her. She'd started out at a base-level accounting job, moved up several times over the years, knew she was trusted and well liked—but she couldn't imagine that anyone on the upper floors knew her, much less was asking for her.

And then there was Graham, standing over a desk as big as a train and more cluttered than a train wreck. He was so handsome he took her breath, but his tie was askew, his hair disheveled and his telephone lines ringing nonstop.

"I need help," he'd said desperately, with the Prince Charming smile that could have won over a stone. "Only I'd better honestly tell you first that I'm horrible to work for. Ask anyone. They'll all tell you I'm a tyrant, but my AA is going to be gone for at least two weeks—and I swear I'll be good as a saint or you have permission to shoot me. I won't force you to take the job. It's okay for you to say no. But Human Resources told me you were the best—"

And so it began. Two weeks. Then five more days. Then five more. On the day after his AA returned to work, Graham asked her out to dinner. She'd been stunned. Until then she had no idea he'd noticed her in any personal way.

But Graham explained that he would never have pressured her by asking her out while she was directly working for him. She'd cautiously accepted his invitation, and after that first dinner had come the camellias. And the gardenias. And the pearls, and the second dinner at the Grosse Pointe Yacht Club, and the evening at the symphony, and on that specific night…

Abruptly Kasey realized how long she'd been woolgathering. Those memories of when she first fell in love with Graham only made her feel more guilty for secretly making this appointment.

Dr. Morran strode in, changing the atmosphere like a charge of lightning. He hadn't rushed her either of the two times she'd brought in Tess before, but the hurry-hurry feeling was there. He was young. Important. Always radiating an intense sense of energy and purpose.

"Hi, Mrs. Crandall…and how is our…" Dr. Morran checked the chart. "How's our Tess doing today?"

"I think," Kasey said swiftly, "that the baby's doing fine and it's the mom who needs treatment. I hope I'm not wasting your time. I *know* you gave her a clean bill of health at her six-week checkup, but I can't seem to stop worrying."

"Take it easy, Mom. Tell me what's on your mind."

Moments later, the doctor was leaning over a naked Tess. Kasey started talking, fast, so fast that she seemed to be gulping in air.

"She doesn't seem to…see. I mean, if we go outside into a bright day or I turn on a lamp, she doesn't even blink. I know, I know, that's ridiculous. Everyone's told me that new babies don't see much, that it takes a while before their vision develops. I'm making too much of it—"

A light was flashed in Tess's eyes. Flashed off.

"…and she's so good. I *know* that's a crazy thing to complain about. Everyone keeps telling me how lucky I am, and

I feel lucky. It's just...when I put her in her crib, she doesn't shift or turn over. Hours later she's in exactly the same position. I *know* I'm being paranoid. What sane mom would be worried about having too good a baby, huh?" Kasey tried to chuckle, but somehow it came out more like a hiccup.

"Her obstetrician was Dr. Armstrong?" When he turned around to ask the question, he wasn't smiling like before.

"Yes." Kasey lurched closer. "What's wrong?"

He didn't answer. He just continued his examination of Tess, but eventually he said calmly, "I think we should probably run a few tests."

"What kind of tests?"

"Some diagnostic tests." Dr. Morran's voice was as smooth as butter. "We'll start by drawing a little blood—"

Kasey suddenly couldn't breathe. "What's wrong? You just saw her. You said she was healthy. You said she was beautiful. You said—"

"She is beautiful. Aren't you, sweetheart?" Still there was no smile for the sweetheart's mother, only compassion and gravity in those quiet brown eyes. "In fact, I just looked up her chart from that visit. She slept through the whole exam, as I recall."

"Yeah, she did."

"Well...it's really foolish to jump to conclusions this soon. Even striking abnormalities don't always show up in babies so young."

Kasey felt as if someone had dropped her in a nightmare and she couldn't climb out. "My God, what are you saying?"

"That it can be difficult to evaluate symptoms or make an

accurate diagnosis on young babies. Did anything unusual happen during labor that you recall?"

"No. Nothing at all, I—" Yet a siren of memories from that night suddenly screamed in her mind. Not the pain. Once she met other moms, she realized everybody went through that pit-awful pain. Yet now she recalled the nurse's voice in the delivery room, her calling for the doctor, sounding alarmed, worried. "Maybe. Yes. Honestly, I'm just not sure."

The pediatrician nodded. "Well, I'll tell you what. We'll run a couple of tests right now. And I'll give Dr. Armstrong a call. We'll get some answers for you."

But Dr. Morran made it sound as if they could have answers lickety split, when that wasn't remotely possible. The lab ran tests, but then they sent Kasey home to wait for results. One day passed. Then two.

"What on earth is wrong with you?" Graham demanded Thursday morning. "You've been jumpy all week. You haven't heard a word I've said—"

"I'm sorry." Kasey kissed his forehead as she served a platter of fresh blueberry pancakes.

"You're not sick, are you?"

"No, no…I'm just having a clutzy week, you know?" Well Graham wouldn't know what it was like to be a clutz, but when she smiled, he stopped looking so annoyed. "Tell me about the Meltzer deal again, okay?"

Once Graham started talking, he seemed to regain his good humor, but Kasey still felt jumpier than oil spitting in a hot skillet. *Tell him about the tests*, her conscience scolded.

But she was afraid. Afraid that he'd never bond with Tess if he only associated the baby with problems. Afraid he'd blame her if something was wrong with the baby, afraid that he'd insist on hiring a nanny, afraid he'd think the baby was more important to her than him, afraid...

Cripes, that was half the reason she couldn't shake the constant anxiety—because she *was* afraid. Not just afraid for her baby, but shook up that there was something seriously wrong between her and Graham. If God were kind, the test results would come out normal—but Kasey was coming to understand that wouldn't fix the other side of this problem.

She was hiding things from the man she was supposed to love more than life.

She dreamed that night. She was standing on top of an extraordinary mountain, a fourteen-carat gold pinnacle, a beautiful place of gauzy silks and golden hues and shiny scents...but if she moved in any direction, she risked falling off. There was a man in the dream, and at first she assumed he was Graham. When she realized it was a stranger coming toward her, she was frightened. He was hazy, unclear, but tall and powerful; he had brown hair with glints of red and deep dark eyes and he was holding out a hand to her, but she couldn't possibly take it. How could she trust a stranger? Especially when even the smallest misstep risked complete disaster. The drop was thousands and thousands of feet down, a crash no one could survive....

She wakened with her heart pounding, her throat thick with panic—only to realize that, of course, it was nothing but a dream. Nothing was wrong. Graham was lying right next to her. A silver moon shone in from the second-story balcony. She could feel the smooshy pillows and luxurious down comforter and Graham's big, possessive hand tucking her tight against him.

Everything was normal.

Everything was fine.

So she kept promising herself as she took Tess back to Dr. Morran on Friday morning. The office had called first thing; the test results were back. Finally, this infernal waiting would be over, and this time, she'd barely walked in the office before the receptionist called her name and shuttled them into an examining room.

"It'll just a minute, Mrs. Crandall," the nurse promised her.

Kasey figured that was worth beans—a minute in a doctor's office meant a good half hour, minimum. Yet she barely had Tess undressed before Dr. Morran clipped in. He glanced at her and Tess, and then closed the door with a frown.

"When the nurse called, didn't she suggest that you bring your husband with you, Mrs. Crandall?"

"Well, yes, she did, but Graham's at work—he's terribly busy—and it's not as though I can't tell him myself whatever you…" Her voice trailed off. "Something's seriously wrong, isn't it?"

Dr. Morran motioned for her to take a seat, and he did the same. The fluorescent light glowed on his tanned skin and handsome young face. "I'd feel more comfortable if both you and Tess's father heard this at the same time. I'll tell you what. We'll make another appointment—"

"Dr. Morran, there's no way I'm leaving without answers. If you think it's necessary, I can have Graham call you, or both of us could come back together at another time. But I want to know the test results right now." She never sounded this forceful—only at the moment she didn't seem to be Kasey so much as simply Tess's mom.

"All right." The pediatrician hesitated. "Did you and your husband go through genetic counseling before the pregnancy?"

"No. For one thing, we never planned on the pregnancy, but besides that, we both come from healthy families—" Kasey quit trying to explain. Her stomach was starting to feel like a ball heated in fire. "I need to know what you think is wrong with Tess. Please cut to the chase, whatever it is, just *tell* me."

"I only wish it were that easy, Mrs. Crandall, but there's no way we can be sure of anything at this point. The baby is too young to make an absolute diagnosis. The initial symptoms have too many variables, could change completely over the next months. We can rule out certain things, but we can't—"

He seemed nice; he looked nice, but Kasey wondered if he had a history of tearing the wings off butterflies. "For God's sake, just tell me what you think is wrong!"

He looked at her compassionately. "You already suspected that Tess wasn't developing normally. There could be all kinds of reasons for this. Eventually we'll be able to run more conclusive tests, but I recommend that we wait until the baby's several months older—even several years older. I know it's difficult to wait when you're worried, but she's simply too young to be positive what we're dealing with. Still, you already suspected about the blindness. Mrs. Crandall—"

It wasn't hearing the word *blindness* that spurred her into action. It was the doctor's whole tone going into that monologue. She knew. She knew he was going to try telling her something grave was wrong with Tess, something unbearable, something hopeless.

And that was what she'd been afraid of—but not really. Her whole life, she'd seemed surrounded by people determined to let her know that she wasn't that smart, not that bright. She'd never trusted that she had an instinct worth spit—so why in the Sam Hill did she have to be right now? Now—the one time in the universe when she desperately wanted to be wrong. Halfway through the doctor's monologue, she scooped up the baby. The baby, then the baby's clothes, their coats, hats, purse, diaper bag....

"Mrs. Crandall, please try to calm down," Dr. Morran said again.

"Shut up."

She'd never been rude. Not deliberately. But right then... right then, her lungs felt crushed and her throat was desert-dry and she couldn't even swallow for fear of choking. She just couldn't stand to hear him say something ugly. Not about her baby. Not about Tess.

"Mrs. Crandall," Dr. Morran tried one more time, standing up, obviously wanting to calm her before she tried to leave.

"Get away from my baby. Don't you touch Tess!"

CHAPTER 4

Jake strode into Dr. Gustavson's waiting room in a buoyant mood. Although he'd been researching the newborn lawsuit mystery for a good two months now, he still never expected the head of Obstetrics to agree to a meeting. God had no reason to talk to the lowly-nobody-reporter of a weekly newspaper.

Waiting, he tugged on his button-down blue shirt—the only shirt he hadn't ruined with bleach or overdrying. He'd even put on a tie. One of the old ones in his closet—which meant it had a conservative stripe, instead of the cartoon-figured ties he put on these days when he was threatened at knife point to dress to a respectable code.

Apparently, though, all this extraordinary effort was for nothing. The waiting room for Dr. Gustavson's office looked like all the other fancy offices at Randolph's—fresh flowers, cool art on the walls, a carpet softer than his mattress. But when the receptionist finally showed him into the sacred inner sanctum, there was no doctor waiting for him, but a businesswoman.

She identified herself as Christine Renaker.

Jake guessed her age at around thirty. Looks to bring men to their knees. Burgundy suit, frail little silk blouse, no boobs, perky heels and, no question, easy to smile for.

"You're PR," he said. He shook her hand amiably enough. She was adorable, for God's sake.

Christine came across with a high-wattage smile and both the sacred S's—sympathy and sincerity. "I know. You hoped to meet with Dr. Gustavson. But honestly—I'm the one who can help you. I'm aware of the questions you've been asking for some weeks now, Mr. McGraw—Jake?" She made it sound as if which name she should call him was a question—which was humorous.

She could call him anything she wanted. Which she knew. And he knew.

Still, Jake started to feel heartened. He'd wasted the tie and shirt for sure—she was too skilled to spill any serious beans. But he must be scraping some serious nerves if they'd sent him a top suit from the PR Department.

"The truth," Christine said, as she motioned him to a chair, "is that the hospital would appreciate the chance to talk to the press. We're glad you're here. Glad you're asking questions."

And cows blew bubbles. She sat next to him, instead of behind the desk, which meant that he got a close-up of her crossed legs and the big, personal smile. For a man who'd been celibate for two years—and who was damn tired of pining for a woman who was forbidden to him—she was worth wasting a few minutes for, even though he already figured she was going to hand him some kind of prepared bullshit. "Okay, so shoot. Let's hear your spiel."

"It's not a spiel. It's the truth. The public needs a better understanding of what's happening in our health-care system. The inference, when the public hears about a malpractice suit—whether it's against a hospital or an individual doctor—is that they start feeling afraid they're getting bad medical care. Reality is that it's an extremely rare doctor who hasn't had at least one malpractice claim against him—"

"You can speed it up. I passed the Research 101 truck a while back."

She nodded. "Good. Then you know we're in a sue-crazy society. And you know we're all losing because of it. Insurance companies continue to settle claims totaling over twenty-five billion dollars a year—even when certain claims are known to be bogus. That money doesn't come out of a rabbit's ear. The bill gets passed on, to you and me."

"Could you get into some specifics? You know what I've been asking questions about—babies. Why Randolph Hospital has had a significantly increased number of claims regarding newborns."

"Again, this is something that the public needs to understand. Which is why I'm glad you're here, glad you've asked." Again, she offered him a smile, this one warmer than a kiss.

Jake didn't glance at his watch, but by then he was pretty sure she'd graduated cum laude from a Catholic school. Her knees were glued together, so to speak. She wasn't giving away anything for free—except promises.

"Obstetrics," she said gravely, "is one of the most commonly litigated areas in any hospital. Moms and dads tend to feel absolute panic when a baby is born with something wrong. They feel responsible. They felt guilty. They feel frightened. They've waited nine moths to bring their darling home, and suddenly they've got this baby that their friends and relatives aren't going to feel so proud of. And out of nowhere, they could be facing thousands, even hundreds of thousands in bills they're in no way prepared for—much less prepared to deal with a baby with special needs. No one plans for this. Almost no one just accepts it. Everyone wants there to be an answer. We want there to be a reason."

When she paused for breath, Jake didn't try to interrupt. Hell, he knew he was being fed the company line. But she was still relaying the exact reason he'd gotten into this, because he could imagine himself in those parents' shoes, imagine how torn up he'd feel if he had a kid in pain and there was nothing he could do to make it better.

Christine continued. "People almost always sue if a baby has a disability—even if both parents go into the pregnancy knowing there are bad risks. Moms taking drugs still get pregnant. Dads with grave histories of genetic disease somehow talk themselves into believing their kid'll escape it. Women over forty don't want to hear that the chances of their having a baby with Down's Syndrome is going to apply to them."

Christine sighed. "The point, Jake, is that the cost of malpractice insurance for both hospitals and individual doctors has raised health-care costs beyond all reason. Our care is better than it's ever been. Medicine is better than it's ever been. Our experience is better than it's ever been—but we don't have answers for every medical problem and we never will."

The woman was so passionate on the subject that, damnation, he hated to cut her off. "You're singing to the choir," he told her. "I don't need convincing about the lawsuit insanity. But the question I want you to address is whether this lawsuit epidemic is forcing doctors to change the way they do medicine."

"Forcing? In what way?"

Jake hunched forward. "Let's say a baby is born with something wrong—it's developmentally challenged, sick, whatever. Nothing the doctor did wrong, but nevertheless, a tragedy for the baby and the family. Could a doctor feel driven—forced—into covering up the baby's real medical situation, even if the baby's problem isn't his fault? But because he can't afford more malpractice claims?"

Christine stiffened. "No doctor in this hospital would do such a thing."

Minutes later, Jake hiked from the office with a briefcase stuffed with worthless papers. He'd learned nothing new. Pretty damn hard to learn something new, when all three hospitals he'd been investigating were too worried about damage control to risk admitting a problem.

As he exited the elevator, moving toward the lobby, he glanced at his watch. Noon. He needed something to eat, then work, and at four that afternoon, he'd promised Danny another driving session.

Jake was unsure whether his son was an honest mechanical train wreck or whether Danny had hopes of killing him. Either way, he needed sustenance before facing any more of this never-ending day. Vaguely he remembered seeing a deli-drugstore across the street where he might pick up a fast sandwich.

Suddenly, though, from the corner of his eye he glimpsed something off-kilter—off-kilter enough to make him stop dead.

The lobby décor included signed oils and furniture that looked designer. No one wandering around ever seemed to look sick. There was probably a rule against it. Jake figured if you looked or did something unpleasant, somebody swiftly chased you into a part of the hospital where you couldn't be seen. For damn sure, no one did anything as inelegant as cry in Randolph Hospital's lobby. It simply wasn't done.

But the woman on the far side of the lobby was definitely crying.

In that first bullet-fast glance, Jake only saw the woman's back. She was crouched on the carpet, wearing a sweater with big bright stripes and snug jeans. From the back, her hair looked as if it'd been put through a Mixmaster on high. Soft, mind you, but wildly, exuberantly untamed.

He knew it was Kasey.

It was embarrassing as hell to recognize a woman—a married woman—by her butt. But what shook him to the core was hearing her cry.

Where he grew up, women believed seriously in pride and control. If you had to cry, then you had to cry—but you always disappeared from sight. Kasey had a life-loving Mae West laugh, but apparently, when she cried, she got into it full bore the same way. She was gulping in air. Choking back sobs. Hiccupping. All while she was struggling to fit the baby into a snowsuit.

The baby didn't want to fit—probably because mom couldn't get those bitsy limbs into the little snowsuit arms and legs when she was crying too hard to see. There were other people in the lobby, but nowhere near Kasey and the baby and the strewn baby debris. Jake couldn't fathom how this mess had all happened. How had the baby come to be naked? Particularly in the lobby? But the point was that people had tactfully shifted away to give her some space. Nobody was looking at her.

Damn it.

No one was helping her either.

"There-there, there-there." She was trying to croon to the baby. Only it wasn't the baby who needed crooning to. Tess wasn't crying. Tess was just lying there looking no more intimidating than any other baby.

Don't touch her. Don't go near her. The mantra had beat like a tribal drum in his head from the day he first saw her. He was climbing out of shame, making something of his life, doing okay—or close enough. But Jake unquestionably understood that he hadn't reached safe, solid ground yet. He had to be smart enough to steer clear of certain types of temptations.

But hell and damnation. She was crying. What was he supposed to do, walk away and pretend he'd never seen her?

"Kasey…" The quiet hand on her shoulder made her head whip around. Her cheeks flushed with embarrassment. She'd clearly never expected to run into anyone she knew. He didn't waste time asking if something was wrong, just said, "What can I do?"

"Nothing. I just…need a minute. I seem to have, um, lost it. I'll be fine in a minute. Really. Don't bother about—"

He tuned out, since she obviously wasn't going to say anything but fluff. He studied the disaster, trying to evaluate for himself what to do—and specifically what to do first.

"Really, Jake. I'm sorry you caught me. But I'm fine. I just got upset for a second—"

"Uh-huh." He'd already heard that. Clues clicked together—hospital, naked baby, mom. So, she'd had a doctor appointment. And she must have heard some kind of bad news. Something that made her run out of there before the baby was even dressed, and upset her enough to bring on the tears. "How about if I drive you home?"

"Oh, no, I've got a car. I'm fine."

She might have a car, but just then his son was more qualified to drive than she was, and Danny's driving had expanded to threatening the greater Metropolitan Detroit area. "You know what? I'm pretty positive there's a drugstore across the street with a lunch bar in back. Give you a chance to sit down, get coffee or tea or something to eat. Between the two of us, the baby'll be fine. A little break wouldn't take twenty minutes."

"I couldn't," she said.

"Then how about if I call your husband for you?"

"No. Please—no."

Back in his drinking days, Jake had given himself credit for being a manipulative, selfish son of a bitch. It was one of those character flaws he'd tried to reform, but sometimes it still came in handy. Getting Kasey and the baby and all the gear across the street—without a moving van—took close to a miracle. And Kasey was still protesting when they got there—but once the waitress plopped down a mug of orange pekoe, she wrapped her hands around it and started sipping.

Somehow in the fracas, he'd ended up holding Tess. That seemed unlikely—Jake couldn't imagine he'd volunteered for the job—but so far the baby didn't seem too annoyed. She just lay there on his lap, her head on the crook of his knee, bolstered by a mattress of blankets, occasionally blinking at him with these big, gorgeous blue eyes.

"She's not going to scream when she realizes I'm a stranger?" Jake whispered.

"No, she'll be okay." There, Kasey tried a smile. God knew it was faint, more a shadow than the real thing, but a smile nonetheless. "You're really this scared of babies?"

"This is nothing. You should see how scared I am of teenagers. When my son turned fifteen, I learned what real fear was. Still…there's something about babies. You don't know why they cry. You can't reason with them. Or explain why they should give you another chance." His knee was trying to fall asleep, but obviously he couldn't move. The baby looked happy enough, but who knew how long that would last?

"Jake…I'm sorry you felt you had to stop. I really am okay."

"You didn't look okay. You look like someone had kicked you in the teeth. You were seeing the baby's doctor?"

"Tess's pediatrician," she concurred, but then added nothing.

Frustration clawed at him. He'd known she was worried about the baby. Knew there were unsettling medical statistics about babies coming out of that hospital. But the last time he'd tried to interfere, he'd only ended up upsetting her and tangling himself up.

It wasn't his business. *She* wasn't his business. There was no way Graham Crandall would appreciate his wife talking to him. And possibly Kasey didn't realize it—or feel it—but Jake knew damn well there was an elephant between them. He couldn't look at her eyes, her mouth, the wild rusty blond hair without wanting to connect. To touch.

Still. He couldn't just say nothing, not when it was obvious something had terribly upset her. So he poked a cautious finger at the baby's tummy. "Did you give your mama hell in the doctor's office, blue eyes? God knows you look good as gold. And beautiful. But maybe you weren't quite this much of a perfect angel for the pediatrician? Did that jerk try to stick you with a shot?"

Hell. He was trying to be funny, but Kasey suddenly ducked her head and grabbed her tea cup. He had a horrible feeling her eyes had filled up with tears again.

A lunch crowd filled every table. The pharmacy itself was a typical drugstore, but back here, someone had created an oasis for tired business people and medical staff from the hospital. The tea was fresh brewed, the sandwiches simple but fresh, the bread homemade.

Jake hadn't glanced at his watch, but he knew he was already late going back to work and that he didn't give a damn—which was not a good sign. Recovering drunks learned to recognize that "don't care" moments led to other impulses that led to roller-coaster rides in the wrong direction. You had to care. Every minute. You had to keep reminding yourself where you'd been—how easy it was to lose your whole life—if you quit paying attention.

But he was paying attention. To the way the lamplight nestled in the curls of her hair, brought out the crushable strands of red and gold. To the way her oversize sweater hinted alluringly at her full, rounded breasts. And then there were her hands, the small, slim fingers. The mouth, so breathtaking when curved in a smile. The eyes, so riveting when dancing with laughter.

The eyes, so unbearable when they looked lost and scared like they did now.

"Kasey—" he started to say.

She swallowed. "Jake, would you keep the baby for just a minute? I'd like to run to the restroom, wash my face."

"Sure," he said, and tried not to look terror-stricken at being left alone with the kid. Tess knew. Babies always knew when their moms disappeared from sight. Kasey'd barely turned a corner before the little one let out a burp the size of a small country.

"Take it easy, Beauty. Don't cry. Don't throw up. She'll be right back. And she's having a tough day, so let's not do anything to make it worse. We'll go look at stuff, okay?"

Well, the kid was too young to look at stuff, but there were no more of those mountain-sized burps once he'd nestled her on a shoulder and started pacing. He vaguely remembered doing this with Danny. He'd been a pretty lousy father when Danny was little—too self-absorbed in his own life—but night duty was one of His Things. So many times the baby wouldn't be hungry or thirsty or sick. He'd just be crying because he didn't want his parents to get any sleep. You just had to walk him so he'd quiet down. Sometimes you had to walk him forever.

The drugstore had one aisle with kids' toys and junk—but nothing for a baby too young to play. Still, it was a place to walk, so he paced up and down the aisle, keeping one eye peeled for the door to the restrooms. En route, his attention really snagged on a ball. It was big. A bright sassy red. Made of soft velvet. The kid needed something after having a rough morning, didn't she? And the ball was the closest thing to a baby toy he'd seen.

So he shifted the baby a little higher on his shoulder, paid for the ball at the checkout counter, and then hustled back to their table. Kasey still hadn't come out of the restroom, but the blankets and stuff had all started to bunch and fall—the way they always did when you were holding a too-young kid.

"So I'm going to put you in the baby seat for a second, okay? Don't cry," he told her. "I'll pick you right back up if it's a problem. But you're about to smother in all the blankets. And I'll get the ball out of the bag so you can play with it. I just need a minute to get it all straight again before your mom comes back. Only don't cry. Promise."

The kid seemed to be looking right at him.

"Don't give me that I'm-the-most-beautiful-woman-in-the-whole-world look. You think I was born yesterday? Been there, done that, fallen down that well before. I want a promise for real. Just say flat out, 'I won't cry, Jake.' Come on. You're almost three months old, aren't you? And female, so don't try telling me you can't talk yet—"

There. Finally he spotted Kasey coming back toward them. Her face was fresh-washed, her hair brushed. Although her expression still showed signs of strain, she came up with a smile for him. Not one of her humdinger smiles, but still, an honest, softer-than-sunshine little one, until she turned her head to check on Tess in the baby carrier. In that same instant, she noticed the spanking-red velvet ball.

She started as if someone had slapped her.

"You don't mind that I bought the ball, do you? I mean, I know it isn't the best of toys. It's practically bigger than the baby. But it's soft and she seemed to like it, and it was such a bright color—"

Hell. He couldn't imagine what was wrong. Just knew something was. Something bad. Whenever he'd hurt a woman, he'd always known perfectly well what he'd done wrong. This was like dying. He'd sworn—*sworn*—he'd do no harm to her of any kind, yet the look of terrible pain in her eyes made him feel guiltier than a thief.

She raised her arms. He thought for a second she was going to hit him. A goofy thought, but he just couldn't make sense of what was happening. First she raised her arms…and then, for no fathomable reason in the universe, she seemed to be flying toward him.

The baby was in the carrier on the table. So was Kasey's mug, a couple of napkins. Tess still had her teensy arms wrapped around the colorful ball. He saw all that, saw a couple of women laughing at the front of the store, saw a guy in a gray-striped suit glowering over his *Wall Street Journal* down a far aisle.

And that's the last thing he knew before she lifted up on tiptoes and kissed him.

Nothing shocked him anymore. He'd have been prepared for a raise in taxes. Prepared for his dad to call and say now I realize what a selfish son you always were. Prepared for all his bad choices to sneak around and bite him in the butt again. Life had forced him to turn into a realist.

But nothing—nothing—could have prepared him for that kiss.

Kasey…God. He had no clue what motivated her to kiss him, but somewhere in the closet of his brain, his conscience was wide awake and already warning him against reacting. She'd been upset, that's all this was. All he had to do, all he needed to do was stay careful and keep control of the situation.

Only...

Only he'd always flunked the course in control and it wasn't that simple, anyway. Her lips smooshed against his like butter meeting satin—two different elements, but both of them soft, pliable, resilient. Possibly all she intended was an impulsive smack—who knew?—but that smashingly exuberant kiss turned into something luring and winsome and deep-deep quiet in the space of a heartbeat.

For one stunned instant, all the oxygen seemed sucked out of the room. All this time, Jake thought he'd needed air to survive. All this time he'd been wrong. Sure, oxygen was necessary. But not like she was.

Her eyelashes flashed up, her gaze meeting his as if pulled by an electric harness. It was a mighty plop to his ego, realizing that she'd never had an instant's awareness of him as a man until then. On the other hand, she figured a lot out in that millisecond.

Confusion and guilt clouded her expression. But so did something else. Sexual awareness made her skin blossom with color, her eyes shine with the startling power of emotion. "Jake..."

As if suddenly realizing she'd been clutching his shoulders, she dropped her hands. As if suddenly realizing she was still looking at him, she gulped in a breath and looked away.

"Jake, I'm sorry. I don't know what I was thinking of. Well, I do. It was the red ball. I know that sounds nuts. It's just that the ball was big and bright and colorful, and after what the doctor told me, I...damn. The point is that I really didn't mean, never meant—"

"Easy. It's okay, Kasey. Nothing happened, nothing's wrong."

"No, of course nothing happened. And nothing's wrong." Her face tilted up to his. She couldn't lie worth beans. Something was real wrong. For her.

"Kasey, I *know* you're married. It was just a quick kiss. A thank-you for the ball or something. There's no problem." She wasn't really listening, but he still tried to get through. "There's no problem," he repeated. "There's nothing I'd do to hurt you. Try to believe me, okay?"

"Sure, of course—"

"Not 'of course.' I'm sorry chemistry entered the picture if it embarrasses you, but nothing will happen. I promise." Still, he wasn't through. Although she was trying to swiftly gather up all the baby stuff, he had to block her path for one more second. "I don't know what happened to you today. Or before. I can see you don't want to tell me—"

She shook her head swiftly, wildly. "It's just that I don't know you, Jake. So I can't tell you something that I haven't even told Graham. It wouldn't be right."

He nodded. "I understand. But just know…you've got a friend if you need to talk to someone." Hell. Whether it was his business or not, he had to try the question nagging on his brain. "Did something happen to Tess?"

"No. There's nothing—*nothing*—wrong with Tess," she said fiercely.

And moments later, she was gone. He watched her from the pharmacy window, dashing outside, her hair flying in the sunlight as she hurled across the street with ninety pounds of child gear and baby, aiming for wherever she'd parked her car in the hospital parking lot. What had crippled her spirit, though, obviously had something to do with her baby.

Jake had sensed before there was something wrong with the kid. But what he didn't get, and couldn't fathom, was where the hell Graham was in this picture.

As he drove back to work, somehow a humorous thought snuck through to the surface. There was nothing humorous or light about that kiss—or about the emotions roiling through him either. But damn. Who'd have thunk giving a woman's baby a big red ball could cause such an outstanding response?

Kasey furiously raked another massive pile of leaves. The groundskeeper, of course, thought she'd gone bonkers. That was the whole point of being rich, wasn't it, to have someone else do the chores? And when that argument failed, Mr. Roberts had tried to tactfully suggest that no one sane raked in a high wind.

She'd given Mr. Roberts the rest of the afternoon off, which was easier than arguing with him. She needed some kind of real, physical, exhausting work while waiting for Graham.

The sharp wind off Lake St. Clair sifted and shifted the last pile of leaves she'd put together, but Kasey just picked up the rake again. Tess, bundled from head to toe in a white snowsuit, was chortling happily in her baby buggy. The last squint of late afternoon sunshine revealed the giant red ball cuddled next to her.

Graham had been on a business trip for these last three days, so initially this had seemed the ideal time to sneak Tess to the doctor. Now, though, he needed to know the results of that doctor visit, and she hadn't wanted to tell him on the phone—particularly when she couldn't handle the news herself.

She'd spent every minute of the last few days with Tess. Touching her baby. Hugging her. Walking her. Loving her. She'd also flashed lights and lamps and flashlights in Tess's eyes over and over. And all over again.

Tess didn't respond to any light.

She always responded to the sound of Kasey's voice. But not to light. No matter how bright.

Kasey kept trying to get a grip, face what the doctor had told her—especially before seeing Graham. Instead, in quiet moments, her mind spun back to those moments with Jake.

God knew why she'd impulsively kissed him. At the time…Jake had just been so wonderful to Tess. The way he'd held the baby and talked to her had squeezed Kasey's heart, as if he'd just naturally found her easy to love. And then he'd bought the ball. The gift wouldn't have thrown her so much if it weren't such an obvious symbol of something the baby could *see*, and that moment kept replaying in Kasey's mind, like a rerun of a movie she couldn't forget. Didn't want to forget.

Needed to forget.

If those moments with Jake hadn't been enough to rock her world, the panic she'd been living with certainly was. The panic kept sneaking up on her like a robber in a back alley, looming out of the darkness, causing her lungs to jam and her heart to lunge. She'd barely eaten in days. Yes, she'd sensed there was something wrong with Tess. But she'd never guessed anything like this. Not... blindness.

For God's sake.

Not blindness.

Anything but blindness.

At the sudden sound of a car, she whipped around. Graham's black BMW zoomed up the drive. Finally.

She never intended to hurl the crisis of Tess's health on his head the instant he arrived. She never forgot Graham's comments about how Janelle had killed off his love by being incessantly needy. But the anxiety and grief and fear had been building in Kasey for three long days. When Graham climbed out of the car, she hurled herself toward him with tears swimming in her eyes.

"Good grief, sweetheart—"

If he'd pushed away right then, Kasey instinctively understood there'd be something irrevocable breached between them. But he didn't. He immediately put his arms around her, so much like the man she'd first fallen in love with.

"It's Tess, Graham. The doctor...they're saying...he said...tests—"

"Just go slower. Whatever it is, we'll handle it."

"They're wrong! They're wrong! She's not seeing well, I can see that, but our baby—"

There was no crisis in their marriage. No breach. Surely it had been in her head. Graham was wonderful. Within fifteen minutes he was on the telephone with medical specialists. He yanked someone's chain to get an appointment with Morran the next day. He poured wine for her, filled a tub so she could relax, listened, talked.

In middle of the night, though, she woke up, suddenly realizing that Graham hadn't actually looked at the baby—much less picked up Tess—since he'd heard the news.

She tried to snap off that thought like a broken twig. My God, what was wrong with her that she was being so constantly critical? He'd devoted every second since he'd gotten home to taking care of her—and he was the same the next morning. There was no question about his staying home. All during breakfast, he used his cell phone to bark notes and delegate work for the day, and then in typical take-charge mode, helped her bundle Tess and the baby gear into the car.

Life was different when Graham was with her. The receptionist jumped when they walked into the office. They were immediately ushered into Dr. Morran's office. And although Kasey had anticipated keeping Tess with them, a nurse showed up to care for the baby so they could talk privately with the doctor.

"I'm glad you're here. Like I told Mrs. Crandall, I really wanted the three of us to sit down and talk about Tess together."

The pediatrician had told her that, but Kasey picked up something different in his tone now—an implication that she couldn't handle the news alone, that he could say more now that her husband was here. It wasn't the first time she'd been exposed to an exasperating macho attitude, but she assumed Graham would take her side.

Graham, though, hunkered down in the office chair across the desk and focused on Dr. Morran. "I want to know the name for whatever condition you feel the child could have. And then whatever tests and procedures we can do to define the problem for certain."

"Evaluating infants is an imperfect science, Mr. Crandall. Some conditions and diseases are cut-and-dried. But when they're not, we often have to wait until the child is older. There are just so many variations in a baby's developmental patterns. However, her lack of vision is an easily identifiable problem. So is the lack of physical responses and reflexes that we'd expect to see in a baby this age. The few tests we've tried so far…" Dr. Morran hesitated, shooting a compassionate look at Kasey. "Well, I didn't want to bring this up to Mrs. Crandall alone."

"*What?* You knew something you didn't tell me?"

"I don't know anything for certain, Mrs. Crandall. And I don't want to upset you—either of you—without knowing something for positive—"

"Forget the 'making nice,'" Graham said flatly. "Just tell me flat out. What is the worst we could be dealing with?"

First there was silence. Then Dr. Morran let out a grave sigh as he sank back. "There are several symptoms, at this time, pointing to a disorder called Leber's Congenital Amaurosis."

"What?" Kasey said. "You never once mentioned that during our appointment—"

"I know I didn't, Mrs. Crandall." And to Graham, "It's a serious condition. An unusual problem, in fact, that can be inherited only if you both have a certain autosomal recessive genetic trait."

"If both Kasey and I have it? So that means that you could test us and then we'd know for positive if it's the problem?"

"Unfortunately, it's not quite that easy. Definitely we can test you, but I'm afraid—even if you both show up with the same recessive genetic trait—that we still won't know for sure. I know it's hard to accept, but in the majority of cases—more than sixty percent—there is no way we'll ever be able to identify the exact cause. Birth defects are complex. Even when there's a hereditary factor for certain, we could still have environmental or chromosomal or lifestyle factors that contribute to whatever your daughter has."

Graham had turned gray. "Something, though, led you to believe that our daughter has this Leber's problem."

"Yes. Leber's is a rare disorder, but blindness was a primary clue. Blindness at birth is particularly unusual when there's no physical cause or trauma or related background in the family. And although Tess is still young, she seems to be showing signs of psychomotor delay. By now, she should at least be turning over, moving around in her crib—"

"Okay. We don't have to catalog every symptom. The point is, what's the deal with this disease? What do we have to do to fix it, or cure it? Is there another medical facility where we need to take her? What medications do we need to start her on—?" Typically, Graham wanted to tick off a list of actions he could direct.

"I'm afraid it's not going to be that easy." Dr. Morran's voice was laced with compassion. "We can't simply try drugs on Tess until we know definitely what she has. But if the diagnosis *is* Leber's, there are some things that you and your wife need to seriously consider."

"Like what?"

"Well, the blindness, of course, is a primary and immediate issue. It's possible she had some sight after birth, but right now, all we see is an involuntary movement in her right eye, and that's it. No responsiveness to light whatsoever. If the rest of her symptoms lead us to Leber's, mental retardation is part of the condition. And I'm afraid—"

Kasey stopped breathing the instant she heard the word *retardation*.

"What?" Graham demanded.

Dr. Morran made direct eye contact with Graham, as if he felt unable to look at Kasey. "We are likely talking developing retardation. Even possibly severe retardation. And between those kinds of mental problems, the blindness, and the physical lack of motor and muscular developments, patients who have this severely simply cannot be cared for at home...unless you can permanently provide twenty-four-hour-a-day help. I realize this is difficult to hear—"

"You sure as hell have that right," Graham said hoarsely.

"But there is no alternative to being honest with you. I realize that Tess isn't hard for you to care for right now. But for a child who has this condition severely, it's frankly the kindest thing to put them in an institution from the start, because getting them used to a home environment only makes the change harder on the child in the long run. I don't mean you need to make any changes now, this minute, this month. We're not even close to that conclusive diagnosis yet. But I do think you should prepare yourselves. Should the symptoms persist in leading us to a diagnosis of Leber's—I wish I never had to say this—but both of you will have to face some hard decisions, and denial will only make the situation worse. For you two. And for your daughter."

Kasey didn't know she'd been holding her breath until a lost sound escaped her throat...a keening sound of pain. Like the wail of wind.

CHAPTER 5

Jake kept telling himself that it could be worse. Many years they had major blizzards by the week before Thanksgiving. This little snow squall was zip by comparison—except to a brand-new driver.

"Hey," Danny said, "I'm doing way better, right?"

Jake weighed his answer. In the first ten minutes on the road, Danny hadn't hit anything. "So far we're still alive," he acknowledged.

"Hey, come on. I haven't stalled once or had to slam on the brakes or anything. What do you want?"

"Good question. I'm thinking…the ability to pray. Or a direct line to God."

Danny looked ready to snap back an argumentative retort, but then he glanced at his dad and hesitated. "That was a joke, right?"

"Yeah, that was a joke, Danny." It ached, that his son couldn't remember the early years when the two of them had known how to laugh together. "Your driving's improved a hundred percent. The learning curve's a lot longer for anyone driving a stick shift, don't forget. And the first snow day is a different kind of test. You have no way to be prepared for snow and ice until you've had a chance to practice."

"I'm sick of practicing." Danny downshifted like a young Parnelli Jones, and turned off the nice, quiet, peaceful Lothrop onto, unfortunately, Kercheval. The shopping district was straight ahead. "I've been practicing for weeks already. When I get my license, I think I should be able to get my own car. I've got that trust fund from Gramps, so really, like that money is already mine. If I had my own wheels, I wouldn't have to ask you or Mom for rides all the time. And I don't see how you could vote against me, when you're the one who left us to begin with."

Jake patted his shirt pocket for his roll of antacids. "On the trust fund, you can't get your hands on that until you're twenty-one. Which you know. Your mom won't agree to your getting a car right now, besides—which you also know. I don't blame you for wanting wheels. I felt the same at your age. But it's not going to happen, so there's no point in beating your head against a wall. And as far as my leaving you..."

Jake had to clench his teeth when a frisky Shitzu ran out onto the road, but Danny saw the dog in time. "As far as my leaving you," he continued, "I didn't. What happened was that your mom kicked me out—and that's exactly what she should have done, because at the time I was a worthless dad and husband both. She did the right thing. What was best for you and her both."

Danny rolled his eyes to the ceiling—which made the car swerve over the middle line. "God, I get so sick of this. You're always so *understanding*. Like being nice now makes up. I got news. It doesn't make up."

Jake let a spot of silence fall. For a while now, he'd intuited what his son was up to. Danny wasn't baiting him solely for the joy of coming across as the card-carrying spoiled brat of the universe. He was angry. Letting out anger that he'd never had a chance to as a little boy. And though Jake may have been justified in arguing with him—or smacking his preciously loved son upside the head—his coming down hard could close a communication door that was finally, finally open. If only an inch.

Jake had to risk opening it a little farther. "Danny...do you want to come to my place on Thanksgiving?"

"Huh?" The change of subject clearly startled the boy.

"You've told me a million times how much you hate T-Day. Old people sit around and dress up and eat forever and it's boring. Well—if your mother agrees, you can come over to my place. I'd pick you up, take you back when you wanted. And I'm thinking about baking a turkey, but otherwise, I had in mind vegging out in front of the ball games. No manners, no napkins, no ties. What do you say?"

Danny didn't answer for several moments, then offered a grudging, "Maybe."

Jake felt like slapping his chest in shock. He'd been so sure he was going to get an unequivocal—and disgusted—no. "Look, I really think it'd be all right with your mother—but when we get home, I'll ask her right then if you want."

"Can't. Because she won't be home when we get there. She's over at the Crandalls'. You know the Crandalls? Like Laura—really cool, long blond hair, goes to University of Michigan—"

"Yes, I know the Crandalls. Not Laura, but her father, Graham. And Kascy. What about them?"

"Yeah, well, like I guess they had a baby a few months ago, but now they found out something bad is wrong with the kid.

So a bunch of women are putting together, like, a surprise party. I guess it's to cheer her up, so they got stuff like bubble bath and junk like that, I guess—oh, and they're bringing over this lady who's a masseur—"

Jake could feel a lump filling up his throat, clogging his breathing passage. Something the size of a sharp boulder. "I believe a woman who does a massage is called a masseuse."

"Yeah, whatever. Anyway, Mom said Mrs. Crandall was pretty depressed. So nobody's gonna talk about the baby. They're just gonna party. Mom took over some wine and stuff." Danny was clearly wearying of imparting this boring neighborhood news. "Anyway, if you were going to call Mom, she said she'd be home like by seven-thirty."

"I didn't know your mom was that close to the Crandalls."

"Beats me. I don't know who Mom's close to. But naturally, I know Laura and all…"

When Danny shifted in his seat, Jake finally caught on why his son had paid so much attention to the whole business. Laura Crandall's name was always said in the same hallowed tones. Every underclassman had drooled in her shadow for her entire senior year.

"Anyways," Danny went on, "that's why I was listening. Because Laura might be home at Thanksgiving and Christmas, you know? So if I ran into her, I'd know about what happened to her baby sister and all."

"Did you happen to hear what was wrong with the baby?"

Danny shrugged, then noticed a young girl in a short skirt and long, flapping scarf, pushing open the door of the Barnes & Noble. She was unquestionably cute, but sweat broke out on Jake's brow. His son narrowly missed the entire row of parked cars on his right. "I didn't hear what was wrong with the kid, but I guess it's real bad because everybody in the neighborhood's been talking about it. Cripes, I can hardly get on the Internet. Mom's been hogging the phone line ever since this thing started..." Abruptly Danny changed gears. "I'm thinking about Thanksgiving."

The thick feeling in Jake's throat just kept growing. God, he'd sensed she was worried about her baby long before he saw her that morning at the hospital...the day she'd kissed him. The day he'd mentally called the Red Ball Day ever since.

Maybe that kiss had blurred his brain, but it also slapped him to his senses. She wasn't just married. She was in the middle of a crisis and vulnerable. Being around a man like him, with a torn-up reputation and ten miles of bad history, could only hurt her. So he'd stayed far out of her radar—but now, concern was killing him. What had she found out about the baby?

"Anyway," Danny repeated, "*maybe* I wouldn't mind coming over on Thanksgiving." And then, thank-you-God, he turned off Kercheval onto Neff, a quiet residential street where there weren't so many people to potentially kill or maim. "The only time I'd want to come, though, is when Grandma and Mom are doing the dinner. There's no point unless I get out of that torture."

Jake remembered those dinners. The white linen. The godawful oyster dressing. Sneaking the dog tidbits under the table while his mother-in-law droned on about bloodlines and D.A.R. history. Although Danny had consistently refused coming to see his apartment, Jake understood that fam-

ily holiday dinners could be even the strongest man's nemesis. "All right. I'll call your mom later, and find out what time
the meal is, so we can try to set up something... Danny?"

"What?"

"That's real sad about the Crandalls' baby."

"Yeah. Mom said she had to be sedated." Danny frowned.
"I don't know if she meant the baby or Mrs. Crandall. But I
guess one of 'em was in such rough shape that they needed
to be drugged up."

Since no one was likely to sedate a baby, Jake all too easily understood that Kasey needed the help of drugs to cope.
What in God's name was going on in that house?

Leave her alone, warned his conscience. *She's none of your
business. None.*

Faster than lightning, he felt the sudden razor-sharp craving for a drink. The urge was always there, but he was long
past that first, ugly stretch when the craving clawed at him
relentlessly. Now, temptation only bit this bad when serious
anxiety entered the picture.

Like Kasey. She was a test, he thought. The kind of test
he'd failed his whole life. He'd always put himself first, grown
up with an unshakable feeling of entitlement, skidded
blithely over people's lives like tire tracks. He'd always
thought it was easy to be selfish. Now he knew better. If he
hurt another innocent person through his selfishness, he
knew damn well he wouldn't survive. This was his shot. His
last shot, his only shot, at becoming a decent man.

And that was exactly why he'd resolved not to call

Kasey…yet now, not to contact her after discovering she was in trouble, seemed equally wrong.

So how in hell was he supposed to pass this test?

Kasey had just stepped out of her closet when she heard a sound in the nursery, and quickly went across the hall. In the baby's room, shutters were drawn against the blustery November afternoon, but amethyst and jade horses were dancing around the baby's musical mobile. Kasey tiptoed over to the crib, where Tess lay on her back, wide awake, the red velvet ball snuggled next to her. "How's my darling?" she whispered.

The baby had looked content before, but at the sound of her mother's voice, she immediately kicked a little and smiled. The big toothless grin made Kasey's heart turn over. The kicking was a new achievement. And finally she was growing some hair—not that Tess needed hair to be breathtakingly gorgeous.

"I got you alone for a couple minutes, love bug, can you believe it? It seems to me we should do something wild. Maybe we could sing at the top of our lungs? Dance up and down the halls to some wild rock and roll, and then maybe pig out on a little milk…you like that plan?"

She cuddled up the baby and soundly kissed her before carrying her to the dressing table for a diaper change. Tess, when consulted with a wardrobe choice, seemed to vote for the red-and-white outfit with the balloons. Dressing her took more kisses and tickles, and when that was done, Kasey gently began to turn the baby, first in one direction, then the other.

"My theory on this, love bug," she whispered, "is that you

could turn over if you wanted to. Why should you want to, right? When you're already happy? But still, it's not doing any harm to practice, is it?"

Day after day she tried to make herself believe the blind and retarded prognosis, but couldn't. She looked at Tess and all she saw was beauty. A gentle personality was emerging. Tess was happy, serene by nature, loving, sweet. She liked music and sunshine. She hated oatmeal and shoes.

All of them were wrong, Kasey thought fiercely.

All of them. The doctors, the tests. The hospital. Graham. She was the first one who'd noticed something was wrong, wasn't she? She'd never denied there was a problem—but she also spent more time with her baby than anyone. "Something wrong" was miles different than the drastic diagnosis they'd given her. It was unthinkable—unbearable—to believe Tess had nothing ahead of her but a doomed future.

"Could you try, Tess?" she coaxed. "Just try. Just see if you might want to roll over on your own. I'll help you halfway, okay, and then…"

Sensing someone else was in the room, Kasey jerked her head around—a mistake, because she got dizzy so easily from the pills Graham insisted she take—but groggy or not, she immediately recognized the live-in nanny in the doorway. Graham had hired Frances O'Hearny the day after they'd seen Dr. Morran together.

"Our baby sure looks content," Frances said jovially. "Such an angel she is."

"Yes." Kasey forced a smile. Graham hadn't asked permission to hire Frances, any more than he'd asked her about the dozen other changes he'd put in motion that traumatic day.

The diamonds in her ears were new. A weekly appointment at a spa was another new gift, and so was the pale-pink cashmere sweater she was wearing.

Graham couldn't have been more thoughtful or caring. He'd done anything a man could do to get her mind off Tess.

Still, when Frances strode in the nursery, Kasey felt a flash of resentment. By anyone's standards, Fran was a new mom's dream. She was plain-faced and frizzy-haired—but she was competent and comfortable and had twenty years of baby-care experience. And now, as always, her voice was kindly. "Well, I hate to interrupt you two, but you've got a telephone call, Mrs. Crandall. I'll take Tess. I left the phone off the hook in your husband's study."

For an instant Kasey considered balking, but then of course she moved; of course she relinquished Tess into Frances's capable arms. "Thanks, Fran," she said, knowing her attitude sucked from the look on the nanny's face.

She headed toward Graham's upstairs study, feeling guilty for being so difficult. So many people had been trying to help her, and instead of feeling grateful, she had the crazy urge to just grab the baby and disappear, hide Tess, rebel against everyone and everything.

Graham's study was his personal hideout, done up with red leather and dark paneling. Windows viewed the lake, where today the water was a broody, moody charcoal and the sky spitting snow. She hunched over the mahogany desk to switch on the banker's lamp and grab the phone.

"Kasey? It's Jake McGraw."

"Jake? What a surprise—hi!" She sank into Graham's oversize desk chair, forgetting the weather, forgetting that broody dark sky. She couldn't imagine why Jake was calling her, but just the sound of his low, masculine voice sent an edgy little hum thrumming in her pulse.

She hadn't forgotten kissing him—but he was an adult and so was she. Her whole world had been torn up that morning, and that's when Jake found her, and helped, and when he'd given that big red ball to Tess, something just cracked. She'd desperately needed someone to hold on to. Just for a minute. Just until she could get her sanity back. Jake couldn't possibly have known the whole picture, but he'd surely seen how upset she was.

That didn't totally excuse her kissing a man besides Graham—much less in her own eyes—but Kasey knew nothing like that would ever happen again. To regret that moment completely wasn't that easy, though. She couldn't remember feeling that rare precious sense of connection and trust for anyone else.

Jake immediately told her why he'd called. "I heard in the neighborhood that your Tess had some rough health news. I guessed there had to be something wrong the day I ran into you. And I know it's none of my business, but darn it, I had to ask—"

She sank deeper into the chair. "It's okay. I don't mind talking about it." Yet it seemed she had to swallow once, hard, to get started. "And you heard right. We got a very scary prognosis on Tess. But it isn't for sure. Right now, we're stuck playing a waiting game. The doctor said she really needs to be several months older before any tests can hope to be conclusive."

"That sucks. I'll bet the waiting's worse than hell," he said gently.

She had to swallow again. So many people had called over the last weeks. Friends, family, neighbors. Everyone had been kind, but they talked about the weather or doing lunch or community projects. No one let her talk about Tess. If she even mentioned the baby, they swiftly cut her off—probably to avoid upsetting her. But she'd felt so isolated that Jake's frank, quiet sympathy seemed to plug straight into her heart. "Oh God, you can't imagine."

He went on, his voice as soothing as salve for a burn. "Kasey…look, I probably have no way to help you. But it bothered me that I hadn't called before." He added swiftly, "Or called your husband."

"There's no reason you should have felt obligated."

"Obligated, no. But I'm not sure if I mentioned that I was studying some lawsuits involving several area hospitals, including Randolph. I'm sure they're unrelated—but could you tell me what's wrong with the baby?"

She rubbed a hand over her face. "They think she has something called Leber's. But they're wrong, Jake. They *have* to be. I just know—"

"Wait. Hold on, let me get a pen. Now say it again?"

"Leber's. Leber's Congenital Amaurosis."

"I'm writing it down, but damn…"

"What?"

"I'm afraid I never heard of it, Kase, I'm sorry. It's not like I wanted it to be one of the medical problems those other babies had. But I guess I'd hoped it'd be able to offer you information, something that might help—"

"It's okay." She hadn't been hoping anything.

"I'll look into it, though. See what I can scare up in research—"

Suddenly Kasey heard the baby cry. She didn't want to interrupt Jake—she wanted to keep talking with him. It was the first time in weeks she'd been able to openly discuss Tess, and Jake made it so easy. But Tess so rarely cried that her maternal instincts immediately kicked in louder than a three-alarm fire. "Jake—I appreciate your calling, more than you know—but could I talk to you another time? I really have to go."

She hung up swiftly and charged into the nursery. Frances had Tess on the changing table, fresh diaper in hand. "I should have known you'd hear her cry, Mrs. Crandall. Nothing's wrong. She just wet her diaper and didn't seem inclined to have it changed, that's all."

Still Kasey shot forward. Tess stopped shrieking when she sensed her mother's presence. Kasey automatically plucked the red ball from the crib and pretended to tickle the baby's tummy with it. That was all it took to quiet Tess.

Frances smiled, but then said firmly, "Now, Mrs. Crandall, you know Mr. Crandall wants you to have some free time in the afternoon, to rest or nap or read or whatever you need—"

"I'm not tired," Kasey insisted. "I'd like to play with Tess—"

Again there was a smile, this one even more kind. "Now, you're not worried that I won't take good care of the baby, are you? She's fine, Mrs. Crandall. And in a few minutes, it'll be time for her bath."

Because the baby was happy, Kasey acquiesced and headed downstairs to start dinner. Yet as she started hurling open cupboards and drawers, finding the ingredients for spaghetti with a walnut sauce and fresh pasta, she felt a bone-deep chill on the inside. No one was fooling her. She knew what was going on.

Graham wanted to separate her from the baby.

That was the reason he'd outvoted her and hired the nanny. The reason he'd spread the word to friends not to talk about the baby. The reason he'd brought her endless presents.

He was trying to help her face reality—the reality of their baby being abnormal. The reality of Tess belonging long-term in an institution. The reality that it would be hurtful—for Kasey and the baby—to become any more attached.

Graham was trying to be good to her, Kasey understood. He was even totally right—because she hadn't faced the reality of those things. Hadn't. Couldn't. Wouldn't.

Refused to.

An egg suddenly dropped from her hand and cracked on the kitchen floor, leaving a spattered, sticky mess. She crouched down with a rag to clean it up, wishing she could cry. She'd always been open and emotional, yet lately she felt so…alone. So isolated. It was stupid to feel this way, when she was safe in her castle, being cosseted right and left—but somehow there was no one she could talk to honestly.

Except Jake. His name seeped into her mind, slinkier than silk, and suddenly she realized that she was daydreaming about long, strong arms holding her—arms that were Jake's, not Graham's. His arms, where she felt secure, not Graham's. Him she hungered to talk to, not her husband.

She darn near dropped a second egg. She cleaned up the mess, feeling as if a shock of pepper had suddenly been thrown into her emotional soup. She was married. To a generous and wonderful man, for God's sake.

What kind of horrible woman was she, to be thinking about someone else? Even for a second?

Quickly she straightened up. For Tess's sake and her own, she needed to show some backbone and take control of her life again. It didn't matter what she thought of Jake. It couldn't.

CHAPTER 6

Jake pulled into his ex-wife's driveway, thinking that there should be a limit on how much penance a guy should have to pay. Yeah, he owed. For the wrongs he'd done, he'd probably never be done mending fences. But he'd rather break a toe, suffer the flu…anything…rather than endure a starched-shirt Christmas party at the Fitzgeralds'.

He climbed out of the car and trudged to the door, his face assaulted by stinging needles of snow. It was colder than a well-digger's ankle—not untypical of December—but the snow was already six inches deep and still coming. If he got stranded in Grosse Pointe for the night because of the weather, he was *not* going to be a happy camper.

He rapped on the door, and since no one in hell could likely hear him for the wind, knuckled it harder.

Paula opened it moments later. "You're saving my life," she said with a croak, which was probably the nicest thing his ex-wife had said to him in three years—but Jake noted wryly that she didn't go so far as to ask him in.

"Danny! Your father's here to pick you up!" she shrieked, and then hovered on the other side of the storm door.

Waiting for Danny, sleet pouring down his neck, Jake

considered that possibly he really *had* saved Paula's life—by divorcing her. There was little animosity between them now. More, an exhaustion. Back when, she'd been as enthusiastic and stupid about experimenting with sex and substances as he had. Paula, though, had dug up some character faster than he had.

He had no quarrel with her. Even when they disagreed— like over issues with Danny—he tried his best to shut up. And right now, with her nose brighter than Rudolph's and eyes squinty with fever, his only inclination was to offer her sympathy. But then Danny showed up. Jake almost didn't recognize him.

His son was wearing a button-down shirt; his hair was slicked back, and damned if Jake couldn't smell some lethal aftershave. More astounding was a smile that seemed to express genuine pleasure at seeing him.

"Dad—thanks. I didn't think you'd go for this," he mumbled.

"Hey, your mom's sick. I was glad to go if it was something you wanted to do." Amazing his nose didn't grow, that lie was so big, but hell. Danny had obviously spent hours spiffing up, made a real effort to look civilized on adult terms. He was clearly dying to attend this godawful Christmas party.

"Can I drive?"

"Sure." The roads were slicker than slides and Danny hadn't mastered night driving yet, but what was life without risk?

Flush-cheeked, Danny slid behind the driver's seat. "Cool outside, huh? With all the snow and all."

"Yeah, cool."

"I didn't think you owned a suit, Dad."

"I used to be a lawyer, remember? I just prefer to wear suits now only for funerals. And fun occasions like this."

"Huh?"

"Nothing, Danny." When his son skidded down the driveway and nearly did a 360, Jake cheered up. Maybe they wouldn't get there after all. "I think you'll find the stick shift was made for this weather. It gives you more control. Just take it easy... You know, you surprised me that you wanted to go to this."

"Because it's an old people party? I normally wouldn't, but the kids get the whole downstairs. And everybody'll be there that went to college. Like Laura. And Jason and Brian."

Laura, Jake thought. Kasey's stepdaughter. Now he understood why Danny was so hot to go. "I take it there'll be alcohol served downstairs?"

"I don't know."

"Sure you do," Jake said mildly.

"Sometimes there's beer. Nothing harder than that."

"Uh-huh. And what drugs?"

"God, you never let up, do you? You thinking about lecturing me, as if you were Mr. Saint near drinking and drugs?"

"No," Jake said, wishing he could kick himself for bringing up the subject. "I only asked out of curiosity...because I remember how Gary Fitzgerald's father used to handle his Christmas parties when your mom and I were young. There was always an open liquor cabinet downstairs. And something to smoke. He liked to think he was being a super tolerant dad by having that stuff around."

"Mom doesn't mind if I have a drink," Danny informed him defensively.

"If you're waiting for me to tell you not to, Danny, it won't happen. You're old enough to figure out what kind of role you want drinking and drugs to play in your life." When Danny swiveled on a turn and kept on swiveling, Jake jammed hard on the imaginary passenger brake. Even if his Honda was old enough for a cane and arthritis, it was still his only transportation, so it was a tad disconcerting to suddenly spin in a complete circle that included a curb and finished up stalled in the middle of an intersection.

"I'm sorry," Danny said guiltily.

"Nothing to be sorry about. It takes time to get comfortable driving in snow." When the gears screamed, Jake tried to exercise his jaw to see if it would still open. "Now that we've got some snow and ice, maybe we should try some extra practicing in a school parking lot on a Sunday."

"Hey. That'd be cool."

A miracle: He'd said something right. Unfortunately, the Fitzgeralds' house was already in sight. The place was postcard-perfect. Snow snugged on the windowsills of the red-brick house. Garlands and ribbons and ten zillion lights decorated the front of the place. And Mercedeses and Lexuses and BMWs lined the street—so many that Danny was going to have to parallel park.

"It's not a real good place to hit other cars, Danny. You want me to do the parking?"

"No. Come on, Dad, let me try. I've been doing fine!"

Yeah, he had. But not on ice and snow. Still, they'd been doing this for a couple months now, so it was going to get easier, right? Soon?

"See, Dad? I told you I could do it." Danny's eyes shone

with triumph. Jake figured they were a full foot away from the curb.

Close enough.

"Once we get inside, you can go off wherever you want…but I'll be around. Whenever you want to go home, just come and get me," Jake told him.

"Okay."

Danny disappeared pronto, leaving Jake trying to figure out a good place to hide. Only then he saw her. Kasey. He wasn't totally positive because he only saw the woman's back in the milling crowd—the slope of her neck, the swish of silky, rust-blond hair—but it was as if his pulse had been riding on a smooth road and suddenly hit a sharp bump. Hell. Why hadn't he thought? Of course Kasey'd be here. She was integral to the neighborhood now. And he should have been okay with seeing her—he felt good about the call he'd made weeks ago. He'd offered to help, but hadn't pushed, hadn't spilled his heart in her lap, hadn't let on the devil-brew of emotions she stirred up in him. He'd just offered sympathy, and for damn sure, she needed some.

But that was just it. She'd gnawed on his mind for weeks now. Was she okay? Were they still drugging her up? How was the baby?

A woman squeezed his shoulder. "Hi, Jake."

A man clapped him on the back. "Hey, Jake, how's your dad doing? And your mother?"

"Jake, you're looking damn good."

There was no place to hide. He'd grown up with most of these people—and most made a point of checking him out just to see if he was drinking again. In principle, he didn't mind, but he just didn't easily do party chitchat the way he used to.

"Jake!" Rona Fitzgerald, draped in red velvet and rubies, greeted him with a smile. "I'm so glad you came. Paula told me she was sick as a dog with the flu, but I knew Danny'd want to get together with the kids. They always have a blast at these things."

Yeah, they did—which was exactly why Jake couldn't avoid coming. The Fitzgeralds were permissive with what substances were allowed downstairs, but no kid was allowed to the party without a parent. That way, if there was a problem, the Fitzgeralds could shift responsibility onto the parents' shoulders. Rona wandered off with her tray.

The place smelled like a pine factory. Garlands climbed the staircase, and live Christmas trees flashed lights and satin balls in every room—even the bathroom. Mistletoe hung from most chandeliers, and even the white Bichon Frise chasing around had a Santa bow on her neck.

Years before, Jake remembered walking into this party— or others like it—thinking this was it. The good life. Everything he wanted. Good company, good friends, beauty, elegance. The irony was understanding that it was a fabulous life—for some. Just not for him. He knew damn well he'd end up drunk if he came back. He had to accept there were certain temptations he'd never be able to handle.

Food, thankfully, he could handle all day and into tomorrow. When he located the bulging buffet table, more people were clustered around it than bees in a rose garden—but that was still when he caught sight of Kasey again. He put some stuff on his plate, hoping that one of those offerings wasn't snails. He couldn't tell for sure, possibly because he wasn't paying that much attention. To the food.

Someone was handing her a drink. "Hey sweetie, how've you been? You look so beautiful, Kasey!"

"Thanks so much, you too…" Kasey accepted the drink.

Jake could see she had four more filled glasses hiding just behind her back—along with two plates of food that apparently someone had tried to push on her. She was wearing a long dress, such a dark green it was almost black, very tasteful and appropriate and totally unlike Kasey.

Every time she tried to move, someone else was in her face, smiling, being infernally nice.

"You've been all right, honey?" That was a husband and wife, flanking her. "We heard—"

"About Tess, I'm sure. We're fine, though. Both of us are fine—"

But the instant she mentioned her daughter—near anyone—the crowd either diverted the conversation or swiftly skedaddled from sight. Jake couldn't fathom why. God knew, they acted as if they really cared about Kasey. Maybe they thought the problem of a handicapped baby was catching? If they let her talk about it, it could happen in their families.

She suddenly spotted him, around someone's velvet shoulder, beyond someone else's jeweled ear. Her eyes lightened and she took a step toward him—but then she immediately stopped dead with a flush on her cheeks. That one instant, when she smiled at him, she seemed so honestly glad to see him. But then it must have occurred to her that rushing to talk to him, in this crowd, with his reputation, wasn't the wisest move she could make.

Leave her alone, Jake's conscience told him.

But he found himself filling a plate, slowly, then moving toward her, slowly, waiting for the hordes chitchatting with her to fade away. And finally it happened—she was alone.

Close up, he thought that somebody was trying to ruin the damn woman. The dress was bad enough, but she'd also lost a ton of weight. She was meant to have plump cheeks, not sculpted ones. Everything about her was starting to look as if she'd been raised in Grosse Pointe or Aspen. Her hair was brushed, for God's sake. Jewels winked in her ears and at her throat. The color in her face used to come from wind or life; now she looked as if a Beverly Hills cosmetic expert had sold her a bunch of damn fool classy products.

If he didn't notice the run in her stocking, he'd have worried that she was a complete stranger. And her eyes gave her away, of course. The first time he'd seen her, those eyes had startled him. Labeling her eyes blue didn't begin to explain the color of them. They were a special blue, like... pansy blue. Velvet-ribbon blue. Soft, woman-blue. Loving blue.

They still were. When he walked toward her, she met his eyes and didn't look away.

"Great party," he said.

"Sure is."

He pushed the food around his plate. Since he could eat almost anything, God knew why he'd stuffed the plate with sushi and octopus and snails. They all looked so...dead. "Man," he said gravely, "do I hate parties."

He earned a chuckle from her—not one of her openhearted Mae West laughs, but still, a good old honest giggle.

"Hoboy, so do I," she confessed in a whisper. Some neighbor with a snowman tie walked up, kissed her on the back of the neck, asked if she was finally ready to dump that stuffed-shirt husband of hers.

When the guy wandered off, an embarrassed flush climbed Kasey's throat. "It's just a joke. He doesn't mean it."

"I used to live here. I know the games, Kase." But he also knew any conversation was on borrowed time and he quickly turned serious. "In the meantime—how's our baby?"

Words poured out as if she hadn't been allowed to talk in a year. She and Graham had taken blood tests, because the only way Tess could have Leber's was if both parents had the same recessive gene. But the test came back and, as they'd been warned, unfortunately the results were inconclusive. Nobody had any other suggestions—except to wait. And nobody seemed to be sure of anything—except that their baby couldn't see—and that Tess wasn't moving around and developing motor skills the way other babies her age did.

"You're scared," Jake said quietly.

Again, her eyes met his. "Oh, God. Beyond scared."

"I'd feel the same way. Scared. And frustrated that I couldn't get any sure answers out of anybody."

"Exactly. Graham called another specialist. A friend of Dr. Morran's. But he said the same thing. The symptoms look just like Leber's, but for right now, there's nothing they can do, just wait and see how the baby develops." From nowhere, those unforgettable blue eyes suddenly looked as fierce as fire. "I don't believe them."

"You don't believe…?"

"The doctors." She pushed a hand at her hair, which finally made some of that formal, classy coif start to tumble. She looked like herself again. "There's no question she isn't seeing right. You shine a flashlight in her eyes, she doesn't even blink. But I know my baby, Jake. I *know* her. She's responsive. When I'm talking to her, playing with her, she looks alert. Normal. But everyone keeps saying that I'm in denial."

"Well. Are you?"

The question seemed to startle her. "God." She shook her head, tears suddenly glistening in her eyes, but there was life and animation in her expression, not sadness. "*Thanks*, Jake," she whispered.

"Thanks for what?"

"Thanks for not just automatically assuming that I'm out of my mind or can't face reality or can't have a valid opinion of my own. Thanks for treating me like a grown-up instead of a doll. People have been so nice that…that I just want to smack them."

"Sounds rational to me," he said wryly.

And then she did laugh. It was that exact sound he remembered from the second time he'd met her—the joy bubbling up from the inside, the life-lover, the kind of woman who danced in the rain…and who'd make love from the whole richness of her heart.

He didn't know where that last thought came from, but it clung to his mind like morning dew on a spiderweb, catching the light, refusing to let go.

And she looked back at him, as if the party had disappeared like the fade-out in a movie, sounds and sights muted, no one in her universe but him. Just him. The way no one had looked at him in a long time, if ever.

He didn't know he'd moved a step closer.

He didn't realize that she'd moved a step closer to him, either, until they were suddenly standing less than a foot apart. Eyes still locked together. The world still locked out. He didn't know what was happening—if he was going to touch her, if she was going to touch him. If she had something more to say, if he did. But that pull tugging him toward her was harder to stop than gravity.

And then suddenly, a voice intruded on that sylvan moment—just someone yelling. The party came back in focus, from a couple loudly smooching under the mistletoe, to the laughter echoing from the living room, to the snowy spill of frigid air when the front door opened.

"Dad?"

Jake reeled, hearing his son just behind him. Danny looked at him, then at Kasey. "Hey, Mrs. Crandall," he said politely. And then again, "Dad, you want to stay, doesn't matter to me, but I'm going home, okay?"

"I'll take you," Jake said immediately.

"It's not like I can't walk. It's just that I told you I'd say when I wanted to leave—"

"I'll take you," Jake repeated. "It's snowing like a banshee, no night to be walking."

Something was wrong. He could see it in his son's face. It was a good excuse to get away form Kasey, and he needed one. If he stayed even a second longer, he wasn't positive what he would have done.

Within minutes, he and Danny collected their coats and

said their goodbyes. Outside, the sting of icy sleet on his face felt good. Woke him up. Hard.

"Somehow I thought you'd want to stay longer. You wanted to see a bunch of kids, didn't you?" Jake asked as they climbed into the car. "The ones home from college for Christmas break—"

"Yeah, they were all there. Arguing about whether U of M or State is better. How great it is to be out of high school—like I didn't know that." Danny ground the gears, stalled, restarted. "I didn't have anything to drink, if that's what you were going to ask."

"I wasn't going to ask."

"Yeah, sure." Danny managed to work the car out of the parking space with only three start-and-stalls. "Laura's got a boyfriend."

"Oh, yeah?"

"Not from home. From Chicago or New York or somewhere. But they sound pretty tight." One quick glance at his dad. "Don't be telling Mr. or Mrs. Crandall. I don't know if she's told them about the guy."

"I wouldn't say anything. Not my business." But Jake got it now, why his son wanted to go home. If Laura Crandall had a guy, then the infamous crush of Danny's young life had moved out of the attainable dream class, maybe forever.

On the drive home, though, Jake kept thinking about Kasey. She had a man in her life. He had to remember that. For her sake—

And for his.

The Fitzgeralds' house had a solarium on the second floor, facing east. This late, this view was magical, with rooftops and trees all the way to Lake St. Clair dancing with Christmas lights and diamond-strewn snow. Initially Kasey stole up there to escape the party noise, but she could see the gambrel roof and second story of their house from the windows, and something about the view started to bother her. She kept staring, trying to identify what struck her as wrong.

Oh, hell. She rubbed her arms, knowing the only thing wrong was *her*. Jake had only left a few minutes ago. She had the strangest feeling that she'd been a pinch away from kissing him. Jake. Not her husband. And in the middle of a public party. For the craziest moment, she'd felt as if she were under some damn fool spell.

She rubbed her arms even more briskly, feeling shamed one second, mortified the next. Why on earth was she having so many impossible feelings lately?

"Kasey, what are you doing up here all alone? I want you to meet some people—the Rutherfords—"

Guiltily she twisted around at the sound of Graham's voice, almost catching her heel in the Berber carpet. "I just came up here because it was so pretty, looking out over the Christmas lights...."

That was a downright lie, which shamed her even more. She couldn't seem to do anything right lately. The whole feeling of estrangement between her and Graham was her fault. He'd been an angel, a Prince Charming for real. She was the problem. She'd avoided him, put Tess above everyone and everything in her heart.

She wanted to quit it. She wanted to do what was right. *Just remember*, her mother kept telling her, *how lucky you are to have Graham. It's tough, the problem with the baby, but at least you have the money to deal with it, and he's a good man who'll stay with you. Don't blow it, don't blow it, don't blow it...*

Her mother's mantra usually infuriated her—partly because it implied Kasey cared about Graham's money, and partly because her mother never seemed to have any kind of faith in her. Tonight, though, that mental refrain struck her as unsettling for a different reason. She *did* feel as if she were blowing it, failing to pull her half in the marriage. Deliberately she smiled at the couple coming up behind Graham.

"Kase, this is Jim Rutherford and his wife, Suz. I know I've mentioned working with Jim, and we were talking about putting a dinner together, maybe next week..."

"That sounds just great," Kasey said warmly. At a glance, she could see that Jim and Suz were the kind of couple who'd been together so long they'd started to look like each other. Both were tall and lean, with gray-tipped hair. Jim had the typical engineer squint, where Suz looked like she'd passed the training course in corporate-wife attire.

"They're both still new to Grosse Pointe," Graham was saying. "Just moved here two months ago."

"But I was working with your husband for months before that," Jim added. "He helped me find the right real estate agent, the right house, everything."

Instinctively Kasey cast a worried glance out the solarium windows again—but only for a second, not wanting anyone to realize she wasn't paying attention. Suz was talking about getting her kids, two high schoolers, then one afterthought who'd just turned ten, Bridget.

"Are your teenagers in Grosse Pointe North or South?" Kasey asked.

"South. And Bridget's at Kerby in the fifth grade."

"I love that school," Kasey said warmly. Yet like a nagging mosquito bite, her gaze strayed again toward the east windows. Her sudden twisting motion made a coaster drop from a table. Graham shot her a glance, as if to ask what on earth was bugging her.

So she tried harder. Suz was more than willing to be drawn out. She came from Bowling Green, attended K College, spent a year in Europe. Kasey read beneath the lines. Suz was at this party to cultivate the appropriate friends. She fully understood that the right connections could have a major difference on her husband's career.

"And you're from around here?" Suz asked her.

"No. I met Graham when I had a chance to work for him a couple years ago. Then…what can I say? He swept me off my feet."

Suz shot her a smile that Kasey had seen before—the one that said Kasey was smarter than she'd first thought, to land a man as successful as Graham. No one seemed to get it. She'd fallen in love with him. He'd fallen in love with her. Neither of them were thinking of money or lifestyles two years ago, and when Graham tucked an arm around her shoulder, acting loving, Kasey was reminded how wonderful they'd once been together.

"Graham mentioned a dinner," Kasey said. "Would you two like to come over, have an evening at our place?"

"This time of year, restaurants are so crowded." Graham's vote was clear. He loved to entertain, but only at home.

"And I love to cook," Kasey assured them, so the couple wouldn't think they were imposing. She was pulling this off, wasn't she? Doing her wife job. Business entertaining had always been important to Graham, and it was one of the few places Kasey had always felt she pulled her full weight in the relationship.

Jim said something. Suz laughed. Yet somehow Graham was frowning at her again. "Honey, is something wrong?" he asked her.

Kasey swallowed. She'd thought she was fooling him, but it seemed she couldn't even fool herself. All three of them had noticed that she was twisting her hands together—and her heart was pounding as if she'd just run a four-minute mile.

"I'm fine," she insisted cheerfully.

But hell's bells, she wasn't. Her gaze tore toward the solarium windows again. Finally, she realized what had been troubling her. One of the second-story windows she could see from here was Tess's bedroom. And that's what was wrong. The windows in Tess's bedroom were all black as pitch.

"*What* are you looking at?" Graham asked, no longer trying to hide his impatience.

"I left a light on. I always leave the light on in Tess's room—"

"Like a light matters, Kasey? For God's sake, the baby's blind. What difference does it make?" As if realizing he'd snapped at her, Graham quickly changed tones and jovially asked Suz and Jim if they skied in the winter—either cross-country skiing locally, or heading for Aspen for the real thing.

Kasey wanted to wince, aware she'd aggravated Graham yet

again, but it was like trying not to scratch a mosquito bite. Something was wrong. With Tess. No, she couldn't prove it; no, there was no way to logically explain it. But anxiety was clipping at her nerves with sharp scissors; she couldn't ignore it.

"So I told John Smithers—"

"Graham…" She touched his arm. She couldn't do this. She just couldn't. "I'll come right back, I promise. But I have to check—"

"*What* do you have to check? There's a baby-sitter right there, who would call us in a second if there was any kind of problem!"

She heard, she heard. As always, Graham was right, completely right. And, God, as she backed out of the room, apologizing, she felt lower than a skunk for being such a pain—but she still took off.

She found her coat on the bed in a back bedroom, but she couldn't find her boots and wasn't willing to waste time looking. She ran. Outside, it was blustering, blistering cold, the snow so thick and sludgy that it immediately sank into her dress shoes and stockings. Tears spilled from her eyes, freezing on her cheeks. She slipped, yet kept running.

If she was nuts, then she was just going to have to be nuts. Frances had the night off, but she'd given Kasey a long rundown on the substitute baby-sitter. Samantha was her name. A grandma-aged lady with kindly eyes. She'd seemed okay on first meeting, and as Graham kept claiming, Kasey couldn't be with the baby every second.

She knew he was right on that, as he was on everything else. But tonight, no amount of common sense could seem to calm her. She reached the back door, struggled with the knob, realized that it was locked—of course—and had to fumble in her evening purse for the key. It took punching all the stupid security numbers on the side before she could finally burst in—and immediately, she heard Tess.

The baby was crying upstairs. Really crying.

She took the stairs two at a time, vaguely aware of movement in the living room—Samantha, sitting up from the couch, looking groggy-eyed and half asleep—but Kasey didn't stop, didn't talk, didn't care.

She peeled off her coat, skidded in the long hall on her slick-damp shoes, kicked them off, galloped into the nursery. Yanked on the light. Almost that fast, the baby's screams turned into hiccups.

"It's me, darling, I've got you, I've got you…." Swiftly she scooped up the baby, noticing immediately that Tess was soaked, but more than that, her little body was hot. Not crying-hot, but fever-hot. "There now, I can see you're sick. Who'd have thought it? You were so happy this afternoon, love bug…"

Funny, but just like that, the anxiety disappeared. Obviously she was concerned that Tess was sick—yet still, she felt a huge wave of relief that she'd listened to her instincts. She'd known something was wrong, no matter how goofy other people thought she was being. And now she had things to do—peeling off the baby's damp sleeper, getting her temperature taken, a new diaper and fresh warm sleeper on…. "We'll get you something to drink in just a minute, sweetie, and then we'll see if you'll go for some medicine…"

At some point she sensed a shadow in the doorway and

turned. There was Graham, still wearing his coat, standing still as a stone, watching her.

"I'm firing the baby-sitter. Don't argue with me, Graham."

"I already sent her packing."

So at least on this, they agreed, but it wasn't enough. "See?" she whispered. "The baby really did need us. I wasn't imagining there was something wrong—"

He nodded. But he also pushed a tired hand through his hair and said quietly, firmly, "So you were right, Kasey. But this doesn't change anything. You can't be with her every second. It isn't good for her, or you, or us. We can't keep going on this way. You have to face the facts."

CHAPTER 7

"I'm sure you can see that my references are impeccable."

"I sure can," Kasey agreed.

"I've worked for some of the finest families in Grosse Pointe."

"I can see that." In fact, Kasey had dutifully studied Mrs. Elsabeth McLaughlin's entire five-page resume.

Right in the middle of the holiday madness, Frances had to quit when her mother fell ill. Graham hadn't pressed to hire a new nanny until the smoke of the New Year passed, but now there was a seven-inch stack of applications on the Queen Anne desk in the front sunroom.

Mrs. McLaughlin was candidate number four. The older woman straightened her collar again, sitting with impeccable posture on the white couch across from Kasey. "I strongly believe that a child should be raised with security and rules. No baby thrives without a set schedule—"

Kasey was listening, but when the telephone rang, she leaped to her feet faster than a jack-in-the-box. Instead of grabbing the receiver in the sunroom, she opted for the privacy of the phone in the hall. As expected, the caller was Graham. "Did Mrs. McLaughlin get there?"

"Oh, yes. I'm doing the interview right now," Kasey said cheerily.

"We can't keep going on without help."

"I know," Kasey agreed.

"I understand why you didn't want the first two nannies, sweetheart, but the last set of applicants looked exceptionally good."

"They sure look that way on paper," Kasey agreed.

"So…you think you're going to hire this one?"

"Um…can't tell quite yet, but I'd better get back to it." When she clipped back to the sunroom, Mrs. McLaughlin was delicately removing a thread from her navy blue skirt.

"I also believe that every child needs exposure to music and the arts, as well as a quota of fresh air every day. A little snow would never stop me from taking the baby for a daily walk." Suddenly there was a careful pause. "I must tell you the truth, though, that I've never worked with a damaged baby before. However, whatever alterations are needed in the schedule, I would be glad to make adjustments for."

"How thoughtful of you. And you're one of the strongest candidates who applied for the nanny position, Mrs. McLaughlin, I really appreciate your coming."

The lady stood up, recognizing the dismissal but looking flustered. "If there's anything else I can tell you—"

"No, no, I've heard enough. I'll let you know in a day or two, all right? And thank you for applying."

Mrs. McLaughlin smiled at Kasey. Kasey smiled back—as she steered the woman toward her coat and then the door. Maybe she hadn't been especially likeable—but her fate had been sealed tighter than glue the instant she referred to the baby as "damaged."

As if their hearts were synchronized, Tess let out a wail just as Kasey closed the front door. She pelted upstairs. Faster than lightning, she changed the baby's diaper and put on a day outfit. "First, we'll get you some breakfast, but then we're bumping this pop stand, short stuff, what do you say? Want to play hookey with Mom? And yeah, sooner or later we're stuck getting another nanny—either that or your dad will have a heart attack. But not her. And for right now, the day's all ours."

Twenty minutes later they escaped the house and took off for the car. Typically Kasey forgot her gloves, but the baby's hands were snuggled in an honest-to-God ermine muff. Blinding sunshine poured through the windshield. Last night's snow had virgined-up the landscape all over again.

Aiming down Kercheval toward the library, Kasey turned up the radio. "Just for the record, Tess, I believe in exposing you to music, too. I just think you should hear Chuck Berry and Bon Jovi as well as Beethoven. At least while we're in the B's. You okay with that?"

The baby blew a bubble in clear enthusiasm for all rock and roll, which encouraged Kasey to turn up the radio. At the first red light, she made funny faces for Tess, thinking that if anyone called her daughter "damaged" again, they just might not live to see the next sunrise.

It was a new thing, this feistiness. She kept waiting for guilt to bite her in the butt—when had she stopped being the courteous, basically kind person she'd always been? Instead, this new stubbornness seemed to have taken root in her character and sprouted like a weed.

The Grosse Pointe library loomed on the left. The snowy weather had chased off the regulars. She found a parking place right at the door.

"You know what we're going to do, Tess? We're going to deny all that reality everyone's so determined we face. We're going to deny. We're going to pretend. In fact, we're gonna pig out on some fairy tales, if that's okay with you."

The plan was okay with her daughter. All plans, Kasey thought a little desperately, were always okay with her daughter. Huffing and puffing, she carried Tess, the diaper bag, her purse and the baby carrier up the stairs into the deserted children's section of the library. Once their coats were peeled off, she settled the baby on her lap with a stack of picture books.

Graham, she knew, would consider her behavior loony tunes. Maybe it was, but because the housekeeper tattled everything she did to Graham, the easiest answer was to leave the house. No one ever bothered them at the library.

She read some Seuss, some Mercer Mayer and some Shel S. Tess listened with an enthralled if not downright brilliant expression. After a while Kasey picked up some fairy tales, but she hesitated when it came to *Beauty and the Beast*. "This one used to be my favorite story, Tess, but now I'm afraid it makes me uneasy. The heroine in the story was raised to obey her father. That doesn't seem a bad thing, does it?"

Tess didn't respond.

"Well, it isn't in principle." Kasey tucked her close. "But I grew up believing that was an unshakeable role. A good woman respected the breadwinner of the house. I was brought up to feel grateful, to avoid causing trouble, to accommodate the 'provider' of the household...."

Tess wasn't fussing. Still, Kasey suddenly felt restless. Leaving their books and belongings—it's not as if anyone would steal anything here—she wandered around the library with the baby, rubbing her back, cuddling her. The head librarian winked a hello at her; she winked back. Snow whispered down on the other side of the big front windows.

Perhaps by accident, she ended up ambling past the adult-fiction stacks into the reference section. It kept itching on her. The whole *Beauty and the Beast* story. Because lately it seemed everyone had been pressuring her to go along with whatever Graham and the doctors told her to do. Everyone, including her mother, seemed compelled to tell her that she was refusing to face her daughter's reality—when *damn it*.

Her daughter couldn't *see*. She'd faced that. She hated it, she was afraid of it, but she knew perfectly well Tess couldn't see.

The problem was that Kasey had grown up wanting to be the heroine in the *Beauty and the Beast* story. It was just now occurring to her that Beauty was so damned obedient that she'd walked right into the beast's lair—long, long before she knew he was an okay guy. It never occurred to the stupid girl to stand up for herself.

Kasey knew darn well she'd never stood up, either. It never occurred to her that she'd have to. She woke up every morning playing by the rules, trying to please her husband, studiously listening to the doctors, hearing the advice of well-meaning friends and family.

Only none of it was working. It didn't matter how much she obeyed, there was no happy ending in sight for Tess unless somehow, someway, some new answers showed up.

The reference section wasn't as comfortable as the kids' section. There were no big chairs to curl up in, just desks and computers and work setups for research.

As much as Kasey was determined to practice denial—hard-core denial—her gaze fastened on the research stacks as if drawn by a magnet. "You think you could be good for me for an hour, punkin? Could you try?"

"You're probably pissed I asked you to take off time from work," Danny said.

"No, I understand you're worried about the driving test." So far, Jake had been having a morning from hell. Barney was on a bloody rampage. The hard drive on his home PC had tried to up and die, right when he was strapped with a deadline. And then Danny called, fretting that some kid in his driver's ed class had flunked the test because he couldn't merge on the expressway. Danny was afraid the same thing would happen to him.

"I just want to go up and down the expressway a few times."

"It's all right," Jake repeated. Which it was. He didn't care about skipping an hour of work; he'd have jumped through hoops for Danny. And they'd been getting on so well. The last two times, they'd both gotten home without either of them suffering fresh injuries, emotional or physical. "There's a patch of ice on the corner—"

When Danny shot him a look, Jake resolved to say nothing more come hell or high water. The fresh snow was slicker than grease in places, but they'd been practicing in bad weather for weeks now. And once they got out of the suburbs and onto the freeway, the roads would be salted and—

"*Dad.*"

Aw, hell. The kid wasn't driving that fast, but the car suddenly fish-tailed. Jake turned quiet and calm. "You're doing fine. Don't panic. Take it easy, just don't jam your foot on the brake, don't…"

Aw, double hell. Once Danny jammed his foot on the brake, the car spun faster than a Tilt-A-Whirl. Terror passed in front of Jake's eyes, red as guilt, gray as pain. The car zoomed over a curb, up a stretch of snow-covered lawn, and crunched straight into a nice, big, old maple tree.

It was a very effective way to stop a car dead.

"Oh, God, oh God, oh God. I'm sorry, Dad. Really sorry. I swear I was paying attention. It was just the ice. I remembered about going with the spin and not fighting it, but I was just so scared—"

"Danny, for God's sake. You think I give a royal fuck about anything but you? You're all right. You're not hurt. Nobody's hurt. Nothing else matters. It's just a stupid car."

Two rotten hours followed. It was too darn freezing to stand outside, but an accident was an accident. Everything took time. The cops came. Danny was an underage practice driver—which meant that one accident risked his chances of driving for the next five million years, not to mention the cost of insurance. Danny, who never showed tears or fear in public, couldn't stop shaking. Jake's eight-year-old car, which truth to tell was hardly a virgin even before this virile encounter with a hard surface, just wasn't worth a major fix-it, yet a major fix-it was what it would need. Onlookers stopped, both to gawk and to help.

The only thing that seemed to fare okay through the deal was the tree. Maybe she'd been hit by cars before. Who knew?

Jake wasn't into conning cops, but hell. He hated, completely hated, seeing his son struggling so desperately to keep it together. "Look, he's just learning to drive, and that patch of ice was impossible to see. It really wasn't his fault—do you really have to report this?"

The cop, thank God, was a dad. Right or wrong, he agreed that, as long as no one else was involved, maybe a report didn't have to go on file. They were both frozen solid by the time they could take off, Jake behind the wheel this time. He turned the key, offered up several prayers when the baby started, then slowly backed up off the lawn and onto the street again.

"Danny," he said carefully, "accidents happen to the best of drivers. No point in wallowing in guilt about it. The best thing you can do with a mistake is try to learn from it."

"Your car's going to cost a ton to fix," Danny said.

"It's all right."

"Yeah, if insurance would pay for it. But you can't put it on your insurance because of me."

"That kind of thing is my problem, not yours. It's okay. Really."

"You're mad at me."

"No, I'm not."

"You have to be really pissed."

"No, honestly, Danny, I'm—"

From nowhere, his son's small quaking voice gained ten octaves and turned into a bellow. "*Damn it, Dad! I hate this! Would you quit putting up with shit from me? It's driving me crazy!*"

Jake's jaw dropped. For darn sure, his son had given him

relentless grief. For darn sure, he'd tried to respond with relentless patience—partly because he owed Danny for all the years he'd been a lousy dad, and partly because Jake had assumed his son needed understanding from him.

But apparently not.

"Look," Danny said in an exhausted tone, "I've been giving you nonstop crap. I'm sick of being mean to you, but I'm even more sick of you putting up with it. You preach all the time about how important it is to be honest, but you're the one not being honest. I wrecked your car. You have to be mad about it. Come on. Just say it."

Jake had to swallow to get past a dry lump in his throat. Then said, "I'm ticked off. I need a new car but I can't afford one. And now, damn it, the repairs on this are going to set me back again."

Danny snapped, "Now say, And you can damn well pay for it."

Jake said quietly, "And I sure as hell think you should help me pay for some of the repairs."

Both fell silent, son looking at dad, dad looking at son, it seemed with different eyes. Jake only wished he really knew what was in Danny's head—and heart—but he had hopes the kid was turning into a better man than he'd been. And Danny—just conceivably Danny was picking up the idea that there might be more to his father than the alcoholic who'd let him down years ago.

Eventually Jake put the car in gear and drove Danny home—but he hesitated when they reached the driveway. "Do you want me to come in and tell your mother?"

"Of course I want you to tell Mom. She's gonna freak. It'd

be a lot easier if she screams at you instead of me." Danny climbed out of the car. "But I'll tell her. It's my problem. I did it."

Damn, Jake thought. That kid was turning into a decent man. Owning up. Standing up. Although Jake strongly suspected that Danny was going to walk straight to the nearest bathroom to hurl.

Accidents could do that to a guy.

He turned down Kercheval, but he was too edgy to go back to work and too wired to head back to his silent condo. He hit a red light at the library, and flicked on his turn signal, thinking he'd aim for home via Lakeshore. Drumming his fingers on the steering wheel, he mentally sifted through the list of things he needed to do—the fix-it places he needed to call for his car, the rental he'd better line up, the article he still had to finish tonight… He glanced impatiently at the red light again and caught sight of a rusty-blond head in the library window.

Kasey.

When he first walked in, the sudden blast of heat felt smothering after the blister-cold outside. And unlike the stereotypical library, this one was hopping and noisy. High-schoolers had obviously just descended on the place to do their homework. Coats and boots were strewn everywhere, the whole place smelling of wet wool and books. He ducked around moms trying to settle their preschoolers and scholarly ladies cluttered around the art and history sections.

He found her in the back. She'd claimed a table in the research section. The baby was propped in a car seat, typically dressed like royalty and draped in soft blankets, and damned if the red velvet ball wasn't between her little hands. His ball. The one he'd gotten her.

He saw Tess. He saw everything. But the only thing that ransomed his real attention was Kasey.

She'd obviously been here a while, because papers and periodicals and books were heaped high around the baby. Somebody'd let her get so model-skinny that clothes were starting to hang on her—but except for weight, she looked more like herself. Her hair was an unbrushed tumble; her shirt a wild geometric print. She wore no makeup, but a winter-red flush colored her cheeks.

As if sensing him, she glanced up the instant he walked in—and immediately smiled. A winsome, radiant smile. An honest-to-Pete, I'm-so-glad-to-see-you smile. And suddenly his heart was thumping and his pulse frolicking like a fuzzy-chinned teenage boy's.

Oh, hell. This was exactly why he'd tried to stay completely away from her. The magnetic response to Kasey was getting worse, not better. A man only got so many chances, and he'd used up all of his. But Jake swore that any man would be thrilled to risk hellfire and torture both for one of those wild, soft Kasey smiles.

"Will you look what the blizzard brought in?" she murmured wryly. "I can't believe the riff-raff allowed in the library these days. You here to do some special work for your paper?"

"Nope," he said. "I'm here to see you."

One look at him and Kasey's pulse started to whistle. Snow glistened in his hair. His face had tired shadows, but it was impossible not to respond to those beautiful, compelling eyes. And she saw—felt—the way he looked at her.

It was impossible to ignore the fact that something "not okay" happened every time they saw each other. Not okay for him. And not okay for her.

But life surged through her the way it hadn't in weeks, just because he was in the same room, just because he was here to talk to. Just because he was Jake. "Me?" she echoed. "Why would you come to see me? How did you even know I was here?"

"I didn't. I was driving past and accidentally saw you in the window. I was hoping to catch up with you sometime. Soon. So when I saw you, it just made sense to try." He shrugged out of his leather jacket. "You got a few minutes?"

"At this point, only a few. I've been here most of the afternoon, and have to be home by five."

"Okay. I'll be quick." He had to move some books to get close enough to buss Tess on the forehead. "Hey, beauty. How's my favorite girl? And what on earth are you being quiet for? Don't you know it's a baby's job to scream bloody murder and embarrass your mom in public?"

Kasey wanted to suck in a breath. He talked to Tess so naturally. He'd said he was scared of babies, and maybe he was. But everyone else treated Tess as if she were contagious. And Graham...she understood why Graham didn't want to get too close, but it still ached. He didn't seem to love his daughter. And his distance motivated Kasey even more to love Tess extra, touch Tess extra, because no one else did.

Even if the baby couldn't see, she turned toward the sound of Jake's voice. She offered him one of her most lethal femme-fatale smiles. Again, Kasey felt her heart catch. Like everyone else, he knew that Tess wasn't perfect, yet he still treated her like she was a…a baby. A human being.

Suddenly his gaze left the baby and pinned hers. "What I wanted to talk to you about was the research I'd done on babies and lawsuits. When you first gave me the diagnosis, I didn't think I had anything relevant. And I'm not sure I do now. But I've come across a few things I thought you might want to know."

"I do." She immediately leaned forward.

"When I started those articles, it was because I'd found an epidemic of lawsuits. So I assumed I'd find a reason—like that there was some new disease hitting babies. Or some procedure being used on newborns that had side effects. Or that we had some terrible doctors that somebody'd better catch damn fast before they did any more harm."

"And did you find any of those things?"

"No. Stranger yet, I found exactly the opposite. I found doctors with extraordinary credentials. Who care deeply about their patients. In the hospitals with outstanding records. But what I *did* find was that there was an odd similarity in the babies' problems."

"What?" Her heart leaped with hope.

"Kasey, this may have nothing to do with Tess."

"I know. You said. But what was the similarity?"

"This Leber's that Tess was diagnosed with—it happens to be a condition that a doctor can't be blamed for."

She frowned. "You're right. It can't. The condition has to be inherited, so there's nothing any doctor could do to save her from this—"

He nodded. "And that's the point. The common link. In fact, it's the only link in the other babies' problems as well."

"I don't understand."

He hunched forward. "Kase, in the last ten years, malpractice premiums more than doubled. And obstetricians carry some of the highest malpractice rates, because nobody can stand it when something goes wrong with a baby. Maybe it's the fear, or the hopelessness, or the panic of new parents. But if something goes wrong with a baby, even when the parents know it's beyond the doctor's control, they still sue."

Tess dropped the red ball. Jake automatically picked it up and handed it back to her. "So. We've got ourselves a mess. Both doctors and insurance companies are set up to lose— unless doctors only take on perfect patients who thrive. Nobody can die. Nobody can have a sickness that modern medicine can't cure. Or they risk huge costs. You with me so far?"

"Yes."

"There's an extra problem with a hospital like Randolph— simply because it's an outstanding facility. They're stuck with a Catch-22, because patients with unusual or difficult problems are likely to want those doctors. So they're more at risk of lawsuits than everyone else. Not because they're bad physicians. But because they're good."

Kasey frowned harder now. "I understand, totally—but I'm still unsure how this could relate to Tess—"

"I'm not sure it does. But let me give you a hypothetical situation." He gestured. "Let's say a baby was born at Randolph Hospital with a heart problem. Let's say this problem could be caused by a genetic defect—or by something that goes wrong in the birth process. Either way, the treatment for the child is the same. But which reason do you think the doctor is going to tell the parents?"

Now her heart did leap. "You're saying that doctors could feel forced to lie?"

"Yeah. That's exactly what I think is happening. I don't believe an ethical doctor would normally choose to cover up the truth, or alter a diagnosis. But with the high cost of malpractice insurance and lawsuits, I think society is essentially forcing them to do just that."

"So…you think there's any chance that happened with Tess? That she really doesn't have Leber's?"

Maybe it was the look in her eyes that made Jake reach over and grasp her hands, warmly, firmly, quietly. "No. Kasey, *no*. Don't get your hopes up that fast. All I'm saying is that many of the lawsuits I studied turned out to have a common denominator. A medical condition that was difficult to blame a doctor for. A medical condition where the cause could be attributed to something else. Or a medical condition where the symptoms could lead to several possible diagnoses."

"But that *could* mean that Tess didn't have Leber's. That she has something with symptoms that *look* like Leber's, but wouldn't automatically have to be so serious—"

"I don't know that, but I think it's worth asking the questions."

As if suddenly realizing how tightly he was holding her hands, he loosened his. "Have you personally seen Tess's birth records?"

She shook her head. "No. There seemed no reason to. I mean, the doctors we've talked to have seen them. And in the hospital, they told me after the birth that the Apgar scores were high. No one led me to believe that Tess's problems had anything to do with the labor or delivery."

"And that's probably right. But you have every legal right to call the hospital and get a copy of those records. They'll give you a bunch of grief, Kase. I know the system. Legally, you're entitled to a copy. You just have to sign a release and…damn it, don't look at me like that."

"Like what?"

"You know like what," he grumped.

Kasey hesitated. He was right. She knew what she was suddenly feeling. A glugging, welling, wild case of hope—for the first time in weeks, maybe months. And it was all Jake's doing—not because of the information he'd brought her, but because he was listening to her, taking her side. The way no one else had in…forever.

She wasn't aware of getting up until she saw his gaze narrow. Wasn't aware of whipping around the library table until he said, "Damn it, don't, Kase," in such a gruff, low whisper that her heart suddenly stalled out completely.

For that space between heartbeats, she was still impulsively going to kiss him. For that space between heartbeats, her mouth was less than inches from his mouth, her eyes less than a ruler's reach from his eyes. It wasn't wrong, not by any values or ethics she knew, to touch someone who'd expressed kindness and caring to her. It was no disloyalty, no infidelity.

But there was suddenly something in that space between heartbeats. A kick of fire that didn't belong. The zest of longing and desire. The hunger for someone to intimately connect to.

She knew she'd felt something sexual for Jake before. But she'd sloughed it off as something an adult woman could handle. Now…she wasn't sure. Worse yet, she saw the echo of the same emotions in Jake's face—the same awareness, the same fierce battle for control.

Kasey swallowed hard. She stopped moving closer, stopped moving at all. As if talking to someone in a foreign language that only the two of them knew, she said, "I'm sorry."

Jake said hoarsely, "So am I. Damn it, Kasey. So am I." And then he grabbed his jacket and left.

CHAPTER 8

Kasey frowned at the clerk in the medical records office. "I don't understand. I had the baby on August first. Right here, in Randolph Hospital. My obstetrician and pediatrician are here. I had all my lab work done here. You've sent me bills, I've paid them. How could you possibly have all my records except for that one day?"

"I'm sorry." The young woman looked exasperated. They'd been wrangling for the last half hour. "But I checked the computer three times. I've got all the patient records except for August first."

"But that doesn't make sense. How could you have everything else but that one day?"

"Like I keep saying, I don't know. All I can tell you is that there's no record of any Crandall in the system that day. Did you check with the obstetrician's office?"

"Yes, of course I checked with Dr. Armstrong. That's where I went first. And then I went to Dr. Morran's office. Everyone sent me back here. All I'm trying to find is the medical information about my labor and delivery. You billed me for the procedures. You have to have the records!"

"I'm sorry, Mrs. Crandall, but there's nothing else I can do. I can't find something that doesn't exist!"

Kasey lifted a hand. "Okay, okay. I'm sorry to bug you."

She turned toward the elevators. There was no point in continuing to fight a lost battle, but she was reeling on the inside. She'd battled different hospital departments for the last four hours, getting nowhere. Were the records really lost?

Or had someone made them disappear to hide something about Tess's condition?

By the time she trudged into the hospital parking lot, it was past four-thirty. The roads were slushy, traffic querulous, horns blaring and streetlights glaring against a gloomy gray afternoon as she drove home. Anxiety drummed through her pulse. She wanted to call Jake—tell him about the lost records, talk to him, see if he had any ideas about where to go from here.

It shook her up how often this was happening. Her wanting to call Jake, not Graham. Her wanting to tell Jake something important, before Graham.

She wasn't falling in love with Jake, she told herself fiercely. She couldn't. Wouldn't. Ever let it happen. Maybe a few cracks had shown up in the palace, but her Prince Charming wasn't totally to blame. She wanted Graham to love Tess. He didn't seem to. She wanted him to accept Tess. He couldn't seem to. But Kasey had spent hours researching families with handicapped babies now. Both parents rarely came to terms with a traumatic problem at the same speed. And some people were just more freaked by a handicap than others—maybe that wasn't admirable, but it was human.

She'd been judging him, Kasey knew. And the minute she

parked the car, she hurried into the house, determined to call Graham—not just to tell him about the lost hospital records, but also to work on the rift between them.

"I'm afraid he's in a meeting, Mrs. Crandall," Graham's secretary told her. "Do you want me to interrupt him?"

"No, no, that's okay. I'll just catch him when he gets home."

She didn't mind waiting. It gave her time to play with Tess and change clothes. She charged upstairs calling, "Robyn!"

The plump college student emerged from the nursery with a half-naked Tess. It was clearly bathtime. "Has she been good?"

"Our angel? Of course she's been good." Robyn had gentle eyes and a round, sunny face. Her Pooh sweatshirt matched her floppy socks.

Kasey had balked at hiring a live-in nanny until finding her—primarily because the young woman had seemed to fall in love with Tess from the start, but also because they made a good team. When Kasey wanted to spend time with the baby, Robyn studied or did other chores.

Tonight, especially, Kasey was thankful for the help. Time invariably got away from her when she was giving Tess her bath, but Robyn was right there to take the baby so she could change. By the time she heard the front door open, she'd battled with her hair and makeup and redressed in slacks and a subdued sweater. She went downstairs to greet Graham, determined to be with him the way she used to be.

He was beat, she could see right off the bat. So she kissed him, poured him a short scotch, and then fussed in the kitchen with his favorites for dinner. Slowly he seemed to relax, and afterward, they ambled into the living room. Graham was the first to start talking.

"You've got something on your mind, Kasey, I can tell."

"Yeah, I do," she admitted, as she curled up next to him on the white couch. "I want to talk to you about something serious—but I didn't want to spring it on you the minute you walked in."

"Well, shoot, darling. I'm fine."

He seemed to be just that. Fine. They used to do their after-dinners just this way, curled up with their fresh mugs of coffee, just talking, with the soft lamplight behind them and no distractions. So she told him about the hospital losing the medical records.

Faster than the click of a trigger, Graham went quiet and his smile died. Finally he said, "I don't understand—why were you asking about the records?"

"To find out if there was anything we didn't know. Anything that might help Tess. Anything that could be a factor in her medical condition."

Graham set down his coffee mug, as quietly as a tiptoe. "You did this without asking me?"

She sensed troubled waters, but wasn't sure why. "Graham, all I did was go to the hospital and ask for our records. I didn't think that was anything requiring a big discussion—"

He didn't let her finish. "I think you should see a psychologist."

"What?"

"Kasey," he said firmly, "you can't seem to accept that the baby isn't normal—and is never going to be normal. I'm not going to insist this minute that we put her in a permanent institutional situation. I understand how hard this is for you, but the more you become attached to the baby, the harder it's going to be, for her and for you. I thought giving you some time would help, but that just isn't working. Look, there's no reason to feel bad you can't handle it."

Her stomach knotted up tighter than a lariat. "I don't feel bad—"

"Everybody needs help sometimes. Especially when a problem is as overwhelming as this one. Sweetheart, this is eating you up."

"Of course I'm worried about—"

Again he interrupted. "She's been to two doctors now. Both extremely reputable specialists in their field. Both of whom consulted with other specialists in the hospital, and Randolph's one of the best hospitals anywhere. And both said exactly the same thing."

"I know that, Graham." God, her mouth was suddenly so dry she could hardly get the words out. "But neither of the doctors were absolutely positive of the Leber's diagnosis—"

"Yes. But they also told us that a definitive diagnosis wouldn't be possible until Tess got old enough to do a more complete evaluation. And neither held out a lick of hope, Kasey, you know that. That's harsh, but it's her reality. Our reality. And it's a reality that we both need to face if she's going to be severely retarded. I resent your going behind my back. Going to the hospital without even asking me."

Kasey didn't know what to say, but at four in the morning she found herself pacing the hall upstairs, unable to sleep. A blizzard-cold wind battered the windows and sneaked under the doors, yet there was a hot ache in her heart that refused to ease.

It was impossible to argue with Graham, when there was every chance he was right. Doctors, friends, family, all seemed to believe the same thing—that she was denying reality, trying to see silver linings where there weren't even clouds. Denial was a common phenomenon with parents of handicapped children.

For that matter, how could she possibly know better than everyone else? She wasn't a doctor. She wasn't an anyone. She was just a mom—and a first-time inexperienced mom at that.

Yet when she tiptoed into the nursery and stood over Tess's crib, she was hit with a wave of protectiveness bigger than a tsunami. Maybe her heart *was* swayed by love for the baby. Maybe that love colored everything she did… But what was going to happen to Tess if Kasey didn't stand up for her?

She closed her eyes, feeling a keening on the inside. Graham had frightened her. Her own husband. The man she'd sworn to love, honor and cherish… But God, tonight, she'd felt intimidated talking to him. Threatened. Still did. So much so that she couldn't sleep and couldn't lie next to him, not this night.

He'd made her feel as if she were a servant—as if she needed to ask permission to call a doctor or go to the hospital or make a decision independently about Tess. And though he hadn't specifically said it in words, Kasey had heard a threat in his voice.

Graham would put the baby in an institution if Kasey didn't start playing by the rules. His rules.

Four o'clock passed. Then five. Then six.

By the time a watery sun poked over the winter horizon,

Kasey was downstairs cooking breakfast—fresh blueberry muffins, hazelnut coffee, an omelet with a dollop of cheese and chives. When Graham wandered into the kitchen, he immediately noticed all the fuss she'd made.

She got a kiss. And a big smile. "What's all this?" he asked.

"I was awake early, just wanted to make you some special treats," she said. When she turned around with a plate, though, she caught a quick reflection of her face in the toaster. For that instant, it seemed that she had her mother's smile, her mother's voice. That *look* that Kasey had sworn she'd never have.

But then, growing up, she'd never understood what motivated a woman to play by the rules.

Now she did.

"This place is a dump," Danny grumped, carrying two whopper-size bags of trash as if his back were breaking under the load.

"Uh-huh." Jake continued punching in computer keys.

Minutes later, Danny passed by him again, this time carrying Windex and Pledge, rags sticking out of every pants pocket like cowlicks. "You used to make millions of dollars as a lawyer, for Pete's sake. Now you got nothing. No DVD. No BMW. Nothing cool."

"Uh-huh."

A half hour later, Danny showed up in the doorway again, this time passing through with a laundry basket and a scowl. "Besides which, you're a slob. Your shirts are all wrinkled. You never said I'd have to learn to iron out of this deal. I'm a guy, for God's sake. This is inhuman. This is like slavery. This is like cruel."

"Uh-huh." As soon as Danny trudged out of sight, Jake let a grin loose. Never mind all the insults. Having his son here, part of his life, was worth gold.

In principle, Danny was working off his debt for the accident. Repairs on the ancient Honda ran a disgraceful $935. Paula didn't want Danny working unless his grades came up, and as Danny had put it, he'd never in hell bring his grades up as long as he had Mr. Anderson for Physics—so that left working off the debt some other way. The deal Danny proposed was $15 an hour for chore-type labor. Cleaning. Cooking. Of course the kid didn't know how to cook or clean, but so what?

Behind him came a thud, then swearing, then, eventually, the sound of a hard rock tune being whistled off-key.

Jake grinned, but he also kept punching the computer keys. For days now, he'd used his free time to hound a certain Internet newsgroup, a place where attorneys hung out. He knew a fair number of the local players from his own lawyering days—enough to distinguish the ambulance chasers from the legit legal eagles. He'd plugged in Randolph Hospital, Tess's symptoms, the docs' names, asked for anything anybody could give him. So far, no cigar, but suddenly...

Hell, suddenly he got a bite. He hit Print, then hunched over the screen. There it was. A case. Seven years ago. Randolph Hospital, Doc Armstrong, a baby born blind, with other physical and mental problems implied. The cause related to oxygen delivered at birth. Too much oxygen? Too little? Why did a newborn kid need oxygen for any reason, anyway? But the point was...

Jake swallowed hard. The point was that the condition was caused by pilot error. Not by Mom or Dad or genetics or chance. But by something one of the medical team had done wrong in the delivery room.

"Dad?"

Jake heard his son, but right then was too busy to answer. He punched off the Internet connection and reached for the landline. Okay, okay, so he shouldn't know Kasey's phone number by heart. But he did. He'd never intended to call her—the last time they were together, they both realized they were flirting with disaster. But this was totally different. This was information about the baby. And if Graham answered the phone, Jake intended to relay the same information.

But it wasn't Graham who answered the first ring. It was a molasses-rich voice with a hint of a lilt and a promise of laughter in the tone. It was a voice that made him think of sunshine and satin. Of sex. Of her smile and her eyes.

"It's just me. Jake McGraw." He pinched his brow as if inducing a little solid pain could obliterate those idiotic fantasies from his mind. He told her about the kid, the oxygen, the lawsuit. "…In fact, the parents won a bundle. This is the same hospital you went to, the same doctor. And the symptoms sound darn close to what Tess seems to have."

For a moment there was an odd silence at the other end, and when Kasey spoke again, he could barely hear her. "I found out something, too. I wanted to call before to tell you…the hospital lost the medical records. Not everything— but all the medical records related to the labor and delivery."

"Damn," Jake said and sank back, cocking a foot on his desk. "I don't believe it. That they really lost them."

"Neither do I."

"It sounds as if they knew they had something to hide. Something that happened during labor or delivery. Hell, Kasey, maybe it really is just like that case with the oxygen."

"That's what I thought the minute you told me about— darn, I'm sorry. I have to go."

Jake heard a click, and the connection went dead. He stared at the phone for a minute, worrying why she'd suddenly started whispering, why she'd cut him off so abruptly.

"Who you talking to?"

Jake swiveled to face his son. "Just a friend."

"A woman, huh? You like her?"

Jake's first instinct was to duck the question, but instead found himself voting for honesty. "Yeah, I like her. But she's married. Off limits. So it was just a friendship call, to give her some information I thought she needed."

"Uh-huh. Sure." Danny sighed. "Well, can you tell me what creemee broolee means?"

"Beats me. How do you spell it?"

"Creme brulee. I think it's some kind of dessert."

"Yeah, it is. But I think that baking something that complex may be just a hair beyond your skill level, sport."

"But you put it on fire at the end. Doesn't that sound cool? If I have to learn to cook, it might as well be fun, you know?"

"Yeah, but the way it normally works in life, you're supposed to master mac-and-cheese before you move to crème brûlée. But hell, if you want to try it, go for it. Just try not to burn down the apartment."

It was over an hour before he smelled smoke. Naturally,

at that first whiff, he tore into the kitchen faster than an electric charge, but right off—thank God—he could see the fire wasn't bad. Bad, now, bad was a definition for the rest of the kitchen.

On its best day, his apartment lacked any claim to fanciness. Minimalism was in, though, wasn't it? He had a couch. A lamp. The dark blue Oriental carpet had been his grandmother's, and his mother—unfortunately—had donated the godawful hand-painted dishes when he first moved in.

He could have lived nicer. In the beginning—after the divorce, after getting substance-free—he was barely eking a living. Still, he'd been stashing savings away for two years now, and somehow hadn't gotten around to filling up the place. The thing was, he had a priceless luxury with the view. Winter and summer both, his desk was set up with an unshuttered, un curtained view of the Detroit River. There were always lights at night, always freighters and boats to watch during the day.

He'd come to love the river, and most of the time he just didn't notice the rest. Who cared if the kitchen was closet-sized with appliances that wheezed and moaned from old age? The Formica counters were pink—which *did* offend him—but picking out new counters always seemed a worse fate than living with what he had.

Right now, though, that sissy-pink was completely covered with burned sugar, cream, egg shells, bowls and dripping spoons. An open cookbook was starting to sizzle at the edges, and the stove…oh, God, the stove. Danny cast him a frantic glance even as he used a dish towel—not the best defense in town—to spank out the sparks. In one second flat, Jake could see his son was near meltdown.

"Hey," he said mildly. "You burn yourself, I'll be ticked, so don't."

"Dad, I—"

"Fire extinguisher. Front hall closet."

"I got it, I got it—"

No big deal. Three more minutes and the fire was out. The stove looked like the inside of a medieval fireplace and the stink could damn near put hair on your chest, but nobody got burned, nothing got ruined that anybody cared about. The kid, though, kept shooting him these anxious looks, until Jake started laughing at the mess.

And when Jake started laughing, Danny first looked shocked, but then he started laughing, too.

It had been years since they'd laughed like this. Free. Easy. The kind of laughing when you're not afraid of someone looking over your shoulder and judging you. The kind of laughing that hurt your stomach and made you hiccup and still you didn't want to stop.

Finally.

Of course, as savored as that laughter was, it didn't remotely help clean up this hopeless Armageddon. "I suppose I'd better do something about this," Danny said finally, but hesitated, as if praying to get rescued.

God knew Jake wanted to do that rescuing. But damn, he was trying to be a better father these days. "This is the thing, Danny. When I was growing up, my parents gave me everything, covered my butt even when I didn't need it. Teachers catered to me. And I know it's hard for you to believe, but I used to be almost as good-looking as you, so I got the girls, too. Problem was, I grew up feeling entitled. Like I didn't have to earn anything. Like I could always duck from consequences."

Danny nodded gravely. "Yeah, and your point?"

"The point is that you wrecked my car. So you need to pay for what you did. I know character is an ugly, boring word. But somehow you've got to grow up having more character than I did. You don't want to make a mess of your life the way I did, do you?"

"Dad," Danny said wearily, "I learned before I was ten not to answer bullshit questions coming from parents like that. They're always ugly. They're always a setup to make a kid eat dirt and learn some crappy lesson that he never wanted to learn to begin with."

"Yeah, they are. I'm sorry."

"Besides which, I like that entitlement idea."

Jake nodded. "I did, too."

"And I like the idea of getting stuff for free. Having somebody cover your butt. Not having to pay the consequences."

"Yeah, I did, too."

"Besides which, all I wanted to know was whether you were gonna help me clean up the kitchen or not. I didn't need the lecture. I just need the answer."

"Well, of course I'm going to help you clean up. Christ, I wouldn't leave a dog to handle this alone."

Another laugh. Another genuine laugh out of his son. Two in one day, and all they'd cost was a destroyed kitchen and a $935 dent. The cheapest prices Jake had ever paid for anything.

He'd have been downright euphoric if answers for Kasey were findable this easily. But when she called three days later, she shook his life up one side and down the other…and in ways he had no way to prepare for.

Sometimes Kasey thought she was making headway with Laura. Over the holidays, Laura had stopped by to see the baby, occasionally stayed for an evening without too much warfare. And this morning, when she'd called to say she wanted to spend the night at home because she had tickets for a concert at Cobo Hall, Kasey had leaped to say yes, hoping for another chance to make friends with Graham's daughter.

Until Laura walked in the door, though, she'd never mentioned that she was bringing a friend. A male friend.

"So where's the pipsqueak?" Laura demanded before she immediately spotted the candy-striped blanket in Kasey's arms. She was just climbing downstairs to join Graham for his pre-dinner drink in the den. "What are they doing to you, Tess? You're growing like a weed. Stop it. I just saw you a couple weeks ago and now you're practically huge," she cooed, and then to Kasey, "This is Murray Pelnik. He's spending the night, too, okay?"

"Of course it's okay. How are you, Murray?" Once Laura took the baby, Kasey went over to shake the young man's hand, thinking, Oh God, Graham's going to have a heart attack.

"Hey," Murray said.

The boy had longer hair than Laura's, worn in dreads. Possibly he'd washed it since the new year. Both kids wore jeans, but Murray's dragged on the ground. His mustache looked like weeds in a desert, and the hemp necklace was a finishing touch on his sense of style. Laura filled in the rest of the bad news. Murray was two years older. Sociology major. Liberal. Non-WASP.

Kasey had her doubts that the boy would survive dinner with Graham.

"I've told you guys before how much I hate the dorm. That's how I got to know Murray. He's got a spare room I could rent, so I'm thinking of moving my stuff over to his place," Laura said blithely.

"Your dad will be so happy to hear that." Kasey's tone was wry.

"Well, I already told my mom. She said it was okay. So if you said it was okay, I'll bet Dad'll agree, too."

And cats sang. Graham had come home an hour before with Rough Day written all over him—which Laura didn't know—but she certainly knew how her dad was going to react to a boy who looked like Murray.

When the kid cupped Laura's behind, walking toward the den, Kasey considered taking up hard-core drinking.

"Hey, Dad, you been busy building trust funds for my sister?" Laura sashayed over to her dad, plopped a kiss on his forehead, then handed him the baby. Tess and Graham stiffened simultaneously. Laura, of course, couldn't realize that her dad rarely volunteered to hold Tess. "This is Murray, Dad. We're going to the Dead Wheels concert at Cobo."

The evening went from bad to worse. Tess chose that particular meal to throw up some rice cereal on Kasey's shoulder. Laura goadingly volunteered that she'd already dropped two courses this term.

"So, where are you from, Murray?" Kasey asked the young man with determined cheer.

"New York. Came to U of M for their pre-law program, but man, I couldn't cut it. The pressure was, like, unbelievable. Life's too short, you know?"

"You're about a year away from graduating?"

Murray waved a fork around, amiably shooting peas down the white tablecloth like baby bowling balls. "If I get around to it. No hurry. Ann Arbor's, like, cool. Lots of political stuff to keep anybody busy."

"What kind of political stuff?" Graham interrupted.

Kasey hadn't had a bout of serious clumsiness since she gave up taking the idiot pills, but now, a piece of blueberry pie managed to slide right off the plate and into the butter. It worked as a diversion for a few moments, but not nearly long enough. Sooner or later, of course, they were bound to get into it.

"You're not moving out of the dorm," Graham told his daughter flatly.

"As usual, you're not listening to me. The dorm is the pits, Dad. You can't eat the food, can't get any sleep. It's not even safe…"

"And living with a boy is better?"

"Hey, Mr. Crandall. I'd keep her safe—"

"You stay out of this," Graham snapped to Murray—which were the only words the two men had exchanged in the last hour—and then to his daughter, "It's illegal to live off campus while you're a freshman."

"Yeah. If they find out. But kids do it all the time—"

"Not you. Not if I'm paying your tuition and room and board."

"Kasey!" Laura appealed to her. "What's your vote on this? Don't you think Dad is being unreasonable?"

Kasey froze. She looked at Tess to save her, but Tess was in the baby seat next to her big sister and seemed enthralled with the fight. And the truth was, she desperately wanted to take Laura's part. On any subject. They'd had so much trouble getting along, and because of Tess the girl had finally seemed to start accepting her—at least a little.

"I don't think you want my opinion, Laura," she said honestly.

"Yeah, I do. Don't you think I should get out of the dorm if it's a bad situation? If I'm really miserable there?"

Kasey looked straight at Laura, not at Murray, and for damn sure not at Graham. "I really don't think you want my opinion," she repeated.

"Yeah, I do. Come on."

Kasey braced herself. "Okay. I don't think this is about whether the dorm's a good place to live or not. I think there's some reason that you're looking for a confrontation with your dad."

"That's dumb. Why would I want to fight with my dad? I just want out of the dorm!" Laura insisted.

"Maybe that's true," Kasey said quietly. "Personally I think you're old enough to make up your own mind how you want to live. But I also think that your dad deserves a say in how you live if you're expecting financial support from him—and you had to know he'd be unhappy about an idea like this."

Laura stood up. "I can see I was a damn fool for thinking you'd back me up. No one ever does in this family."

Later, long after the kids had gone to their concert and the house was quiet, Kasey stepped out of the shower to find Graham already in the bedroom. He was just emptying his suit pockets, the change going into the mahogany box on the bureau.

"I appreciate your taking my side," he told her.

She saw the look in his eyes, guessed what he wanted, and felt an odd sense of sick panic. "I wasn't trying to take anyone's side. I just wish I could help you two get along better. Graham, I honestly think Laura is seriously troubled about something."

"She's not troubled. Sometimes she's just like her mother. Spoiled. Always needing something, always demanding attention. But that's not the point." He peeled off his shirt. His skin was tanned from sunlamps, toned from the biweekly racquetball game he never missed. He stepped into the lamp light. "The point is your loyalty. I counted on you. You came through."

She slipped into bed and curled up under the covers, facing the antique Champleve clock his parents had given them last year. The clock was striking, but its color and style matched absolutely nothing in the house—but then, that was exactly how she felt. As if she didn't fit. Anywhere. Not in this house. Not in the life she was trying to live.

She'd sensed that before, yet always before had shushed away the thought before it could surface. Any marriage took adjustments. Her background was so different from Graham's that living together was always going to require some extra fine tuning. So she'd told herself a zillion times—yet at that moment, she suddenly felt as if she'd exposed a raw sore to the naked air, and her heart was thudding, thudding.

Graham hung his pants on the butler stand. Turned out the light. "When it comes down to it, that's what really happened to my marriage to Janelle. She never came through for me. I could never count on her. Her needs were always more important than mine. I didn't mind her leaning on me so much, but her loyalty wasn't there."

Kasey kept feeling the lump in her throat grow thicker. Nothing he said was new. He wanted her to honor his needs, be loyal to him above everyone else, be nothing like his ex-wife. That was always what she'd thought a good wife would do as well. Before.

Cool air shivered over her skin when he lifted the sheet. He climbed in, sighed with earthy pleasure as he stretched out. And then he turned. Clamped a hand over her waist.

That was his signal for her to turn around, that he wanted sex. Yet tonight, she didn't move, didn't breathe.

Didn't turn to him.

She wasn't sure what she'd have done if Graham had pressed, but he didn't. There was a sudden sharp silence on the other side of the bed, Graham clearly aware that she hadn't responded to his signal. She sensed his surprise—and his annoyance. But a long day eventually caught up with him, and he dropped off.

Not her. She couldn't sleep worth beans. The downstairs clock chimed one, then two, and still she lay in the dark, her heart beating wildly as if she were afraid. In principle, nothing traumatic had occurred this night...yet her heart seemed to think it had.

It seemed all her life, she'd tried to please someone else. Her mom. Her dad. Employers. Graham. If you were a good woman and played by the rules, everything would turn out well, right? Wasn't that the promise she'd sold herself?

Only her baby wasn't all right.

In the morning, she knew she was going to call Jake again. She knew there were risks, asking for Jake's help, being around Jake—but she had to know more about the information he'd uncovered on the Randolph Hospital cases.

If Graham found out, he'd be seriously upset, Kasey realized. He would see it as disloyal. He would see her behavior as directly going against him. And she was afraid of turning that corner.

But she was afraid of failing Tess more. If there was the remotest chance in the universe that something might help her daughter, she had to try. No matter who was mad at her. No matter what anyone thought of her. No matter what the consequences were.

CHAPTER 9

There was barely enough space to turn around in Jake's cubicle, so when his boss blocked the aisle, no one could easily get past him. Barney just stood there, waiting for Jake to look up from the computer.

It didn't seem a good moment to invite conversation. Barney had nearly bitten off the cigar chomped between his teeth, and his narrow eyes looked beady and mean this afternoon.

"What?" Jake sucked in finally.

"I told you I liked the medical lawsuit series on the babies. So I don't get it. You've been writing nothing but crap for three weeks now."

"I've been writing the stuff you told me to write. Doing the work you pay me to do."

"That's what I said. Writing crap." Barney heaved up his belt and took another chonk on his cigar. "Are you drinking?"

"No, but if I keep working for you, I might consider taking it up again."

That won a grin. The whole problem with the rest of the staff was that they didn't get it. Barney loved being insulted. "So the point is…why haven't you yanked my chain about taking on something else controversial? No ideas? No time? What's the problem here?"

Jake sat back. "I could have sworn you just yelled at the whole staff to only spend work time for research and projects that were budgeted."

Barney grimaced, as if facing a spoonful of castor oil. "Well, yeah. I have to say that. This paper doesn't make millions, you know."

"You have mentioned that, now and then. I believe you also told me exactly what you wanted me to do."

A sausagelike finger stabbed at him. "Quit giving me grief. That was all before I saw you could do some real work. I mean, who'd a guessed, you being a lawyer and all? So don't be sitting there bored. You find an issue or cause you want to get your mitts on, then come see me, we'll fight out the budget for it."

He was gone. Jake stared thoughtfully after him, but eventually settled back to work. No matter what he did later, right now he had deadlines on two projects—both exactly the kind of work he'd been hired for. The first was a trial involving custodial rights for an elderly man; the original reporter didn't have the legal background to differentiate between power of attorney and medical powers and custodial powers. Easy work for Jake; it just took time. And then the phone rang just as he'd grabbed his red pen.

"McGraw," he answered curtly.

"Jake, it's Kasey. Crandall."

As if she needed to identify her last name. Smells of ink and marker and paper dust suddenly faded. Clanging phones, clattering printers suddenly muted. There was always a rush in a newspaper office, even a small one like this.

But not in his head. Not once he heard her voice. "Glad you called. What's up?"

She hesitated, just for a moment's breath. "I don't want to involve you in something that could be awkward...but I'd appreciate the chance to talk to you. I don't need more than an hour. I'm just trying to plan a course of action for my daughter. And as much as I've read and studied on my own— you're someone who really knows something. I'd just like to fly some ideas by you and hear your perspective—"

"Kasey, I'd be glad to. When do you want to meet?"

"Whenever you could. But during the day would be a lot easier, if you wouldn't mind—"

"Sure. I can do a long lunch, if that'd work for you."

"That'd be perfect. But you're the one working, so you pick a location that's convenient, okay?"

He thought, then said, "Frankly, I think the best place to meet is my place—primarily because I've still got mountains of papers and studies there, left over from the articles I wrote on the lawsuits. It's also not too far a drive from your house. But if that could be a problem for you—"

"No. That's fine. Although I'll have to bring the baby."

"Well, of course you would." Jake couldn't imagine Kasey leaving Tess unless threatened at knifepoint. "How about Thursday? Noon?"

Once he gave her the address, he hung up, yet the conversation promptly replayed in his mind. Something serious must have happened for Kasey to initiate the call. He'd heard it in her voice. She hadn't sounded afraid, exactly...but there was a timbre in her voice, a shaky determination.

His conscience echoed the same old mantra: *Don't hurt her, don't hurt her.* Of course, his conscience no longer needed that reminder. She'd stunned him in the beginning, because he was so unprepared for that kind of charge—the kind where a woman looks at him and the man goes *whoosh* deep on the inside. It was impossible not to want it, that life force, that feeling, that craving. Still, a grown man knew that explosion of chemistry was different from something that really mattered.

She really mattered.

And Jake damn well couldn't use the excuse of her being the wrong kind of temptation—not if she needed help. Not if she needed him.

Kasey easily found a parking place, but then paused to study the river apartments. She'd wondered what kind of place Jake lived in. The brick apartments looked as if they'd once been expensive and exclusive, but now looked comfortably worn. There wasn't a single BMW in the lot. Balconies needed painting; a cat snoozed in a window.

Tess gurgled, immediately making Kasey turn around with a smile. "Okay, punkin, we'll get you unhooked. And then we'll go see Jake."

It took a minute to detangle the baby from the car seat. The windchill was bitter—which meant that Tess was so swaddled in a snowsuit that only two pink cheeks and a red nose showed. Her arms stuck out like a stick figure in a cartoon.

They headed up the walk, Kasey negotiating the slick spots in the crusty snow. She didn't hear the apartment door open, yet Jake was suddenly standing there in his shirtsleeves. "Hey, gorgeous. Come on with me. Good thing I was watching for you guys, huh? Your mom didn't tell me she needed a bulldozer to cart all the gear."

The baby was taken out of her arms, and Kasey felt a sudden, sharp hurt on the inside. Jake so easily reached for the baby, the way Graham never did.

That thought barely surfaced before it was followed by an engulfing wave of emotion. Sure, she knew she liked Jake. Sure, she knew there was attraction fringing those feelings, but she didn't envision walking in his door and feeling the slam of a bullet in her chest.

A soft bullet. It was the way he looked at her—when damnation, she wasn't wearing anything special, just a yellow sweater and jeans. She had hat-hair. She had yellow socks. She was as ordinary as chicken soup.

Yet Jake somehow tricked her into feeling alluring.

It was such a crazy feeling that she started talking. Fast. "I promise not to take up too much of your time. I realize this is the middle of your work day—"

When his gaze cut back to the baby, she started to breathe again. God knew, his tone was as easy as sunshine. "It's okay. When I'm researching an article, I regularly run all over the city, so I'm often away from my desk for an hour or two. Come on, though, let's get you two settled in. I made coffee. And some gourmet sandwiches."

"Good grief, you didn't have to feed me."

"Well, I had to do something for lunch anyway. Don't panic. My version of gourmet sandwiches is PB and J, and my best coffee's instant. Give me two shakes and I'll bring it in."

Kasey was still smiling over his defining peanut butter sandwiches as "gourmet" when he disappeared off the open doorway to the right—the kitchen, she assumed. Quickly she pulled off the baby's snowsuit and got her snuggled into her carrier with a teething ring, and then she ambled around for a few minutes, exploring.

His living room windows were naked of curtains, and looked out over the Detroit River. The view was mesmerizing, the water gleaming like tarnished pewter, sunlight trapped like diamonds in the crevices of the ice-crusted shore. From the look of his desk, Jake worked for long hours with that view, because files and books framed both sides of his computer.

Her gaze took in the old Oriental rug, the long, worn couch, the books heaped in battered barrister bookcases. Built-in shelves on the north wall held a few personal things. Photos of his son and parents, a railroad lantern that had to be a hundred years old, a polished piece of malachite. A sock was partially hidden under the couch, a shirt cuff peeking from behind the front hall closet doors.

She stared blindly at the sock for a moment, suddenly realizing that something extremely odd was happening to her. Something she'd never expected. Without even thinking about it, she'd pushed off her boots at the door, felt her shoulders lose their stiffness. No, Jake didn't have much, but from the peanut butter to the almost-hidden sock, she felt…at home…the way she hadn't felt at home since she could remember. This was not a place where she had to please anyone. Where someone's temper was at risk all the time. Where she had to try, 24-7, to meet expectations.

Jake showed up in the doorway with two steaming mugs. "I'm not sure how I can help, so how about if you start by telling me what you and Graham are doing specifically—"

She took a quick breath. "Jake, I need to be frank with you. Graham doesn't know I'm here. Anything I'm doing for Tess, I'm on my own."

He shot her a look of confusion as he handed her a mug, and then located a distance away in his desk chair. "Well, whether Graham's directly involved or not, you must have some help with Tess—whether it's family or friends or—"

Again, she gently interrupted. "No. I really meant it when I said I was alone. For sure, I've got friends and neighbors, and lots of family—but no one who I can turn to for this."

He seemed taken aback. "Why?"

The question sounded blunt, but not unkind. She struggled to explain, because she couldn't ask for his confidence without his understanding why she needed it. "All the friends I grew up with…I'm living the life they dreamed of. That's how my mom and family feel, too. They think I've been extraordinarily lucky to land in Camelot—and that no woman with a brain would throw out Prince Charming."

She thought Jake might smile at her silly fairy-tale images, but he didn't. She added hastily, "I didn't mean to imply that I was leaving Graham or anything like that. It's just that…no one seems to agree with me. They've been wonderful about helping me…but only if I do things by certain rules."

His expression looked even more confused. "What kind of rules?"

She pushed a hand through her hair, hating to embroil him any further in her life or her messes, but needing to be honest with him. "I'm supposed to accept that Tess is handicapped. I'm supposed to adjust my life, and the baby's life, to accommodate her never being normal. For all I know, Jake, they're all right and I need a psychologist. For all I know, I'm suffering from the hard-core denial everyone keeps telling me I have."

"Okay."

"You know what?" Damnation, who knew all this stuff was going to burst out? "I don't CARE anymore if I'm right or wrong. This isn't about me. It's about Tess. It has to be about Tess. She's blind. She's not developing the way a normal baby would be. I *know* all that, I'm not denying it. But I'm not convinced she has Leber's, or that her situation is as hopeless as that prognosis."

"Okay," he said again, even more gently.

"Several doctors have confirmed that diagnosis. So now Graham is strongly opposed to Tess seeing more doctors or putting her through more tests. Obviously I don't want to put her through painful tests, either. But I can't just sit here and wait. Hoping they're wrong. Not knowing. I just...Jake, for God's sake, they're all trying to tell me that my baby has no future. None. Zip. Zero."

"Okay."

"If you say 'okay' one more time, I swear I'm going to smack you. It isn't okay. Nothing's okay. I'm not sure what I'm doing is right. All I know is that I have to do something. I have to try."

Jake said quietly, "I'd do the same in your shoes."

Who'd have guessed he'd be this infuriating? "Damn it. Don't be sympathetic or you'll make me cry. I mean it. *Don't*."

"Hell. I'm sorry. I could shout and yell, if you want."

"And don't make me laugh, either." She scowled, then rubbed her forehead in both embarrassment and frustration. "I figured out a long time ago what was really going on. People can't handle a baby they think of as 'damaged.' They just want her to disappear. They want the problem out of their sight. It's not that anyone is deliberately mean or cruel. They're not. But they're uncomfortable, so they tend to back away." She sighed. "I really *do* get it, because I want to run from the problem, too. I'm scared, too. My stomach drops every time I think of Tess in an institution. I don't want to face it either."

"But you are facing it," he said.

"I'm not sure *what* I'm doing…except trying to make sure the baby gets every chance she can. Even if people are unhappy with me. Even if I'm completely wrong."

"Okeydoke. Let's get into it—but you need another PB sandwich or some milk, tough lady?"

"Um…no." She was going to laugh. In spite of everything. He was just being so damned…endearing. But then he glanced at Tess, noticed the baby was snoozing solidly, and suddenly went into work mode.

"First, do you have some specific plans about what you want to do?"

"Yes and no. I can't just travel around the country with the baby—especially knowing that Graham is opposed. But I want to take her to at least one specialist who doesn't practice at or have any association with Randolph Hospital. One of my questions, though, is whether I should be looking at doctors who deal with birth defects or doctors who specialize in eye problems."

"Good question. I can get you some advice on that." He snatched a legal pad from his piled-high desk. "What else?"

"I want a better understanding of the physical problems Tess has. I read about other children with Leber's who weren't given the dire prognosis she was. Maybe the difference is in how the baby is treated, whether there's intervention early on. And whether she has Leber's or not, I'd like to know if there are exercises, therapy, medicines, something that could make her as strong as it's possible for her to be. The thing is, because the doctors we've been to already closed those doors, at least for now, I don't know where to go to ask those questions—"

"Aha. McGraw can come to your rescue on that one." Again he spun back to his desk, shuffled through an Ever-est-sized mountain of folders and emerged with one. "When you called, I started to put some information together. One of the things I found was a physical therapist who works with babies. I don't personally know her, but she's got two pages of credentials there. She's not a doctor and she doesn't do tests. She does swimming, massage, exercise, only works with babies. No way to know if you'll like her, but I think she's the kind of person you were talking about."

"She is. God." This was exactly what Kasey hungered for. Someone to talk to—but who wasn't a doctor or family with a set viewpoint or agenda.

"Then I put together another file. You know about the lawsuits I looked into. But after that, I cross-referenced sites across the country where lawsuits stemmed from similar medical symptoms—like blindness in babies, or problems with oxygen use in the delivery process. I also made a list of sites on the Net—"

She waved a hand. "I may have the ones from the Internet. I've been poring over Leber's sites for weeks now."

"Okay, so maybe that's a waste of your time, but..."

There were no buts. Nothing was a waste of her time. Jake didn't even start running down for another half hour, and every word he told her was more soothing than a balm for a burn. No one had treated her like this in so long. As if she were real, not breakable china. As if her ideas mattered. As if he valued what she had to say.

A man who valued her opinion. What a concept.

"Aw, hell." Jake glanced at his watch, then reluctantly stood up. "I'm sorry, Kase, but I'm stuck. I've got an article still due this afternoon, so I really have to get back to the newspaper."

"And I never meant to take up so much of your time. I can't thank you enough." She bounced to her feet, too. Tess was still snoozing in her carrier, but Kasey suddenly couldn't remember where she'd put everything. Coats, blankets, purse. And now she had papers and files to gather up. "You've given me so many things to follow through with. You can't imagine what this means to me."

"Well, there's one more thing."

"What?" She picked up Tess's snowsuit where it had fallen on the floor, then tilted her head, curious as to what he meant.

"This."

When he touched her hand, her brow crinkled in further confusion...yet at some level of consciousness, she knew what was happening, what was going to happen. He tugged with that hand, gently enough, but with enough force to propel her toward him.

Tess's snowsuit slipped between her fingers to the ground.

She was suddenly close. Close enough to see the lines denting his brow, his beautiful old eyes, the intentness in his expression. But then his mouth touched hers, took hers. The taking started out tentative, gentle, testing, the way kindling could hiss and shimmer and tease the promise of fire without producing any real warmth—yet suddenly there it was. Not a spit of flame, but a burst of it. Not a kiss, but a complete conflagration.

The desperate thought hit her mind that she'd surely felt this with Graham, surely felt more than this with the man she'd married.

It was a crazy time to lie to herself. Especially when Jake wasn't asking for lies. He didn't seem to be asking her for anything. She could have broken free from that kiss, that embrace, any second she wanted to.

Kasey told herself she wanted to...but that was just another fib.

The room spun. The Detroit River turned from a dull gray to sterling. Papers fluttered. Sunlight burst in the windows. The baby's breathy little snores turned into music, a jungle beat, a thrumming, wild, infectious drumming. And still he kissed her, his mouth warm and evocative, his kisses igniting a thousand promises, impossible promises.

Big hands framed her face, sipped from her mouth, her tongue, then moved. Fingertips traced her jaw, her throat, then clutched her shoulders—which was a darn good thing, since her bones had turned to jelly. The erection pressing against her abdomen was another shock, another source of fire, pulsing with its own heartbeat.

She smelled danger, excitement, like the click-click up the track to the top before the roller coaster zooms down. You know it's coming. You know it's only going one way. And nothing's happened yet—but you know what will. What could. What might.

A groan tore from her throat, softer than a whisper. He caused it, his lips sliding against her neck, pushing aside the V-throat of her yellow sweater, sampling her skin, treasuring it. Hands, slower than honey, roved down, shaping her sides, her ribs. And then one hand, hiding under her sweater, slid up, up, to cup a breast so aching hot it hurt every which way from Sunday. Hurt good.

"Jake…"

"Shhh." His voice wasn't an admonition. More an answer, a sound of reassurance, followed by another kiss, a deeper one, involving tongues and teeth and pressure. Heat fisted low in her belly. There was a name for it. Longing. A longing, fierce as fire, to be naked with him. A longing to be taken. A longing to be sucked into this gale force and never let go.

He knew her somehow. He kissed her as if he'd always craved the taste of her, touched her as if he'd always understood what sizzled her senses, caressed her as if he knew her heart.

His level of tenderness alone seemed to stun her. Through men, through marriage, she'd had no idea she could want like this, yearn like this. That taste and sound and touch could be as explosive as a whisper, as shocking as a shadow. That one man could induce such feelings, such hunger, such longings.

With a helpless groan, she wound her arms around him, took all his kisses back, took more, took everything she could reach and claim. She sensed a smile in the shape of his mouth, but not for long. He matched flame for flame, wild for wild, rough earthy kisses for more rough earthy kisses. Lips, breasts, abdomen, pelvis, all rocked against each other, wooing, calling, teasing.

And then it was done.

On a sudden harsh breath, Jake jerked his head up. He squeezed his eyes closed, as if fighting for control, but when he opened them his gaze focused intently on her face. His bones looked carved in granite, but his eyes were hot and wild with desire. Still, he took the time to slowly trace the line of her jaw with a gentle finger.

"I'm relieved that happened, Kase. For your sake and mine both."

Desire still owned her. She just couldn't suddenly come through with coherent conversation. "What do you mean?"

"I meant that I've been worried as hell about this. About the sex, the chemistry. I knew it was powerful for me from the day I first saw you." His hand gently dropped. "It's not that I wanted something to happen, Kasey. But I did want to prove to you that you could trust me. Yeah, this has been between us, and yeah, it came close to getting out of hand— but it didn't. It won't. I don't want you afraid of being with me, of letting me help you with Tess. I swear I won't let anything go too far. I know exactly who I am."

Again she felt confused. Her body was still beating, bleating in want for him. It stunned her to realize that they could have made love, that she wouldn't have stopped it. Right then, though, she struggled to understand what Jake was trying to communicate.

"I'm an alcoholic," he said.

She frowned. "I've heard you define yourself that way before. But I don't think it's fair, Jake. I understand that you had serious problems with alcohol—"

"Have. Not had. Being sober doesn't make the problem disappear. I'll always be an alcoholic. It'll always be part of who I am."

She touched his cheek. "I wasn't trying to make light of it. But when you've mentioned it before, I thought... you were trying to make me run away. As if you think I'd judge you for having a problem."

"No. But I have to judge myself constantly." She could see him groping for the right words. "And that's why I really need you to understand that I would never willingly hurt you, Kasey. Not through my being careless or selfish. Because I'll never make it out of the hole if I fall in that pit again."

She looked at him. "I think you're being terribly hard on yourself. People hurt each other, even when they're both trying their best. You can't hold yourself responsible for someone else's choices."

"Yeah, I can. Because I have to. If I turn back into the man I used to be, I know there won't be any more chances." He took her hand, walked with her to the river windows, to the frozen landscape below. "All I'm really trying to say is that I want to help you. With Tess. However I can. But I don't want it to be a problem for you to be with me. And that's partly why I'm relieved that we just—"

"Kissed?"

"We more than kissed." He took her hand, squeezed it, let it go. "What matters is that we both know that chemistry is a real problem. But also—you know that I stopped it. I'm promising you, Kase, that you can trust me."

She opened her mouth, wanting to discuss, to argue, to return a promise to him—but then painfully realized that, of course, she didn't have the right. She had no way to be there for him. No way to offer him help in return. Not as long as she was a married woman.

In that slash of a second, Kasey understood that she'd been denying this looming problem—just like the denial-expert others had accused her of being. But this wasn't about Tess. This was about hiding—for too long—from deciding what her marriage vows really meant to her.

It was almost seven when Kasey heard the front door open downstairs. She'd been waiting for Graham—he'd called to tell her he'd be late for dinner—yet even expecting him, the thunk of the door closing made her jump. She took a quick, bracing breath, then called down, "I'm up in the nursery, Graham! Dinner's ready—I'll be down in a couple of minutes."

As if sensing her unease, Tess let out a sudden cry, yet she was easy to soothe. The baby was fed and changed, and just needed a little more rocking before going readily to sleep. Kasey had just laid her in the crib when she sensed her husband in the doorway.

Graham was still wearing his navy suit from work, his hands on his hips, a leg cocked forward. One look and Kasey felt her stomach churn. Her life increasingly felt as if it were spinning out of control. She was no longer sure of herself, of her husband, of her marriage. The only thing she was certain of was that the life path she'd been aiming down was terribly wrong—and she had to find some way to make it right again.

"How was your day?" she asked.

"Fine." He was still glancing around the nursery. "Where's Robyn?"

"I told both Robyn and Gladys to take off early tonight." Tonight, she just wanted the house to themselves. "I hope you're hungry. I made lamb chops with a fresh mint sauce. A Waldorf salad. Baby petatoes with tarragon and pepper…"

"That sounds good. Although I'd like a drink first." But he was still looking around. Not at her. Not at Tess, although his daughter was growing more beautiful by the day. His attention seemed drawn only to certain items in the nursery. The jeweled mobile. The dresser lamp with the colored-glass shade. The sun catchers hanging in the east window.

"You're getting worse, Kasey," he said absently.

"Pardon?"

His voice hadn't seemed accusing, but now his eyes cut to hers with sharp perception. "She can't see. When are you going to get it through your head? This is bullshit. That dangling crap in the window, the Tiffany lamp, the mobile—what the hell good is all this color supposed to do?"

He didn't wait for an answer, just turned around and left. As she heard the ice-quiet thud of his footfalls heading downstairs, she found herself swallowing past a throat suddenly gone bone-dry.

A memory of Jake holding her, kissing her, flooded back into her mind. This afternoon she'd felt rich. Rich as a woman, as a mom, as a person. Inspired about all the things she could try for Tess. Exuberant about life. And just high again. High the way she used to feel high on sunshine and being a woman and peanut butter sandwiches and on just feeling happy to be alive.

Now that was all gone, as if someone had slapped her out of a daydream. She was back to tiptoeing and a churning stomach. Those symptoms were becoming more familiar every day. She couldn't seem to stop feeling afraid of Graham, her own husband. Couldn't seem to stop falling for Jake. Couldn't seem to be a good wife anymore—not on her own terms, not on anyone's terms.

Gently she draped a blanket over Tess and then headed downstairs, mentally lecturing herself to get some spine, and pronto. Yes, she was afraid Graham would take Tess away from her, but there had to be a brake that would stop this roller coaster she was on. She had to find a way to talk to Graham. Frankly. Honestly.

Downstairs, she poured Graham his favorite Jameson, then served dinner and a dose of serious wife-listening at the same time. He had had a rough day. There'd been an argument at a board meeting, a clash over financial planning. She heard him out, expressed sympathy and suggested ways of coping with the VP nemesis who gave Graham so much trouble. And when that was done, she served lemon meringue pie and cappuccino in the living room. He settled in the white leather chair with his feet up and watched his traditional half hour of CNN, while she finished cleaning up in the kitchen.

By the time she joined him, she'd checked on Tess, and

Graham seemed more relaxed. So was she. She'd always honestly liked hearing about his work, liked business, and he always seemed to enjoy telling her about his corporate battles. When he wound down, she switched on a soft background lamp, poured him another drink, and then asked if they could seriously talk.

His easy mood immediately clipped off. "I should have guessed something was coming," he said impatiently. "Okay, what is it?"

It wasn't how she wanted to start, with him already sounding exasperated, but still she plunked down on the white leather ottoman at his knees, determined to see this through. "I just feel...we need some air cleared between us, Graham. You're unhappy with me. I'd have to be deaf, dumb and blind not to realize that you're no longer happy with the marriage, with me. You can't want us to keep on this way."

He sighed—as if a teenager had just brought him a problem on a par with a new zit on her face. "Kasey, for God's sake. We're fine. All marriages have stresses. Did you think ours could be any different? Now what's the real problem here? You're not getting enough attention?"

"No, of course not." His comment stung like a wasp bite, because she was so aware of his comparing her to his ex-wife. "Graham, I'm not complaining. I'm concerned. For both of us." She grappled. "You don't seem to like being with me anymore. I feel less and less sure why you even married me."

"For God's sake, Kasey. This is the kind of sophomoric conversation college kids have when they're analyzing their *relationships*. I married you because I loved you. Why else?"

"I don't know why."

He lifted a hand impatiently. "So does this conversation have a point?"

She'd hoped it would, but talking already seemed like trying to wade through mucky quicksand. He was already ticked. And, now, so was she. Quietly, carefully, she said, "This is what you wanted from a wife then? How you thought it would be between us? It doesn't bother you that we're not… close? The way we were?"

"You're the one turning away from me at night. Not the other way around." Graham didn't raise his voice. He lowered it. "Look. We're going through a rough time. That's no surprise. We got hit with a bomb, for God's sake. No marriage could go through a traumatic crisis like Tess without everybody getting some fallout. It hurts me, no different than it hurts you, to have a child who isn't normal. We just have to weather past it to get to the next place."

He made it sound as if Tess were something one could get over like chicken pox. She hunched forward. "Graham…do you love her?"

He didn't roll his eyes, but again she caught the impatience. "Love Tess? Of course I love Tess. But I can still accept that she's never going to be part of the family like a normal child—which you can't seem to do. If you want things to be good between us again—it's easy, Kasey. Just accept reality."

Kasey clenched her hands together. "And what if I can't, ever, accept that Tess isn't going to be okay? Would you want a divorce?"

That seven-letter word seemed to echo in the suddenly silent room as if she'd farted in church. He folded his paper, put down his drink. And then he stood up, as properly and rigidly as a Marine. "Make no mistake," he said, "there'll be no divorce. You think I'd let people believe I would walk out on a wife and a handicapped child? It won't happen. Not in this life. Now I don't know what the hell started all this—PMS?"

"Graham, I'm just trying to have a serious talk with you. I feel we have problems—"

"We don't have problems. You have problems. All I want is the wife I married. I don't want every waking moment spent talking about Tess. I want you to start putting your life—and our lives—back in perspective. And if you can't do that with the child in the house, Kasey, then I'll have to start immediately searching for appropriate institutions that can give Tess the care she needs."

Jesus. She'd hoped to have an open conversation between them. Now she felt as if someone had slugged a fist in her stomach. Fear, big as panic, shadowed her heartbeat. Despair clogged her throat.

He'd threatened to put Tess in an institution before…but before, she'd believed that loving her would stop Graham from really doing that. Now…she didn't feel love coming from him. She only felt the line being drawn in the sand. Behave. On his terms. Or risk losing her daughter.

CHAPTER 10

Ignoring the buzz of phones and faxes and printers all around him, Jake sat back at his desk, poking a pencil from end to end.

If Kasey wanted more help, she could have asked. Instead, two weeks had passed without a call, so obviously the woman had come to her senses. Whatever she planned to do about the baby—and that selfish son of a seadog she'd married—was none of his business. She was a smart woman. Smart enough to realize that an ex-drinker was a lousy gamble—even for a friend.

"Hey." Barney knuckled the wall of his cubicle, then hiked up his pants and chomped down on his ever-present Cuban. "What does it take to get your attention? You think I'm paying you to sit around here daydreaming?"

Jake looked up, but he didn't take his boots off the desk. "Nope."

"Well, I been standing here two full minutes, maybe three. First of all, I need—"

Smooth as a greased wheel, Jake handed him a sheaf of papers.

Barney glowered even darker. "Okay, so you fixed up the article on the Brink murder trial. And you even got it done early. But I also need—"

Smooth as another cog in the same greased wheel, Jake forked over another clipped set of papers.

Barney grunted around the cigar, then shut up momentarily while he perused the printed sheets. "Okay," he said with exasperation. "So damned if you didn't make that dipshit corporate lawsuit into something a few of us might even be able to understand. And ahead of schedule on this one, too. But if you're thinking you're so hotsy-totsy that you're due a raise—"

"Your offering me a raise never crossed my mind. Trust me," Jake said wryly.

"The hell it didn't. I saw that article you put on my desk this morning." Barney pushed against the door frame, as if a few seconds of ergonomic exercise might produce an effect on the watermelon hanging over his belt. "This piece, on the young drivers and accidents, wasn't nearly as good as the series you did on the babies. But I think I'll put it on the front page of next week's feature section." He added gruffly, "Don't be thinking I thought it was great or anything. It was okay."

"I know," Jake said, deadpan.

"You know. You know. You know nothing." A fat finger wagged at him. "You think I haven't figured out what's going on? You keep coming through with all this work. Next thing you'll be asking for a raise, or God damn it, you'll threaten to go back to lawyering."

"How many times do we have to go through this? I don't want to practice law again. Ever. You can take that to the bank."

"Like that helps. I don't trust banks." Barney hiked up his pants. "Hell, I'll give you a little raise. Thirty more bucks a week. Coming right out of my retirement fund—just so you know. But I expect more pieces like you been doing. Maybe a piece every two weeks. Real stuff, nothing sensationalized. Like you did the others."

Barney didn't wait for agreement, just turned around and stomped off. Jake almost grinned. His boss had been fretting himself into an ulcer over that not-asked-for raise for weeks now. The short diversion had roused Jake from a looming dire, dour mood besides.

On impulse, he grabbed his Rolodex, fanned the cards until he reached the name of a certain physical therapist, and then dialed on his cell. The woman who answered had a voice like a boom box—big on the bass and the volume. Jake mentally pictured her as over six feet and well over two hundred pounds, the kind who could give a speech to 10,000 without a microphone.

Lily Raflleeken seemed to recognize his voice, too. "Yah, yah, she called. She's coming two mornings from now, Thursday. Now you can quit bugging me, huh? I promised I'd take good care of her if she called. I figured she wasn't interested, didn't hear from her in these two weeks. But she did. It's all okeydoke, Mr. McGraw."

Thursday morning, driving with a map in his left hand, Jake tried to justify his skipping work to track down Kasey and Tess. Couldn't be done. There *was* no justifying this. When he identified the address and pulled into the driveway, he was so pissed at himself he could hardly think. Back when he took a daily swim in alcohol, he'd been outstanding at selling himself excuses. Now there seemed nowhere to hide, much less from himself. It was damned annoying.

He jammed his hands in his pockets as he headed up the walk. He'd researched the therapist, but hadn't personally seen the place before. The original owner had made extravagant accommodations to make life easier for his handicapped wife. After they moved on, a physical therapist had bought the place. The result was far more secluded and comfortable than the usual physical therapy facility—which Jake thought would matter to Kasey.

A note on the back door instructed PT clients to come in, sign in, and either wait in the waiting room or follow the arrows toward the pool. He slowly ambled toward the pool area, still trying to talk himself into leaving before Kasey ever saw him. The place was old-world elegant, with grotto-like walls and pampered plants flanking a flagstone walkway.

When Jake stepped inside the pool area, he felt engulfed by the warm, tropical air. Plants and trees surrounded the pool, making it seem more like a private lagoon than a utilitarian therapy center. Arched, tinted windows hinted at the landscaped grounds beyond—rock gardens and flowered berms, all tucked inside a high stone privacy fence.

There were only three people inside the pool area, all clustered in the far corner. Kasey was kneeling at the pool's edge, watching Tess in the water with the physical therapist.

In a single glance, Jake realized he'd been dead wrong about Lily. She was smaller than a minute, so God knew where that big booming voice came from. He also noticed that the baby was chortling and splashing and having a blast. That was it, for noticing those two.

Kasey was the only one not dressed to swim. She looked...different. Her shirt was pale, her hair pulled back in a tidy ponytail. She'd skinned down again—had to have lost another 7-8 pounds—and her face was tanned, nothing she could have gotten in Michigan this early, so she must have been away.

He could have left right then. She hadn't noticed him yet. He could still escape and not risk either of them getting in any more trouble.

But he didn't go.

The tan made her eyes look startling-blue. Her concentration focused completely on Tess—she was watching the baby with the fierceness of a mama lion for her cub. But she was hunched over in such a tight, tense posture. It was the posture of someone who was scared, someone who was trying to be invisible.

In certain ways she was more beautiful than the woman he'd first met, but she definitely wasn't the exuberant, joyful woman she'd been months ago…and the roar of a silent DAMN filled his mind.

The look on her face was breaking his heart. The frail courage. The stubbornness. The fierce protectiveness. For God's sake, Jake had a sudden terrible feeling that he could kill for her without a qualm. Him. A man who barely had the guts to kill a mosquito, a man who'd been running from trouble his whole life.

He ambled forward, not making a sound, but Kasey's head suddenly whipped around—as if wary anyone might discover her and Tess here. Their eyes met. For her, probably, cymbals and fireworks didn't go off, but damned if they didn't for him.

"Hey," he murmured.

A slow smile. Maybe it wasn't that wildly uninhibited grin he'd first fallen in love with, but it was still a natural smile, the kind that burst from a spirit that was—or had been—so wild and free she stole his heart. "Hey," she murmured back. "You here for some PT, too?"

"No. Don't shoot me, but I admit I'm here to spy. It bugged me that I'd recommended Lily and then didn't know if it worked out okay for you and Tess. I had to see for myself."

"Then you can relax, Rambo." Kasey nodded her head at the two in the pool. "She's a marvel. Lily. The first few minutes we were here, she tossed the baby in the pool and I thought I was going to have a conniption."

"Yeah?" Jake couldn't hold back a grin.

"But it worked out. Tess came up gasping, but she wasn't scared—more shocked that anyone would do such a thing to her. And since then the two have been getting on like two pals in a sandbox. Lily said not to forget that babies are born in water. They know water from the womb. They have every reason to love it." Kasey added, "And look at Tess."

He looked at the little naked squirt, but he didn't understand what Kasey wanted him to notice. She had to explain.

"She's not naturally mobile, Jake. She doesn't move like other babies. But in the water, I could see right away that everything was different. She can do more things. Build up some strength and skills. That's what Lily said, too." She sighed. "I just wished I could have come two weeks ago, when you first brought this up."

"Everybody gets busy sometimes—"

"I wasn't busy. I was in Monaco."

What was he supposed to say to that? "Terrific place, huh?"

"Yeah. Terrific. The trip was a gift from Graham. Ten days away from the baby. Sun, casinos, diamonds, yachts. Anything I could possibly dream of on a vacation. Except for being with my daughter."

She didn't sound unhappy or complaining, but there was a blankness in her eyes he'd never seen before. Now Jake understood the tan. He also understood why she hadn't pursued the appointment with the physical therapist until now. But something must have happened with Graham to make her look this…fragile, this different. "Kasey…" He started to ask, but she'd already started speaking again.

"You know what she said? Lily? Get her talking, she can't stop, and brother, is she against doctors. I have no idea what she really knows, but she did make me think. She says she's never seen a baby diagnosed—not one baby—with anything a doctor could be blamed for. Amazing, huh?"

She was. With those soft-fierce eyes and the pretty-pale clothes that didn't suit her.

"She also says almost every baby can benefit from swimming and exercise. No matter what's wrong, the right kind of exercise can help make the child stronger. Even if they can only do one thing, they can be helped to do that one thing in a stronger way. Cripes. The woman had me crying before I was here ten minutes. She says the younger she gets her hands on a baby, the more potential that child can have."

Okay, Jake kept telling himself. *You shouldn't have come, but that's spilled milk now. At least you haven't touched her. In spite of all the five million tempting reasons you want to, you haven't touched her.*

"From now on, we're coming here three times a week. No matter what. No matter what. Nothing is going to stop me from coming here after this. Not now that I know how great it is for her—"

Okay. But he couldn't swear he could keep refraining from touching her if she didn't quit talking. "Kasey, I tracked down an attorney I think you should speak with."

There. She was diverted. Her expression changed to surprise, momentarily shaking off that look that made him want to tear out his heart. "Well, thanks on that, Jake, but honestly, the only person I ever wanted legal advice from is you. A friend I could trust. If I just needed a lawyer, there have to be five hundred in the neighborhood."

"This one's different. He's a guy named Ned Jeffries. I knew him from years ago. He won't charge you, Kase, because he owes me a debt. And he's got a solid medical background. I think you'll find he has a perspective about Tess that you can't get anywhere else."

She seemed hesitant, but he handed her a slip of paper with the name and information on it. He left quickly after that, so there was only that one second when he touched her—one brief second when her fingers grazed the heart of his palm.

But in that millisecond, her eyes shot to his like a light seeking its source. Those fingertips touched, hesitated, held, clung. Most milliseconds lasted a millisecond. This one spun on for an hour of years, a shadow of mornings, a whisper of lifetimes. I love you. Jake knew his eyes said it. Knew he felt it. Knew he was tired of trying to deny it.

But putting her at risk was out of the question. No matter how much he disliked Graham—or sensed that the marriage was rocky—he continually intuited that Kasey was in an emotionally volatile situation. He couldn't love her and want to make anything harder for her.

He could help her. He would help her. As long as there was no threat of his hurting her.

Kasey had never been in the office of a certifiable kook before. According to the framed credentials, Ned Jeffries was a lawyer, but he sure didn't resemble any lawyer she'd ever met. One whole shelf of a barrister bookcase was devoted to a mama cat and her kittens, who apparently regularly came to work with him. Children's crayon artwork was taped to the elegant wainscoted walls. Amid the pricey lawyer tomes were a pacifier, a half-empty box of diapers, and various Red Wing hockey memorabilia.

Ned shook her hand hard enough to threaten her shoulder socket, and motioned her to the only clean seat, while he hunkered back in his desk chair—a hefty man, way too young to be balding and losing his waistline, but who cared? He obviously didn't.

"Jake and I went to law school together. He was top in his class, and I wanted to hate him for it, but fact was, he was the only reason I passed the bar. We fight about politics every time we see each other, but what are you gonna do? He's too blockheaded to see reason. Coffee?"

"Thanks." Whatever Kasey had expected, it wasn't a man more comfortable to be with than a brother.

He poured her a Spider-Man mug of coffee, and chose the Lion King mug for himself. "Jake sent me a ream of information on your daughter. Primarily he suggested that you needed a solid understanding of what your rights are. Truthfully, Jake could give you that information as well as anyone on earth…but I suspect he thought you might want to hear from an unbiased outsider."

"I'll listen to whatever you have to say."

Ned got straight down to business. "You have ample grounds for a lawsuit, Kasey. When Dr. Morran asked to see the birth records, I believe he already guessed that something happened during the birth process to cause your baby's disabilities. The hospital claiming to lose those records is no excuse. No one is going to believe that they miraculously lost the records of a handicapped child. The court will force them to deliver."

Kasey sank deeper into his overstuffed client chair. "Suing never crossed my mind."

"And that may not be your choice. But you still need to know that you could win such a lawsuit. If you can afford to care for your daughter, that's fine. But most people would find it an overwhelming financial burden to support a child over a lifetime who needed constant care. So at least know that we could get compensation for you. There's no doubt in my mind."

She bit her lip. "I'd like to say I'd never sue…but that isn't true. If I had no other way to support Tess, then I'd have to reconsider. But right now I'm not in that position. And right now I don't know if anyone's responsible for Tess's situation. If she doesn't have Leber's, if it could be proven that an overdose of oxygen caused her condition…well, then I'd be worried if this could happen to other babies, too—"

"Yes. That's exactly the point. A lawsuit can prevent it from happening again, if it draws attention to an unsafe practice or a careless doctor. I just advise you to keep the door open, and to know, absolutely, that you have legal options. However...there is something else I discuss with every parent in your shoes."

"And that is?"

"I want you to be very clear about what you can win—and what you can't win. No amount of money is going to change your child's prognosis." He said gently, "A lot of people go into a lawsuit subconsciously believing that winning means hope. That winning money will somehow equate to winning a different outcome for the child. A lawsuit can definitely enable the child's financial security...but it can't help a crippled child walk or a blind child see. It can't change the things that tear your heart out with a special baby."

When she walked out of the office, it was almost four. Outside, the wind was screeching and screaming and shaking the tree branches. She needed to pick up the baby from her mom's and get dinner made before Graham got home. The snow was long gone, but except for a few brave crocuses, the landscape still had that winter-bald coldness. She hunched in her coat, as if trying to hide from the bitter March wind, shivering.

Until she saw Jake. His lanky form was standing by her car. Her step faltered, and then she sprinted toward him. It had been two weeks since she'd seen him—two weeks that felt longer than five years.

He put up his hands in a gesture of humorous innocence. "I know, I know, it looks like I'm spying on you again. But this time, I swear I was in the neighborhood, researching something at the courthouse. I often stop to see Ned, and when I saw your car in the lot, I figured you were here. So I just waited, hoping to hear the meeting went okay."

"More than okay. It bites to admit it—you know I didn't want to talk to an attorney—but you were right. Ned was terrific. He gave me a ton of advice and information, like what records to keep. What to listen for when I take Tess to different medical resources. And not to close my mind against suing, but to just keep finding out the facts."

"Uh-huh. And in the meantime, why in hell are you looking so skinny?"

"I'm not skinny. For Pete's sake, doughnuts glue right to my thighs. Or they used to." Never mind how she looked; he was the one who looked good. More than good. His hair was wind-tousled, cheeks burning from the cold, eyes full of life. "You've got a real friend in Ned."

"He's given me hell for twenty years at least."

"So he said."

"How's my baby?"

"Loving her swimming lessons and therapy. She's with my mom right now. How's life going for you?"

"Trouble." He sighed. "If I don't shape up really fast, I'm going to start making a serious living again. Boss gave me a raise a couple weeks ago. Now's he given me a decent office. I'm going to ruin my reputation as a derelict alcoholic if this keeps up."

"Oh, God, not that. How are things going with your son?"

"Yes and no...teenagers are a predictable source of torture. No matter what you do right, they're still mad at you. When you're that age, a parent is like an insufferable vegetable. Maybe you're stuck eating it, but nothing can make you like it." He reached over to turn up her collar. "Danny tolerates being with me sometimes. Which is better than we were doing before."

"I'll bet it's way better."

"It is, but I don't kid myself. We've still got miles to go. He's still got a lot of anger."

It was so crazy, she thought. Both of them standing in the cold, drafts of wind biting all around them, the hour growing later. Still he kept making talk. So did she. And even if it was just talk, it seemed more of a real conversation than she'd had with anyone else in a blue moon.

"Maybe you did the best you could at the time, Jake."

"Naw. And the kid knows I didn't. But…that's yesterday's pastrami. Best I can do now is keep plugging. He's getting his driver's license tomorrow. May I suggest staying off the roads?"

She chuckled. But she also remembered Jake talking about his alcoholism, his implying that she didn't understand what it really meant. So she kept her voice light, but still asked, "So…how's the drinking today?"

He stiffened, as if he suddenly felt wary. "It's there."

"Like always?"

"Like always," he affirmed.

"And is there a chance you'd let someone help you, Jake? If sometime you felt the urge and it was beyond what you felt you could cope with?"

"This isn't something anyone can help with," he said quietly.

"Yes, they can. It has to be better to have someone in your corner than to have no one. I'm not talking about someone judging, looking over your shoulder all the time. But just someone on your side. Someone who wants you to win." Maybe that was going too far; she wasn't sure how willing he was to talk about it. So she swiftly changed subjects. "I found a doctor I'm taking Tess to. He's in Chicago, a pediatrics neurologist named Frazier. He's worked with Leber's patients before."

Jake lost that stiffness immediately. "Terrific. So when's the appointment?"

"Two weeks from now. It's the soonest I could get." She added quietly, "But I'm afraid Graham doesn't know about this. If he did, he'd be adamantly against it. So I'll be going alone."

Jake immediately cut to the chase. "He'll find out, Kase."

"Yes, he will. But not until after she's seen this specialist."

He hesitated. "You mentioned before that he was against taking Tess to any more doctors. But you've learned more since then—that the hospital lost the records. That other circumstances could have caused the symptoms. I don't understand why Graham would be against seeking more help for the baby."

"He isn't against giving her help. But so far every medical person she's seen has given her the same diagnosis, so Graham feels it's cruel to put Tess through more tests just to find out what we already know. And no one—so far—has given us any reason to hope. Or to believe there's a chance of finding out anything different until she's older. So he feels I only want to pursue this because I can't face the truth—that the baby belongs in an institution." Kasey hadn't put it that baldly before, not to Jake. But it was a relief to get that *insti-*

tution word out and said. "My mom feels the same way. So does everyone else. They think I'm too attached. That I'm being as blind as my daughter about the truth."

Again Jake touched her, straightened her collar for a second time.

"But you're determined to go."

"Yes. I am." Sickness welled in her stomach, the same acid that had been roiling there for weeks now. "If yet another specialist confirms the Leber's diagnosis, then maybe I can accept it. But I need to be a ton more positive than I am now before condemning Tess to a life with no future."

Jake said gently, "You don't have to defend yourself to me."

She'd hoped she didn't. Still, the panicky sick feeling refused to completely go away. "I'm afraid." The words just sneaked out.

Jake went still. "Afraid? Why, Kase? For the baby?"

"Yes, for the baby. Everything's for the baby. But also...I don't know how Graham will react. I know he'll be angry with me for going—I don't care about that. But...I need to come home with serious hope for Tess. New facts, not just pipe dreams and maybes. Or else...I just don't know what Graham will do."

"Wait a minute. If you're afraid for one minute that he would lay a hand on you—"

"No. I never meant to imply that. In fact, I never meant to spill all this either. It'll just be tough, that's all I meant to say." She'd never have spilled so much if Jake wasn't so impossibly easy to talk to.

But Kasey didn't want to always lean on him. She wanted him to know that he could count on her as well.

And before that could happen, Kasey understood that she'd damn well better figure out if she could count on herself.

CHAPTER 11

For two weeks Kasey dwelled on that last conversation with Jake. But this morning, she opened the back door, took one sniff outside, and quickly grabbed Tess and a blanket. Tomorrow they were headed to Chicago—time enough to deal with worry and crises. Today was just too wonderful not to savor the fresh air.

The first of April was hardly warm, but she could smell hope in the air, sweet as yearning, soft as love songs. Hyacinth and daffodil buds pushed up in the flower beds; new greens were exploding on the maples and oaks. A lone sailboat gusted across the lake—obviously a madman with spring fever as bad as Kasey's—and Tess, swaddled on the blanket next to her, seemed to catch her mom's infectious silly smiles.

They lolled almost an hour...until Kasey saw her mother's car bounce up the driveway. She bolted to her feet, knowing full well that her mother never visited without calling first, unless she had an unusual reason. Like Armageddon. A second coming. A Buddy Holly revival.

A daughter flirting with disaster.

Ellen had barely climbed out of the car before she started in. "I can't believe you're serious about this trip to Chicago—

and I'm not leaving until I've talked you out of it." She sashayed over to her granddaughter, immediately crouching down to tickle Tess. "How's my darling snookums this morning, huh? Are you happy to see grandma, punkin-wunkin?"

Ellen's tone was lullaby-sweet, her pastel plaid jacket as cheerful as spring. Nothing in her voice or manner let on to the universe that she was less than happy. Her mom was an expert at hiding her feelings, but the expression in her eyes was bald-naked furious, and meant to be seen by her daughter.

"Mom, I never meant to make this your problem. I only told you about the Chicago trip so you'd know where we were, just in case something happened—"

"Something *is* happening. You're going to this doctor without your husband knowing." Ellen tickled the baby's cheek with a soft blade of grass, but the anger in her eyes was steel-cold. "I can't believe I raised a daughter this stupid. You can't lie to a husband about something like this. There are lies you can tell and lies you can't. This is a can't. When Graham finds out you did this behind his back, what do you think is going to happen?"

It was an old instinct, wanting to defend herself against her mother's criticism, wanting to please, feeling a wail of anxiety for having disappointed her mom. Yet now, because her whole life was such a mess, her mother's judgment seemed a paltry problem, easy to answer with basic honesty. "There'll be hell to pay," she admitted.

"More than hell. What is *wrong* with you, girl? You'd risk throwing away a fabulous man like Graham, and for what? There are a hundred reasons why a woman goes behind a man's back. Some of them are good ones. But not this. If he throws you out, how are you going to be able to support Tess? It would cost a *fortune* to raise a handicapped baby alone!"

"I know it would. But I have to put Tess first. The only thing that matters is what the baby needs, not what Graham thinks. And I have to believe that Graham will be okay if another doctor sees the baby with fresh eyes and comes up with a different opinion—"

"Shut up," Ellen snapped. "You don't know what any doctor is going to say. What you *do* know is that Graham gives you everything. Every time I see you, you're wearing a new piece of jewelry. New clothes. You've got a house nicer than a castle, and servants taking care of it for you. He takes you everywhere, Monaco, Korpu—"

"Korfu."

Ellen threw up a hand. "Wherever it was he took you for that long weekend. Who cares where it is? The point is, he takes you to exotic places, this month, that month, buys you everything, gives you the good life... He's the kind of man a woman dreams of. Yet do you appreciate him? Kasey, how can you be so foolish and ungrateful?"

Kasey closed her eyes. "I'm not trying to be either. And I'm not doing this to deliberately upset Graham. For that matter, if I felt I had absolutely any other choice, I wouldn't be doing this without telling him—"

"Then DON'T. DON'T do this." Ellen stayed crouched by the baby, but she plugged her daughter with a sharp stare. "I've covered for you when you go to all the physical therapy appointments. I didn't mind, but this is different. Kasey, he's going to know you're gone as soon as you leave the house, for heaven's sake. You don't buck a husband on something as serious as this!"

"Mom. Stop." Kasey sank down into the cool spring grass. Suddenly the sunshine felt icy and the lush breeze had a bite. "I'm not asking you to cover for me. I only told you so that someone would know where Tess and I were, in case of an emergency."

"That's not the point!"

Kasey nodded. "It's not the point for you. But for me, the point is that I was afraid. Unless I made up a story, I was afraid Graham would try to stop us from going to Chicago, afraid he would go so far as canceling the appointment—"

"Which is his right! He's the child's father!"

Kasey motioned to the baby, and lowered her voice to a whisper. "Please, please, look at her. Tess is so much stronger than she was. She can almost sit up. I know, other babies sit up long before this...but she is getting some motor skills that the doctors first claimed she'd never have. She responds to music. She loves to be read to. I know she can't see; I know there are other physical things wrong...but I still believe she's got a shot at a life. She's not—"

Ellen interrupted impatiently. "You think you're smarter than the doctors?"

Kasey gulped. "Yes. *Yes*, damn it. I do know her better than any doctor. Better than anyone."

Ellen muttered an *oy vay* the same way her grandmother would have done. "Now you listen to me, Kasey, and listen good. You think any mother could easily accept that her baby isn't perfect? I understand how hard this is for you. But that's all the more reason why you have to be smart. It's not like Graham is cruel or irresponsible. He'll take care of the baby financially in a way you couldn't possibly on your own. You're risking everything."

Not everything, Kasey thought desperately, but she was risking…Camelot. Her gaze brushed across the landscape, her wonderful house, the lake, all the sights and sounds and textures of the neighborhood. Not that long ago, this had been a treasured dream. The dream she'd never thought she could have, and had once wanted so fiercely. "You think I want to?" she asked quietly.

"Then why are you being so stupid?"

She tried again. This time more softly. "I love her more than my life. I love her more than anything I ever imagined. And the problem is that there's no one to stand up for her if I don't. Graham has already written her off. So has everyone else. It's damned inconvenient to have a damaged child."

When Ellen started to interrupt, Kasey stubbornly pushed on. "This is how it is. Either I fight to give her a chance, or she won't have one. Maybe I'm wrong. Maybe I'm completely, terribly wrong. Maybe she has the worst case of Leber's that any child has ever had, and in a short period of time she's going to turn into a vegetable. But I can't just sit back and accept that. Do you understand? I can't. I *have* to fight for her. I *have* to try."

Ellen heaved an exasperated sigh, but then she fell silent, as if Kasey's rant seemed to finally quell the fight in her. Kasey watched her mom look around, but the two of them had always viewed the world from different eyes.

Ellen looked over the house and grounds with a prideful gaze—not pride for herself, but pride for what her daughter had. She'd told everyone what Kasey had managed to land herself, but Ellen really saw it as her doing—her raising and counseling and disciplining her daughter so Kasey could have this wonderful life.

Kasey watched her mother's face. Ellen said nothing, but they knew each other the way only mothers and adult daughters could. It took time for Ellen to work a problem through, to change her mind when she positively, absolutely didn't want to see another point of view. Finally, though, she said roughly, "I think you should do what your husband says. What he wants. Because I think—I really believe, Kasey— that that's the best way to insure Tess's future."

Kasey nodded. "You could be right, and I could be completely wrong. But I don't know what else to do but live my own life, Mom. And that means that I have to protect Tess any way I can."

"Well, I think you're wrong. Dangerously wrong." Ellen made a gesture that would have done a disgusted Italian proud. "But I'll help you if I can. If I can cover for you, I'll cover for you. If you need me to lie for you, I'll lie for you. But I'll hate it. I don't agree with you at all. In fact, I just wish I could smack some sense into your head."

For the first time in eons, Kasey impulsively reached over to hug her mother. Ellen stiffened, but then seemed to accept the embrace. When Kasey pulled back, though, her mom's cheeks were as pink as fake rouge. "What's all this for?" Ellen grumbled.

"Just a thank-you. For taking my side. I didn't expect you to."

"For Pete's sake. I'm your mother. Even if I wanted to kill you, I'd take your side." Ellen, flustered, struggled to her feet. "I can't believe you doubted that for even a second."

A few minutes later, her mother left, claiming she had a dozen chores to do. When the old bumptious Plymouth disappeared from sight, Kasey scooped up the baby and headed inside to tackle chores of her own…yet she suddenly had the oddest urge to cry.

Her mother's offer to help had touched her, but it was more than that. Until recently, she'd never believed for a second that she'd ever live her mother's kind of life. She'd always been troubled by how Ellen jumped to cater to her dad. Kasey never believed she'd jump for any man—or that she'd have to.

Yet over the last few months, she had slowly, unwillingly, come to realize that Graham was not the man she thought she'd married. She'd believed she was so lucky, so blessed, to find someone to love her the way Graham seemed to. But love couldn't exist without trust, and Graham had tarnished her trust—close to irrevocably. She could no longer share with a man who she was seriously, heart-deep, afraid of.

Her mom's lifelong criticizing suddenly made more sense. Kasey understood that's what Ellen had always tried to do—protect her daughter from this kind of fear. Ellen only saw men through one lens.

And maybe she'd have done the same…if she hadn't met Jake.

With Jake, from their first conversation together, she'd never once felt the need to hide who she really was. Quickly, though, she squelched that thought. It didn't matter if she'd fallen gut-deep in love with Jake. Didn't matter if she'd finally discovered everything that mattered—or could matter between a man and a woman.

Jake wasn't hers. And God knew, she had enough to worry about without pining after a man who was forbidden to her.

The next morning, Kasey decided O'Hare was really another name for hell and it had simply been misnamed for an airport.

"There-there, there-there," she crooned to Tess, who had cried through the whole flight from Detroit. There was no problem with cabin pressure now; they were on the ground, but the baby still wanted the universe to know that air travel wasn't her cup of tea. Kasey was thinking about crying herself.

It seemed a pretty appealing idea. Just sit down. Dump everything. Cry her eyes out. If people stared, so what? No one knew her.

"There-there, there-there…" Desperately she patted the baby's back and tried to sound soothing, but she was starting to run out of *there-theres*. Tess weighed a ton. Travelers were jostling them. When she'd planned this, it seemed obvious that hopping a plane to Chicago would be easier than a ten-hour round-trip car ride with a baby.

Wrong. Even for a two day-stay, she'd needed a hefty-size bag, because babies required a ton of gear. More immediately, Tess had to have a car seat. And a diaper bag. And some toys for the flight. And then there were jackets and snacks, not counting one ticked-off baby…

Tess's small fist smacked her in the nose. Tess wanted down. Now.

Only Kasey couldn't let her down. They still had to pick up the suitcase, then get a taxi, then check into the hotel—

which was thankfully walking distance to the hospital where Dr. Frazier practiced—and then get over to the office by two that afternoon. In the meantime, it had to be at least a ten-mile walk between the plane and Baggage Claim—maybe twenty.

Oh God. She shouldn't have come. A bleak mood built over her head like a pending gloomy storm. She wanted to do this, but she had no illusions about what she was risking. Unless this doctor produced some good news, God knew what Graham would do.

The more Kasey considered it, the more crying her heart out seemed an outstanding idea. Uplifting. Inspiring. Just give up, for Pete's sake, and howl in unison with Tess...

From behind her she suddenly felt a tug on the diaper-bag strap. It was the wrong time for a thief to test her. She spun around, prepared to belt the creep with everything she had—give or take the small problem of her arms already being completely full—and suddenly there was Jake.

His eyes met hers. Down went the volume on the airport and the people and the loudspeakers. The fluorescent lights softened. The stale air freshened.

She wanted to gulp him in like chocolate after a long fast. Or forget that. She just wanted to look at him. The disheveled dark hair. The old deep-dark-sexy eyes. The long, lanky body, the way he stood, the way he looked, the way he breathed. And his initial expression reflected nerves—he obviously wasn't positive she was going to be thrilled at seeing him—but then, there it was. That slow-burn, slow-honey smile just for her.

"You're in such a mess I don't even know how to begin. But how about...gimme Tess."

She handed him the baby, who cut off an operatic high note at the sudden change in ownership.

"Now, hand over the big bag."

She handed him the diaper bag. Then her purse. By then a jacket and baby shoe had fallen to the ground, but it didn't matter; she had a chance to pick those up, straighten her hair and almost, almost, get a lid on her emotions. "I can't believe that you were flying into Chicago at the same time we were!"

"Well, I wasn't exactly." He hefted Tess another notch. She'd suddenly decided to be content, now that she'd garnered a man's complete attention—just like the femme fatale she was. "I had a Chicago work trek planned for a while. Doing a study on urban kids, a comparison of Chicago and Detroit teenagers, how much their lives are the same, how much they're different coming from similar urban environments. So I had to make a trip here."

Kasey was impressed. It was the lamest excuse she'd heard in a month of Sundays.

"And I picked now, because, well, I happened to call your house early this morning. I wanted to tell you about another lawsuit I'd come across. And Gladys—I guess she's your housekeeper? She was having a stroke about you and the baby taking off for the airport and Mr. Crandall not there and she didn't even know you were going. I knew you had this appointment, just didn't know the exact details, but not hard to figure out today was the day…"

The luggage conveyer finally started rolling around, causing a traveler stampede. Jake grabbed her arm and said to Tess, "What the hell has she been feeding you, beauty? Bricks?"

Kasey still couldn't seem to move. Jake had surprised her

before by showing up when she needed a guardian angel. But driving a few miles out of his way was hugely different than crippling his work week with a trek to Chicago. "You actually showed up—just to help us?"

"Hell, no. Didn't you hear what I said about the research I had to do?"

"Yes. I heard you." Kasey, fascinated, watched a flush shoot up his neck. He'd never tried lying to her before. And once he'd started, he seemed determined to paint himself in a blacker light.

"I don't do anything for nothing, Kasey. You can take that to the bank."

"Uh-huh." She couldn't argue with the dolt. Besides which, to pretend she didn't need the help was crazy. At least with two adults, the next two frazzling hours went smoother. Jake took care of the rental car, transported them to the hotel; she got them settled and ordered lunch, and then Jake carted them to the doctor's office. At Dr. Frazier's, though, Kasey balked at stealing any more of his time.

"It'd be crazy for you to wait for us, Jake. If you have work to do in the city, go, for heaven's sake. I have no idea how long this'll take. And I can handle it from here. Honest."

"Okay," Jake agreed. "I'll call your room later, see how it went and how you two feel about dinner by then." The baby got a kiss. "Give 'em hell, Tess, and you tell me if anyone doesn't treat you right."

Kasey watched him stride down the hall. It seemed her daughter shared the same sudden sense of silence and loss, because Tess let out a winsome calling sound after him, as if to ask *where's my Jake going?*

Kasey wore a smile when she pushed the door into the Pediatrics Neurology Department, but she lost her smile fast. This wasn't like a regular doctor's office, and the babies here weren't like regular babies. Some never quit crying; some had deformities that made them unsettling to look at. Fear seeped into Kasey's nerves. What Tess might have to face in the future could be just as terrifying as what some of these other babies faced right now. She cuddled the baby close to her pounding heart until the nurse finally called her name.

"Mrs. Crandall and Tess."

She all but sprinted into the examining room, yet even so, barely had Tess undressed before Dr. Frazier strode in with a staff of medical students who trailed him like shadows. The doctor looked more regal than a king and treated the students like toilet paper.

Kasey greeted him. He didn't respond. She readily got the message that she was a parent—a complete no-one in this scenario. The group clustered around the baby for the examination as if Kasey were as relevant to the situation as a dust bunny under the bed.

Tess wasn't usually affected by indifference, nor did she usually need attention to be content. But she hadn't liked the airport this morning, and she seemed to sense the doctor's coldness.

"If you'd let me closer, I can—"

No one was going to let Kasey closer. In fact, the doctor impatiently instructed his nurse to "give the mother" some place to go until they were through.

"I'm not leaving Tess—"

"The babies tend to do better if the mothers aren't here," the nurse assured her.

"No. You don't know her. She'll stop crying if you just—"

But no one was interested in her opinion. Kasey was escorted into a private waiting room, where she huddled in a chair and tried to convince herself that it really didn't matter if Dr. Frazier was a cold-hearted jerk. In fact, maybe it was a good sign. If the doc was this highfalutin important, then surely *he* could help Tess if anyone could. It didn't matter if he personally was a creep. She didn't care. Just please God, make him good, please God.

Minutes passed. Then an hour. Finally a nurse came to fetch Kasey, but not to take her to the baby. Instead she was ushered into Dr. Frazier's office, where the doctor sat behind a polished zebra-wood desk.

He wasted no time on pleasantries. "I won't have test results for several days, but I'll give you what I've got. First off, I can't completely negate my colleagues' diagnosis of Leber's. It's certainly possible, but I've found the condition misdiagnosed before. It's one of the causes a doctor often looks to when a child has congenital blindness. But personally, I'm wary of coming up with a Leber's diagnosis conclusively until the child is past three, preferably four or five. Too many symptoms can change and develop as the child progresses. After age four, I could probably talk possibilities with you."

"Four?" Kasey interrupted. "Are you saying I have to wait until she's four before knowing for sure what's wrong with her?"

"I didn't say that."

"Dr. Frazier…" Maybe Mr. Choke-Collar was unpleasant, but Kasey had risked too much trouble coming here to waste the opportunity. She leaned forward, blurting out one of the hardest questions she'd saved up. "Could I have done anything to cause Tess's problems?"

"Certainly. Certain drugs taken during pregnancy, certain injuries, certain problems during the labor process…but I read her entire file, Mrs. Crandall. Assuming the information is accurate, I have no reason to suspect anything prenatal as contributing to her condition."

"Then—"

"There could be a number of reasons for her various symptoms. One is cerebral palsy—"

"She doesn't have any palsy. Or any symptom like that."

Dr. Frazier sighed, as if disbelieving she'd had the nerve to interrupt him again. "Cerebral palsy is a broad term referring to injury to the brain in a way that affects control of muscles. It includes a whole spectrum of defects and disorders. This kind of damage to a child's brain could happen before, during or after birth, and can cause a wide range of difficulties—from hearing and vision disabilities to mental retardation to muscular problems. For instance, a normal infant lifts its head sometime between one and three months. A baby with CP might not do this until after their first birthday—"

"Tess can already do that, and she's still months from her first birthday."

He gave her another look, communicating what he thought of as yet another interruption from the peanut gallery. "Another example is that a child normally crawls somewhere between six and eight months. A CP baby might not start crawling until twenty-six months. That's not—"

"So if Tess has this CP—" Kasey grappled "—she could still do everything? It just might take her longer?"

"Mrs. Crandall, you keep trying to put words in my mouth. I didn't say that. Further, I am not trying to leap into a cerebral palsy diagnosis for your daughter. Another possibility is simply an underdeveloped brain."

"Underdeveloped, meaning—?"

He poured himself a cup of tea. "Two thirds of birth defects have no definite cause. In fact, it is absolutely impossible to identify the precise cause in sixty percent of the cases. So if you're counting on an absolute sure diagnosis, it may never happen."

Kasey gulped. "All right."

"However, I've seen cases of an underdeveloped brain several times. It's a mystery. Everything develops normally in the fetus but the brain...such that the child is born behind. The infant can seem retarded, both physically and mentally. Yet they catch up. The immature brain simply seems to show up in the form of delayed development, yet by the time the child is eight or nine, they might well be in a regular classroom. By the time they're seventeen, possibly no one would be able to tell there'd ever been a problem."

"Oh, God. That sounds so hopeful."

Dr. Frazier sighed. Again. "You want definitive answers, Mrs. Crandall. You want hope. But the medical community doesn't always have answers about birth defects. It'd be nice if things were that cut-and-dried."

"Nice?" Kasey repeated.

As if sensing he'd struck some kind of wrong chord with her, he squinted across the desk. "Would you rather I lied to you?"

"No."

"Good. Because I'm tired of parents who only want to hear one thing—that their child's going to be perfectly all right. We all wish that, but lies won't do you or your child any good. Right now there is no knowing for certain what's wrong with your daughter, or what her future is. Period. That's the only truth I can give you."

Kasey tracked down Tess, stumbled down the hallways, past the desk, past the waiting room and finally outside. Tears starting building in her eyes, feeling like the weight of a river. It was just…Frazier had been so cold and uncaring. And she was so exhausted. And it seemed as if she'd been holding on, holding on for weeks, counting on a promise of hope for Tess that no one seemed able to give her.

A tear squeezed out and then another, exasperating her, infuriating her. Outside, it was starting to rain, and she had to get Tess back to the hotel. The baby would be hungry soon. She needed to be fed, bathed, rocked, loved. She'd had a terrible day, too, so this was no time for Mom to fall apart. Yet those tears kept squishing out, smooshing out, until she walked blindly into a tall man's chest.

Long fingers squeezed her arms, steadying both her and the baby. Then that familiar tenor. "Well, hell. What a miracle that I keep running into my best girls. And I was just thinking, Tess, that you might like to go dancing tonight…."

He lifted the baby, then stole the diaper bag.

"But your mother isn't included," Jake told Tess. "She can go put her feet up for a few hours. We don't need her. I don't suppose you brought any high-heel sneakers and a red dress in your diaper bag, did you, kid?"

He never made out like he noticed her crying. Never made out that he had any notion this was the longest day she could ever remember.

"We'll leave your mama with a bottle—a bottle of wine, that is. But you and I are gonna do up the town right. Chicago is…well, Chicago. Lots of jazz. Lots of smoky nightclubs. We'll go somewhere with some bluesy sax, order some mac-and-cheese and milk. Does that sound like a plan or what?"

Damn him. He was carrying everything, including the baby, yet he somehow still had a hand free to grab hers. The street they were crossing had about ten lanes of furious traffic. Drizzle oozed down, just enough to curdle her hairstyle and splash in the eyes. Rain or no rain, it was still light out— that early spring evening light, all shadows, no heat, all glare, no softness.

"Would you quit looking at your mama? This is between you and me—we don't have to go dancing if you don't want. We can just stay up late and do everything wrong. Sound good, beauty?"

He was trying to hustle them across the street, carrying all her stuff, his voice lazier than a summer morning in Georgia and sexier than anything she'd heard in months. And something just snapped inside her. She knew what she'd been fiercely, violently trying to deny for ages now.

Jake was everything that had been missing in her marriage. He was laughter. And fun. And the joy of being with someone, the joy of being there for someone. He was the person she felt safe with. The person she felt dangerous with. He was the only person who'd made her laugh since the day Kasey had realized Tess had problems.

And on this day, this horrible horrible day, for him to come through and keep coming through for her was just more than she could handle.

His hands were completely full, but hers weren't.

Horns blared. Brakes squealed. But when she cupped his head in her palms to make him bend down, she only felt his smooth cool lips on hers. Screw the horns, screw the traffic. She kissed him with her eyes closed. She kissed him with everything she had, and then a little more. She kissed him, knowing Tess was between them, knowing full well that a city of several million people wasn't going to stop forever while she drank from the silky, sexy well of Jake's mouth—but damned if she didn't need to do it. Kiss him right. Kiss him well. Kiss him the way she'd needed to kiss him all this time.

And when she finally ran out of breath and drew back, she saw his eyes, not such old eyes at that instant. But hot-black eyes, as young as desire, as sinking deep as hunger.

She heard a cacophony of whistles and catcalls, approving that midstreet kiss. Jake seemed to approve it, too.

But then of course she came to her senses—she was a mother now; she had no choice about coming to her senses. Still, that moment still simmered and shimmered inside her as if a jewel had suddenly come to life.

And in that instant, she knew something irrevocable had happened. Not in the Chicago street. But in her heart.

CHAPTER 12

It wasn't fair. Convicts on a chain gang never had to work this hard. Jake's fingers pounded the computer keys at a hundred miles an hour. Four mugs were lined up next to him, filled to various degrees with cold coffee. He'd brushed his hair yesterday. He'd had breakfast. He was pretty sure.

He was never supposed to turn into a workaholic, much less a productive member of society. This was all a mistake. Somebody had him confused for someone else. Any day now, he was going to wake up and be himself again.

Under penalty of death, Jake would never admit that it was helping. The long hours. The absorbing work. The intense concentration required...

Pound pound pound. Pour another mug of coffee. Pound pound pound. His stomach started to hiss and growl again. His stomach was turning into an annoying prima donna; damn thing wanted real food, not just liquid sludge. And he was going to make a real meal. Pretty soon.

Suddenly...it stopped. Not the stomach roiling, not the story about the schizophrenic prosecutor, not the smoking computer keys. But suddenly Kasey poked into his mind again. Like magic, she was just…there. An image of her laughing, her hair all tangled, her wide smile full of life.

For weeks now, he'd been meeting her at Lily's place, knowing she was stuck with idle time while the physical therapist worked with the baby. For weeks now, he'd touched her hand. Unearthed his worst jokes to try and make her laugh. Sat with her in the spring grass, always carrying a thermos of latte because she had a weakness for good coffee.

For weeks now, he'd woken up every morning with a hard-on—which was probably the reason Barney kept heaping an unmanageable workload on his head. His writing was different. It was easy to make the words come out tight and fast and biting when a guy was trying to outrun a bullet. Sexual frustration was a mighty motivator.

The telephone rang.

He wanted to ignore it. Wanted to wallow a few minutes more in those images of Kasey, and no, nobody could live forever in this emotional limbo. But having some of her was better than having none. Worrying about her was damn near killing him, but at least he was seeing her often enough to—

The telephone rang again, and out of sheer impatience, he yanked the receiver off its cradle. His mood changed from manic to serious in a mini-blink.

Paula's voice was pitched higher than a shriek. Jake hadn't heard his ex-wife this wrung up in years. "Danny's been suspended. And I've had it, Jake. This one's on you. Damn it, you have to do something to turn this kid around, starting with getting over here right now!"

It took forty minutes to get to Paula's house and claim the kitchen for a one-on-one meet with Danny. The kid skulked in with a new scalped haircut, jeans hanging lower than his butt crack, and eyes so belligerent he looked ready to take on all comers—including his dad.

"The way I hear it," Jake said tactfully, "you're up shit creek."

"Like I care what you think."

Jake raided the fridge, came through with two Dr. Peppers. It gave him a second to get a grip—not easy to do when his heart was sinking like a dead fish in an aquarium. He'd thought they'd made such headway, but now, hearing the disgust back in Danny's voice, he didn't know what to say, how to reach him.

He sat on the stool across the counter and pushed a can Danny's way. "I was told you were suspended from school for three days."

"Yeah, so?"

"So…your mom wants you grounded from driving for a month. "

"Like I care." The eyes cared, though. God, the kid did love driving.

"Danny, shake the attitude. Tell me what happened."

"Why, what's the point? You're going to believe what everyone else says anyway, so why should I bother?"

Aw, man. It was so tempting to pour a bucket of cold water over his kid's head. Instead, Jake said, "I don't know what I believe. All I know is that I haven't heard your side. The story I was told was that you were caught with a bottle of liquor in your gym locker at school. Sounds pretty hard to deny."

"Yeah, well. I'm not denying it."

Jake hesitated, thinking that sitting on a hive of red ants had to be easier than this. "You know…I could have sworn you had a bird's-eye view what drinking could do to a family. Last I knew, you had no interest in turning out like me, you had the sense to watch yourself near that kind of thing."

Danny gave him the rolling-eyes routine. "I don't drink and I don't do drugs."

"Okay," Jake said quietly, and waited.

Eventually Danny jerked off the stool and started shuffling around the kitchen, hunkering a look out the side window, opening and closing the fridge. Anything to avoid face-to-face contact. "I'm not saying this happened. I'm just giving you a hypothetical. But let's say I had a friend who'd been in trouble. So much trouble that he couldn't risk getting his ass in a wringer another time—because if he did, he'd get kicked out of school for good."

"Okay."

"And let's say, maybe, like, I had a choice. It wasn't my problem. I could get in a lot of trouble if a bottle of liquor was found in my locker. But not as bad trouble as him. Maybe I'd get caught. Maybe I'd get suspended even. But mostly everybody'd just be mad at me. Not worse than that."

"Okay," Jake said again.

"Hypothetically, now, this friend, he said he'd get some help if I did this for him. Because he was drinking before school almost every morning, you know? Like he was really, really messed up. It's just nobody could get him to talk about it before, much less do anything."

"Okay," Jake echoed again.

"The way I see it, you can't just duck out, not do something, just because you know you're gonna get hurt. If it's right, you still have to step up." Danny spared him a glance, before glugging down his Dr. Pepper. "Lots of people get themselves in messes. You did. You really fucked up. You hurt a lot of people. Like me."

"Oh, son, I know."

"But at least when you could, you didn't hide behind it. You didn't duck out. You didn't blame anybody else. See? This friend of mine—this hypothetical friend. Maybe I should have let him hang, you know? But it seemed to me that I had to try. Just because he's all messed up right now doesn't mean he isn't a good guy. It's not like he's *evil*, Dad. I mean, come on, what would you have done in a situation like that?"

Jake said, "Probably—exactly what you did."

Finally, his son lost some of that furious starch in his shoulders. Not all of it. "I'm not telling anybody his name. Or telling anybody else this story either, because they'd guess right away who it was. So don't you tell, either."

"I won't."

"If I can't drive for a month, then I can't. And if my friend keeps on drinking like he has been, then I'm gonna feel fifty times worse for covering for him. I keep worrying what could happen if he doesn't stop. Like that he could crash a car and kill somebody or kill himself. But maybe this could turn him, you know? Maybe somebody really showing up on his side could make him think about getting help. And there was nobody else who would do it for him."

Late that night, back at his own place, Jake couldn't sleep. He stood at the window, watching the freighters in the Detroit River, their lights shining like white stars against the satin black surface. When he'd come home after talking to Danny, he'd automatically gone in the kitchen and opened the cupboard over the fridge. It was the place he used to keep his liquor stash.

He'd wanted a drink. Badly.

He'd poured himself a glass of milk, but he'd known what he was dealing with. The habit was entrenched in his soul. When times were tough, he was always going to want that drink. It was part of who he was, part of what defined him—and always would be.

His son, though, was going to be all right. Not yet. Danny wasn't at a good point in his life and wouldn't be for a while. But Jake saw the seeds of a good man, no matter how exasperating the damn kid was sometimes. For darn sure, Danny wasn't going to be the kind of man who reached for a crutch every time he stubbed his toe.

Jake gulped more milk, still blindly watching the freighters, trying to get his mind around the craving.

For two years, he'd been afraid of precisely this. Afraid that he'd crash and burn—or take up suckling a bottle again—if he allowed too much stress in his life. And yet here it was. His whole life had turned into a mountain of stress, forty times more complex than he'd ever had before—and being in love with Kasey was the core of that mountain.

This limbo just couldn't go on forever. He couldn't love her and not want to make love with her. Yet he couldn't break up a marriage and live with himself.

He had no way to live with her.

And no way he could imagine living without her.

He clunked down the blasted glass of milk, turned away from the crystal lights. His son seemed to think there were times when a good man stood up, no matter what the consequences. And damn, but Jake believed that, too. For himself, he'd been struggling to be a man he could face in the mirror again. A man of honor on his own terms. But by those terms, he needed to be there for Kasey—not to take love from her, not to cause her more trouble—but because she was in trouble and he was in a position to help her.

But damnation, how in God's name could he live this way much longer?

Kasey chased over to the kitchen doorway—where the baby was basking in the afternoon sunshine—bent down to smooch Tess, then galloped back to the oven with her hot pads.

The cherry cake was finally done. She pulled it out, setting it next to the apple muffins and snicker doodles and Parmesan meat loaf. She wasn't remotely hungry, but in times of stress, cooking had always relaxed her.

As she started to whip the potatoes, her spirits lifted. Depression had been relentlessly shagging her heart, but not at this moment. It was one of those rare oh-my afternoons. The baby was babbling, the May sun dazzling, the winsome smells of sweet lilacs and daffodils wafting in the open window.

Graham suddenly strode in, wearing his typical Saturday garb of Dockers and polo shirt. She assumed he popped in to ask her about dinner—until she saw the expression on his face—and then every muscle in her body instinctively tensed.

"Kasey. What is this?"

"What's what?" So maybe nothing had been right between them. Maybe every day their relationship seemed to
slip another notch. But Kasey kept searching her heart for a
rule book that would give her clear answers on what to do—
what was right for the baby, for her, for Graham. What she
wanted to do and what she needed to do seemed a universe
apart.

Graham slapped down a pad of paper. Kasey immediately
recognized it as the mini calendar she generally carried in her
purse—the place she recorded Tess's appointments with Lily,
for instance.

"You've been going to this physical therapist behind my
back? Taking Tess to this person without asking me?"

His tone was sharper than ice. She could never seem to
think when he talked to her like that. Her nerves started rat-
tling and then so did her mind. She tried to calmly set the
table. "It wasn't like th—"

"I thought we had this out a month ago, after you came
back from Chicago. I believe I made myself glass-clear that
I didn't want the child put through any more unnecessary
tests."

Kasey pulled in. No matter how harshly these confrontations had escalated, she still kept believing there had to be
a way to communicate in a more honest and kinder way—if
she could just find it. "There are no tests involved. This is a
physical therapist who works with babies, Graham. And Tess
loves it. She swims and gets massages and—"

"You lied to me."

Again Kasey clenched up. Even now, it was hard to believe that she was afraid of this man she'd once loved—or

thought she'd loved. It was even harder to believe that a marriage once happier than a dream had become a war zone. Everything in Kasey told her to get out… Yet deep inside, she still felt guilty for her part in the failing marriage. She wanted to face that, not run away. And she had to find a way to face Graham that didn't risk the baby. "Graham, could you try, really try, to listen to me?"

"When you lie to me? Why should I listen?"

"Please."

His mouth formed a thin line, but temporarily, he quit talking.

"I haven't put Tess through any more tests or any more doctors, because I knew you were opposed," she said carefully. "But I could see she was benefiting from the physical therapy. I didn't tell you because I suspected you'd be angry. Just like you are." She lifted a hand in an honest gesture, a plea. "I swear, I've never done anything to deliberately upset you. It's not like that. Could you try to believe that I know our daughter? Really know her, the way no doctor or outsider ever could. I can't prove that she'll be all right, but I have to keep trying to—"

He stiffened, finally spurred to interrupt her. "Kasey, get this straight because I'm tired of saying this and I won't do it again. The only reason you keep pursuing miracles for the child is because you're too weak to face the truth. And this is your last chance. Do not go behind my back again. Make no mistake. You're taking risks, with the child and with me, that will have strong repercussions if you try it again. Do you understand me?"

She couldn't speak. He sounded like a judge in a courtroom, not a husband or a father.

"Do you understand me?" When she didn't immediately respond, he lowered his voice and spoke quietly and precisely. "Do you understand that I could divorce you and get custody of Tess? You wouldn't have a prayer of winning against me in a court of law. I've got the money, the influence, the power. Don't kid yourself, Kasey. If you keep pushing me, you'll lose Tess. I guarantee it."

Again she couldn't speak. There wasn't much to say when a man ripped out your heart, but in the sudden gray silence between them, Kasey put a frame on her darkest nightmare. She could live with whatever was right or wrong with Tess. She could sleep with a man she was afraid of, if she had to. She could do whatever she had to do...to keep Tess. To keep her daughter, she'd do anything, anywhere, anytime.

He knew. Abruptly he pushed away from the counter. Something was bubbling over on the stove. Tess started to fuss from her carrier in the doorway. The sound of children's laughter echoed from the neighbor's backyard. Graham announced, "We'll be having dinner at the Whitakers' next Wednesday. And I'll be bringing Rod Grinson and his wife for dinner Friday evening. We're expecting to go to their cottage the week after that. Do you hear me?"

"Yes."

"You're not going to be 'asleep' the next time I turn to you in the night. I've had enough of that, too. Are we clear?"

She meant to answer that time. She understood exactly what was expected of her, exactly what he was threatening. But for one brief moment, she couldn't swallow, couldn't breathe. She had a terrible feeling that unless she drew a line in the sand, she'd lose herself. No matter what was right or wrong. No matter what she was risking.

"Are we clear, Kasey?"

"Oh, yes," she said. And then walked directly past him, toward the door, where she picked up Tess and swiftly walked outside.

A week passed, then two, and then May folded into June. This early on a Sunday, even the churchgoers were still asleep. The grass was still dew-drenched, the robins tugging worms from the ground, the sun washing the trees in soft yellow light. Kneeling in the dirt, Kasey worked with a spade and trowel, planting a border of pansies.

Tess hurled a rattle. This was a game intended to make Mom stop working and immediately fetch the toy, which Mom—as trained as any golden retriever—immediately did.

The baby got her tummy snuzzled for being such a royal pain, which made Tess giggle. The morning was still too cool and damp to have the baby on a blanket, so she was set up next to Kasey in a stroller, wearing OshKosh overalls and a T-shirt with hearts. Her hair was coming in thick and curly now. Kasey thought—with no bias at all—that Tess was so gorgeous she could model for a living. And she was making new sounds—nothing that remotely sounded like language, but they still managed to communicate happiness, frustration, sleepiness, hunger.

"Agh bama? Agh da?"

"I was just thinking the same thing, punkin." Again, Kasey handed her the rattle, pushed a little dirt off her forehead, and went back to spading in the velvety pansies. Wet earth perfumed the air. Bees buzzed in the last of the lilacs. The grass was softer than satin, just cut, downy as a mattress.

Heartache pushed at her consciousness, but Kasey firmly banished it. For now, she specifically had Robyn or a baby-sitter in place whenever Graham was home. For now, she worked at acing the corporate-wife job. For now, she only saw Jake when she took Tess to the PT sessions, and she never allowed her mind to dwell on her feelings for him. For now, if she had to lie, cheat or steal, she'd do those things, too. In silence. Whatever it took to keep her baby.

For a moment Kasey stopped spading and just stared at the soft, floppy pansy in her hand. She wasn't proud of her silence. It knifed, inside, that she couldn't find a way out of this impossible situation. And it ached, that she'd found a very special man at a time in her life when there was no possibility she could ever be with him.

But right now, Tess was growing and thriving and happy. There was nothing that mattered more, and there couldn't be.

"Hey, Kasey. You got a minute?"

Kasey swiftly pivoted around, recognizing Laura's voice even before she saw Graham's daughter loping toward her from the back deck. There had to be a catastrophe. It wasn't even eight, yet Laura was not only awake but dressed, wearing jeans with a top that almost covered the bottom of her bra, makeup, shoes, the whole nine yards.

"I always have a minute," she said. "You going some-where?"

Technically Laura lived at her mom's during the college summer break, but somehow she seemed to hang out here most of the time. Because she liked being around the brat, she told the adults.

"Yeah, actually. I've got suitcases packed in the car. I'm leaving."

"Leaving? For where?"

Laura crouched next to Tess's stroller. Her gaze wandered over Kasey's appearance—the smudge on her cheek, the dirt-crusted knees, the straggly T-shirt. There was a time she wouldn't have resisted commenting on Kasey's hopeless lack of taste, but lately Laura seemed to hang with her, just to talk, just to be. And sometimes to confide. "I'm not going back to U of M in the fall."

"Oh?"

"The whole thing's stupid. I'm wasting my time and Dad's money. I want to go to school, but not until I figure out what I want to do, you know? So I'm going to Colorado."

Kasey sank back, startled. "Your dad never said."

"Yeah, well, that's because Dad doesn't know. And neither does my mom. I left them both notes. I got a friend there, she's living with a guy—a nice guy, Jeremy—they've got a house. And I've got a job lined up, waitressing, like, in a coffee shop. So I figured I'd do that over the summer, then see what's what after that."

The girl shot her a wary look, as if waiting for an explosion.

Kasey said, "Your dad's going to have a stroke. So's your mom."

"I know. That's why I'm doing the gutless thing and leaving notes instead of talking to them. Especially Dad."

Tess let out a sudden yelp. Instinctively Kasey pulled the

stroller closer so that the baby's face wasn't in direct sunlight. "Then why are you telling me?"

"I don't know." Laura hesitated. "I don't expect you to agree with me, either. But I've been home for a couple weeks. Watching you and Dad. You're not happy, are you?"

Kasey had done her best not to let Graham's daughter see how much trouble there was in River City.

"You can't win with him," Laura said patiently, as if she were the mom and Kasey was the child. "If you do things his way, everything's fine. But that's the only way everything's fine. I don't get it. Why you keep putting up with it."

Again Kasey wasn't sure how to answer. No matter what Graham had done, she didn't want to put him down to his daughter. "Originally, I married your dad because I believed I loved him. The doubts were always on the other side. Why he put up with me, why he married me."

Laura snorted. "Come on. You're smart. Fun. Beautiful. And besides all that kind of crap—you're eternally grateful."

"Grateful?" The word seemed to come from nowhere. Again, Tess let out a sudden yelp. Again, Kasey instinctively pulled the stroller closer, which seemed all that was necessary to quiet the baby.

"You have to know how often my mom comes over here." When Kasey nodded, Laura went on. "So you know she comes over for money, every time she runs short or needs something special. And every time, Dad writes her a check. Making him look really generous, right?"

Kasey frowned, listening but unsure what Laura was trying to say.

"You don't get it, do you, Kasey? Dad has tons. And my

mom spends on stuff she can't afford to—which is my mom's fault, no one else's. But the thing is, Dad doesn't mind giving her money. Ever. She just has to ask. He could have settled more money on her at the time of the divorce, right? But no, he never did that. Because then she wouldn't have to ask him. She wouldn't have to be grateful. And Dad wouldn't come across as the generous, magnanimous ex-husband."

"Sheesh, Laura, don't you think that's harsh?"

"Hell, no. I think it's reality. He *loves* it, that you want to please him. That you came from a poorer background, so anything he does, you're always grateful. Everybody thinks he just adores you, because he's always getting you stuff, taking you places, acting like the doting lover. Gag me with a spoon."

"Look—" Kasey started to say.

"I can't believe you don't see it." Laura picked up the rattle for Tess. "As long as you treated him like a god, everything was copacetic. Same for me. When I kowtow full-time, I can have anything I want. Free education. Trips to Europe. Unlimited clothes. All I have to do is constantly be grateful…" She bounced to her feet. "I really want to get going. I want to be on the road before he gets up."

"Laura, I wish you'd talk longer about this. I don't know if your spending a summer in Colorado is right or wrong. It's not for me to say. But you sound so angry, honey. And I think—"

"*Kasey. Look at Tess.*"

"What?"

"*Look.*" Laura had lifted the baby out of the stroller to hug her—a guaranteed way to win a smile from Tess. This time, though, something was wrong. When Laura first lifted the baby, Tess cried louder. Yet when Laura turned around, the baby quieted faster than the flip of a dime. "Holy shit. Holy cow. Do you see what's happening?"

"What?" Kasey saw that the baby was oddly fretful, particularly when she normally adored attention from her big sister. And Laura was acting goofy—walking forward with the baby, then back. Then forward. Then back. Even stranger, the baby started a cry-stop-cry-stop pattern seemingly in response to what Laura was doing. "Honey, what on earth are you—?"

"She can *see!*"

"What?"

"*Watch her.* She's bothered by the sun in her eyes, see? When I walk into the sun, she throws up a hand and kind of cries? Then when I back up into the shade, she stops. It's about *sun.* It's because she can see. The bright light is bothering her."

Poor Tess. Kasey grabbed the baby, and put her through the same experiment, lifting her to the sun, then shifting her to the shade.

The baby squalled and tried to twist when the bright sun shone directly in her eyes.

And settled contentedly when she was put in the shade.

That is, until she got sick to death of the game and tried to kick both her mom and her sister.

Laura said suddenly, gruffly, "Don't, Kasey. Darn it. Don't."

Kasey hadn't realized she was crying until she felt Laura's skinny arms suddenly wrap around her. And Graham's daughter might not realize it, but she was crying too. It was Kasey who stood up, though, lifting the baby high into the sunlight and twirling around on the grass in a joyful dance.

All of three of them were laughing as they piled into the house. Kasey, not thinking, galloped straight for a telephone, where she dialed and bounced Tess at the same time.

Laura said, "Who are you calling?"

"Ja—" Kasey gulped, her pulse still chiming celebration bells, but it took that moment to register that her first instinct was to tell Jake. Not Graham. It wasn't the first time she'd had that urge, yet it was yet another warning that she couldn't continue in the purgatory she'd been trying to survive—yet this was obviously not the moment to tackle that. She quickly put down the phone and smiled for Laura. "Let's tell your father."

"Kasey, it's not going to change anything. As far as my leaving. But I do want to be with you to tell him about Tess, too, okay?"

They both clamored upstairs, calling Graham, Kasey more subdued as she realized how much Laura hungered to share a good moment with her father. They tracked Graham to his upstairs office and simultaneously spilled what happened... and then showed Graham, by switching a flashlight on and off in the baby's eyes, yelping joyfully when the baby tried to bat it away.

And Graham...for once, for the first time in so many months, hooked Kasey to his chest in a warm, natural hug, and drew both his daughters into the fold with them. A family. That's what Kasey once thought this would feel like, be like. It's what she had assumed that Graham wanted and ex-

pected from their relationship. And that he seemed thrilled
at Tess's news made her desperately want to feel reassured.

After dinner that night, though, when Laura had left and
Graham had taken the newspaper to the back deck, she
brought out a pitcher of sun tea. And he said, "Try not to
make too much of it, Kasey."

He had to mean Tess, because he'd already blown a gas-
ket about Laura leaving home, and that was long hashed out
now. "The baby can see, and you don't want me to make too
much of it?"

The newspaper crackled when he opened it to a different
page, but his eyes only shot to hers momentarily. "It's wonderful. But because she has some sight doesn't mean that she
has normal vision. For that matter, it doesn't mean that any
of her other symptoms are any less serious." When Kasey
failed to respond, he added, "I just don't want you disappointed again. She's had a change in health. That's great. But
all that's actually happened is that she's responded to some
light."

When she still said nothing, he shot her an impatient
look. "What's wrong?"

"Nothing, Graham." But there was. It suddenly struck her
as amazing—and frightening—that she was sitting here,
drinking tea with a man she was afraid of, a man she'd lost
all respect for. She refused to believe he wanted Tess to be
unhealthy. But pretty damn obviously, he had no reason to
be happy if Tess got better, because that could mean losing
power over her and the baby both.

Laura's words from that morning came back to haunt her.
When Kasey had strived to please Graham, they'd had no

problems. When Graham was the focus of her universe, they had no problems. He really didn't know her or value her in any other way.

Kasey wanted to criticize him, but in the deepest part of herself, she thought it was past time to face some hard truths. Their problems weren't solely because of the kind of man Graham was...but because of the kind of woman she was.

She'd always been the kind of woman who expected not to be counted. Who expected to feel grateful and never deserving. Who could be relied on, in any crisis, to shut up and behave.

The kind of woman she was—or used to be.

CHAPTER 13

When Kasey arrived at the hospital in Boston, it was a far different scene than the hospitals she'd encountered before. Knowing Graham couldn't fight her about this appointment definitely made the trip less stressful. So did all the research Jake had done ahead for her.

Even so, she opened the door and was startled into laughing. "Did they make this place for us or what, punkin?" The baby seemed as enthralled as she was. The place looked less like a medical facility than a giant day care. Cartoon characters decorated the ceilings. The waiting rooms held more playpens and cribs than chairs. A baby was crawling down the hall, giggling as a nurse pretended to chase him. A toddler had clearly escaped from another office—judging from the fact that she was stark naked—and was negotiating around chairs and strangers' faces with a fierce look of concentration. Somewhere a child cried in pain...but somewhere else a pair of babies were babbling laughter.

This was exactly what Jake had researched, exactly what she'd been told to expect—that this was a clinic for babies with problems, no matter what those problems were. It was a place not just to talk about futures, but to create futures. A place that didn't dwell on what a baby couldn't do, but on what he could.

She'd barely signed in before a smiling nurse came out to greet them. "You're Kasey Crandall? And your Tess is here to see Dr. Eames. Come on through—"

"You don't want me to wait?" Kasey couldn't believe she'd been identified that fast, much less that they could take her so quickly.

Nurse Redmond—Elaine, according to her name tag—chuckled. "This place caters to babies. Not to doctors, not to nurses, not to moms. We want to get 'em when they're happy and fresh. Which means that we all nap when it's naptime…and for darn sure, we don't make the babies wait if we can help it. Is she going to panic if I try to pick her up?"

"I'm not sure. She's getting a little 'stranger anxiety' these days, but generally she likes people."

"Well, we don't want to start her off crying. Let's just see." The nurse waggled her fingers and cooed to Tess, but the baby snuggled against Kasey's neck. "That's okay, darling. But you just wait. I'll have another chance to win you over." To Kasey, "All through the next two days, you can either stay with her or hand her over to us—whichever strikes you as working best for Tess at the time. We're used to making rolling readjustments, and I'm your liaison person, if you come up with questions or need help during your stay. Okay?"

"Okay."

"Something tells me she's extra fond of that big red ball?"

"Yes. They're inseparable—"

"No problem. In fact, that's great. It always helps if a baby has a comfort toy. I'll tell the staff as we go. The small details like that can help us reach the baby. Now…is the baby's father with you?"

"No. I'm alone." Graham considered his work too important to interrupt for something like this. He'd have hired a chauffeur or escort, if she asked. She hadn't asked.

Jake would have come in a blink, if she'd asked him—which was the reason she hadn't. Time after time, he'd already been there for her, taking time from his work, coming through at her lowest moments. Unless Kasey could give him something freely back, she refused to take advantage of him again.

The nurse escorted them down the hall. "Okay…I need you to give me Tess's general routine—bathtime, naptime, meals, that kind of thing. Also, there's a kitchen on every floor where you can prepare food or bottles… there are also private rooms with cots so parents can catch naps when their babies are going through tests. Sometimes everybody just plain needs a time-out. Also…"

Kasey drank in the setup. They passed through a room painted in rainbow colors, followed by a room decorated in a vibrant plaid. She saw a small child with an artificial arm smacking another child with an artificial limb. A legless baby propelled herself in a walker clearly engineered just for her.

Every sight wasn't full of hope, every scene didn't promise smiles. Tragedies hid in the corners; some parents looked beaten, frightened, lost. Yet Kasey felt her heart lifting. It wasn't like other places. The children reigned. And every child seemed to be treated as if he were no different than other children—they were handed out love, scolds, bribes, affection, swarms of praise. And patience. No one, anywhere, seemed to be short of patience.

By six that night, though, Kasey was worn-tired, goofy-tired, lost-it tired. The evaluation program she'd signed Tess up for involved two long days of tests, with a comprehensive team assigned to the baby—a neurologist, pediatrician, counselor and specialists in all areas of birth defects and child development. Dr. Eames was the head honcho. Kasey met him early, but he also connected with her at the end of the day.

No one seemed to have told Dr. Eames that he was a god. He was wearing sandals with socks, a Yale sweatshirt and baggy-kneed cords, and he sucked on cinnamon sticks almost nonstop.

"So," he finished up, "that's the schedule for tomorrow. We should be done by three, but that depends on Tess. If she gets tired and cranky on us, we'll do a nap, then finish after. But that's the plan, okay?"

"Okay."

"Now you know how to get across the walkway to your hotel? So you don't have go outside unless you want to?"

"Yes."

"Mrs. Crandall."

"Yes?"

"You're going left. The covered walkway's down that long hall to the right."

She laughed, but truthfully by then she barely knew left from right. She wasn't sad or upset. It was a terrific place. She just felt more wrung out than a leaf in a tornado.

She remembered the hall now. It was the one with the balloon figures on the walls, the toy store near the reception area. The hotel had several restaurants, shops and movies, she'd been told, but at the moment, all Kasey wanted was room service and the nearest mattress. Unfortunately, Tess was bouncing and babbling ten for a dozen on her shoulder, acting as if she had the energy to party the rest of the night.

She saw the man striding toward her from the other side of the walkway and immediately recognized Jake, but that was only because she was so tired she was delusional. It was almost funny, really, to dream up the only human being she actually wanted to see—even when she was too tired to think, even when her hair hadn't seen a brush in several hours. For that matter, even when it had.

"Hey, beauty. I was just thinking—hoping—I'd run into a good-looking woman cute enough to pick up."

The five-ton baby was suddenly lifted out of her arms, kissed soundly and thoroughly. Tess wriggled all over with delight.

"Yeah, you're happy to see me, too, aren't you, darlin'? I swear you were born with fantastic taste in men—"

Kasey had to interrupt him. "You can't possibly be here!"

"Yeah, I know." He drank her in one long lazy sip. The too long absence bleated between them, an ache that couldn't be said or seen. "My boss even raised hell. Oops. I'm sorry I said 'hell,' Tess, I'm not used to being around chicklets. I'll try harder, okay?"

"Jake—"

"I'll be damned. Is that the red ball I gave you ages ago?" The baby, naturally, had hurled it on the floor so a grown-up could pick it up for her. Jake was the new sucker.

"She glommed on to that ball from the first day you gave it to her," Kasey said.

"I thought it was a mistake then. Your mom got all emotional over that ball, didn't she, princess? But then, you couldn't see at the time. You two sure proved the whole world wrong, didn't you?"

"The whole world *was* wrong," Kasey whispered.

"Not you. Not you, Kase. You believed in her from the get-go." He held her gaze for one long, fierce heartbeat…but then he was back to his nonsense. "Let's get this show on the road, okay? Just steer me where we're going. I'm assuming your room. And once Tess is fed and you've got your shoes off, I was thinking you might need a break. I've got a room two floors up. She'll come with me, won't you, sweetheart? So if you need some rest—"

"Jake. How did you even know—?"

"Robyn. I was excited for you two. For Tess. For the fantastic news about her seeing. But then I couldn't seem to let it go… I figured Graham had to be pretty damn thrilled, too." A guarded note seeped into his voice, but it was gone faster than lightning. "But I also figured, knowing you, that you'd want a doctor to check out that change in her vision right away. So I called. And Robyn spilled the beans about where you were…"

He kept it up, the idle chitchat, but he also kept them herded toward her room. Because the hotel catered to patients' families, her room was like a minisuite—one bedroom had the usual accoutrements for her, but there was also a tiny anteroom set up with a crib for Tess.

When Kasey checked in that morning, she'd simply dumped their stuff and hightailed it over to the hospital with Tess. No housekeeping fairy had shown up in the meantime.

Suitcases were still stashed open on the bed, debris strung out in the bathroom. A sweater had slunk from a chair to the floor.

Jake moved like a well-oiled machine. Carrying the baby, he started a hot bath, came out to grab a phone, ordered dinner for two—and when she failed to figure out in thirty seconds what she wanted, he ordered for her and the baby both. The TV was switched on, the drapes closed, and then she was hustled into the bathroom with a robe and all that steaming hot water for a soak.

When she emerged with her cheeks still pink from the steam, room service was just carting in steaks and red wine for two and a mashed turkey and milk dinner for one. Tess was wearing one of her more elegant pj's—red hearts with red-heart feet, her night diaper on, settled in Jake's lap as if she were stuck there with Velcro.

An hour later, Tess was drooping like a wilted rose—a plump wilted rose. Jake carried her into the little side room with the crib, covered her, and gently closed the door. Kasey hadn't tried to bring up anything personal yet. There'd been no chance, and Jake still had questions.

"What time do all the tests start tomorrow?"

"We're supposed to be over there before eight, and—"

"Like I mentioned, I've got a room upstairs. Haven't been in it yet—in fact my suitcase is still in the rental car. But I can get an alarm set, get a breakfast going with you two by, say, seven-fifteen."

"Jake, you don't have to—"

"You're seeing Eames. I mean, I researched this place, know you get assigned a whole team. But Eames is your main doctor? And he talked to you about the basic plan?"

"Yes, we're hoping the bulk of tests'll be done by midafternoon. Then they set up a summit meeting with Dr. Eames and the whole team. They could want us to stay another day. But after the initial exam, he was pretty sure we'd be done with the tests he wanted by tomorrow."

"Okay. And how's it going so far?"

She told him. And then he asked another question, and she answered that. As he wheeled out the room service cart, he asked yet another question, keeping her occupied yet again. And then he stood up.

"Kasey, you have to be completely beat after a day like this. I'm in room 425. You want me, call. But the baby looks out for the count tonight, and I suspect you need some crash time yourself—"

When he strode toward the door, she was so startled, her jaw almost dropped in shock. "Damn it. You just wait a minute, buster."

"Huh?"

She hiked toward him and jabbed a finger in his chest. Hard. "You're happy with this?"

"Happy with what?"

"Damn it. You've come through for me and through for me and through for me. I'm sick of it, Jake. You never ask me for a damn thing."

He raised an eyebrow, as if the question completely confused him. "What am I supposed to ask you for?"

Another poke. This one harder yet. "You act like you don't need anything from me. Like you don't expect anything. Like it's completely normal, for you to just show up and show up and show up. Helping me. Helping Tess. Being there for us. You're frank about your problems with alcohol, but then I can't get a single chance to do anything to be there for you. I've had it, Jake!"

"You're mad?" he asked carefully.

"Mad doesn't come close! This is ridiculous!"

"Okay," he said, again very cautiously.

So cautiously that she finally blew. She tugged at his shirt collar with both hands and surged up on tiptoe. It was enough to put him within kissing distance, and then it was done. She did it. Kissed him. Took his mouth and kept it and kept on the way she'd wanted to ever since the day she'd kissed him on that busy street in Chicago.

He tasted like mints and coffee and him. As if he were afraid she'd break, his hands carefully clutched her shoulders, not forcibly holding her, but more like making sure one of them—or both of them—didn't fall until he figured out what in God's name was going on.

She could have told him exactly what was going on, except that she was done talking. They'd talked for months. And kissing him like this—hot kisses, hot wet kisses, hot wet kisses involving tongues and teeth and greed and hunger—was exactly what she'd been trying not to do. She was married. Her whole life she'd believed that it was wrong—fiercely wrong, by anyone's ethical and moral standards—to break one's marriage vows.

Only nothing had been simple in her life these last months, and this wasn't either. Jake loved her. He'd shown her love in a thousand ways, giving her support and caring and kindness completely selflessly. So how could loving him possibly be wrong?

It wasn't. Not in her heart. What was wrong was coward-ice, and it seemed like her whole life, she'd snuck around, being accommodating and grateful and hiding behind doing the right thing so she'd never be hanging out there on a frail limb. Only right now she was hanging on such a frail limb that it could crack on her at any second. And probably would.

She no longer cared. There was nothing wrong with lov-ing Jake. Nothing. Nothing wrong with loving someone who deserved love, expressing something from her heart and soul that was real and true and honest.

A button pinged when she yanked at his shirt. Perhaps a woman in love was naturally endowed with some extra strength. God knows he was naturally endowed with some extras, judging from how hard he was kissing her back and how hard his erection was pressed against her robe.

"Now, Kasey—"

Obviously it was a mistake to let him up for air—although she definitely felt gratified to hear his voice coming out thicker than cold glue. And his hands on her shoulders, now, weren't treating her like precious china but seemed to be clenching and unclenching as if he were grappling for con-trol.

Jake, being Jake, would find that control if he were deter-mined enough…but Kasey had the advantage of knowing how strong he was. He would never ask—ever—for a thing from her, so she totally understood they'd never make love if she didn't take the initiative. Jake wasn't going to push her into anything in this lifetime.

So she pushed him. Possibly if he'd been steadier, her mini-push wouldn't have had any effect, but as it was he toppled on the quilted spread of the king-size bed. Her suitcases were still gaping open, taking up most of the bed space, but not for long. She shoved. The suitcases crashed to the floor, and then she crashed on top of Jake and zoomed down to take his mouth again. This time she intended to take it good. To take it ruthlessly. Ravishingly.

Aw, hell. To take it any way she could get him to give it to her.

His mouth let itself be taken; his mouth really liked being seduced. She squirmed on top of him, settling in, breasts and tummy up against his chest and abdomen, well aware that she was courting mayhem. He groaned under her mouth, a groan of need if she'd ever heard one. She push-pulled at his shirt. Fingers scrabbled to find his pants zipper.

It was hard to strip a man when one was lying on top of him, but for darn sure, she wasn't giving up any kisses just because getting him naked was challenging. Clothes tumbled, tucked, bunched. So did the bedspread. She seemed to bunch in and around him, too, but oh, where bare skin suddenly touched bare skin, it was worth every elbow jab, every zipper tooth that fought her, every anything.

She remembered this joy.

What she remembered most was how she used to be. Joyful. She couldn't wait to roar out of bed every morning to start a new day. She hated to go to sleep and miss even seconds of life. She used to love life with an irrepressible exuberance.

The way she loved him.

Jake.

He'd helped her find herself again. The "herself" that she'd somehow lost over the last months. She'd been afraid and ashamed for so long she'd almost forgotten there was more to life than the current disaster she was in. She was more than that mess. Or she could be.

And Jake…he knew her. He knew her disasters. He knew the doormat side of her. He knew the part that giggled when he nipped her neck. The part that made her feel lush and female when his hands splayed on her fanny, pulling her into him, rubbing, making her ache, making her want.

Making her soar.

She clutched her hands around his neck and kissed him, eyes closed, her heart storming, her pulse belting out love songs about longing and belonging. Lights flashed on and off from behind the drapes, reflecting a Boston night so far away it might have been the other side of the universe. Lamplight pooled on his face, then on hers, when they rolled back and forth, seeking some way to be comfortable on a mattress that was suddenly fighting them. There was no comfort to be had between two bodies this hungry, this frustrated.

Yet she wanted to know him in different ways, in all ways. He was sleek and long, her Jake. Not perfect. She examined the creases around his eyes. The sleek shoulders, the long, strong torso and rough chest hair. He had a scar on his right side—appendix? She found a scar from a motorcycle burn, another mark from a long-healed break. His fingers were long, a city man's hands and yet not. He had no blue-collar type of callouses, yet there was character in his grip, in his wrists, tenderness in the meeting of his fingertips to her fingertips.

"Are you…" Jake seemed to lose his voice, and then tried again. "Are you planning on playing all night?"

270 LUCKY

"I'm not sure."

"For a while there I thought I was going to be in for a slam-bam-thank-you-sir kind of experience. I thought you were in a hell of a hurry, but then you seemed to digress. You're not really that interested in holding hands at this minute, are you?"

"I like your hands, Jake."

"I like yours, too." He cleared his throat. Again. "I like…all of you."

"I like all of you, too. And I am in a hell of a hurry," she assured him.

"Good. That's good."

"I would love to give you a slam-bam-thank-you-sir kind of experience. But I can't seem to stop looking at you. Touching you. You think there's something wrong with me?"

"Absolutely not. There's nothing wrong with you in any way. You're beautiful from every direction and backwards from Sunday. Trust me on this."

"I do trust you, Jake."

There. That look in his eyes. The one he usually guarded so carefully. Love turned his old eyes young.

She pushed at his hair. "Do you mind if I hurry this along? I realize you're a man, and men like endless foreplay and all. But I can't just sit around for hours without feeling…frustrated. I'm sorry."

"It's okay."

"We're going to need protection."

"I have protection in my wallet. I have no idea where my wallet is, but—"

"Something tells me you can find it."

"I'd say the odds are outstanding," he agreed.

He was teasing, but that boyish smile of his didn't last, not once she'd sheathed him and got serious. This wasn't like a poker game, because she wasn't playing, in any way, yet she was anteing up everything she was. Everything she'd held back. Every vulnerability and flaw she'd been afraid of revealing. Everything she could lose.

They came together like a forest fire—all fire and heat crackling out of control, and then, oh God, there it was. A spear of joy, shooting through her, propelling a rapacious, greedy need to give. She tried to give him pleasure so rich, it hurt. Heaven knew she hurt from the fierce love of him.

Later, ages later, her eyes were still closed from satiation and exhaustion, yet she could feel his hand stroking, stroking, stroking velvet caresses down her back. Seconds ticked on the bedside clock. He wasn't sleeping, she knew, not just because she could feel his slow, soothing caresses but because she sensed his eyes were open in the darkness. She tucked up tight against him.

"If you're going to feel guilty," she said quietly, "I'll never forgive myself."

"You're the one I was afraid would have a problem with guilt."

She lifted her head. Studied those loving eyes. If she could just hold the memory of his gaze, she'd have something to sustain her forever. "You didn't do anything wrong. You didn't seduce me. You didn't ask me to do anything I didn't want to do. I asked to be with you like this. I wanted you, wanted this."

"And I wanted you, wanted this—for months. But I know you, Kase. You couldn't have planned to sleep with me while you were married to someone else."

"I didn't plan it. And I do have to fix my life, Jake."

"I'm not asking you for anything."

"Maybe you should. Maybe you have a right to ask. If you want me."

"Shut up, Kasey. You know damn well what I want. What I can't ask for."

She searched his face. "This is what I know. That this was right, between us. But it wouldn't be right a second time. This wasn't an accident. It was a choice. A choice I could never regret, a choice I'll always treasure—"

"Damn it. Don't you even try saying goodbye to me."

"Jake, I swear I'm not. But my life, right now, is a train wreck. I have to solve my situation with Graham."

"You're still afraid he'll take Tess away from you?"

"That's exactly why I stayed with him these last months. Fear. But the problem's gotten bigger than that." She grappled to find the words. "It took me forever to understand how I got into that marriage, why I was attracted to the kind of man Graham is, why I didn't see what he was really like. And that part isn't about Tess. It has to do with fixing the part of myself that caused the problem."

"Nothing in you needs fixing, Kase."

She looked at him quietly. "Jake, you told me I didn't understand about your drinking. You told me you had to handle it alone, that no one else could really get it. I didn't agree with you. I still don't. But I do understand now that I have a problem like you did. I need to be strong, I need to be sure of myself—so that I can offer you strength. So that you can know for positive you can count on me."

She saw him squeeze his eyes closed, then open them again. He said slowly, "No matter how you're trying to wrap the words up, I think you're really trying to say goodbye. And I won't fight you. Not this minute. Because we both need to put all the energy we've got on tomorrow—and don't even try to argue with me on that, Kase. Whether you hear good news or bad news from the doctors tomorrow, I'm going to be there for you."

Kasey walked into the meeting the next night, she was almost staggering tired. Initially they'd thought the hour would be three; instead it was almost 8:00 p.m. One test had to be rerun; another time Tess had gotten too fretful to complete a different test; and then another took an extra hour to get the results back.

She sank into the chair in the cream-and-coral conference room. Jake settled next to her—the way he'd been next to her all day—and when Tess started up with a petulant cry, he simply got up, sank to the floor cross-legged and played quietly with her. Kasey was left to concentrate completely on the medical team's comments to her.

Maybe she'd built up so darned much hope—and fear—that she'd somehow put a wall between herself and the words. Maybe their words mattered so damned much that she couldn't tolerate hearing bad news. She asked questions. She knew she did. She listened to each member of the team. She knew she did.

Yet it seemed she could only pick up certain words. "No conclusive diagnosis, but…"

"Absolutely not Leber's."

"Normal vision. Probably not for a year or two yet. But the causes of the initial blindness...normal vision...she'll have normal vision...she'll have normal vision..."

"...develop a comprehensive program of physical and mental therapy for each six-month stretch, until..."

"Absolutely not Leber's."

At some point, the words finally traveled the long, painful path from her brain to her heart and she surged to her feet. She was only a step away from Tess and Jake. And by God, if her tough, cynical, stubborn lover didn't have eyes filled up like a well on the brink of overflowing.

The medical team was still talking, but there were smiles all around as she crouched down and awkwardly, fiercely hugged Jake. Possibly her eyes were as soggy as his, because his face was blurry for that instant. And holding him—she felt as if she couldn't have survived if she couldn't claim that hug.

But then she turned to Tess, who was lying in the fold of Jake's knees, with a rare little scowl on her forehead. The baby was sick to bits of tests, doctors, needles and strangers. Any excuse and she was likely going to deliver a first-class normal tantrum.

Kasey, trying to squeeze back the tears, lifted her wannabe tyrant as if she were the most precious thing in the universe....which, of course, she was. Her baby. Not perfect. Not all things solved. But her baby was going to see. Her baby was going to have a life. Anything Kasey had been through, anything she had to go through, was worth this fight. And Tess, as if sensing her mother's ferocious wave of love at that moment, seemed to—at least temporarily—give up the tantrum idea.

Kasey felt a hand squeeze her shoulder, knew it was Jake's. And eventually she stood up with the baby and started to settle in the chair for the last of the meeting...only to turn toward Jake to share another smile with him. And he wasn't there.

The door was quietly closing at the far end of the room. He was gone.

CHAPTER 14

Kasey opened the car door and felt the immediate gust of hot air. By five o'clock, you'd think the heat might have started to lift—but no. It was too hot to move. Too hot to breathe. Too hot to even complain.

Tess grumped when Kasey lifted her from the car seat—along with her purse and a bag of paperbacks Ellen had insisted on giving her—all of which stuck together like sweaty glue. "I know, punkin, I know. Go ahead and snarl. That's what I feel like, too."

It had been a long month. The wonderful news about Tess made Kasey all the more aware that she had time now—time to concentrate on fixing her own life. Unfortunately, knowing what she needed to do didn't make it happen instantaneously, and fixing oneself, she'd discovered, was low-down lonely work.

To add to her grumps, her mother had begged for a visit this afternoon. Normally she wouldn't have minded, but Tess had a front tooth coming in and was testier than a crab. Kasey chugged toward the back door, wishing to heavens it would rain. Late this morning, ominous, dirty clouds had clustered in the west, and then stalled. The atmosphere was thick and unrelentingly oppressive. "Well, we'll be in the air-conditioning in a minute, love…we can relax and chill out, I promise—"

Sweat drooled down her neck as she juggled the bag of books, pushed the key in the lock and opened the door, the whole time trying to comfort one increasingly pissed-off baby.

"SURPRISE!"

The herd of voices all screamed at once. Kasey dropped the book bag. Even Tess was distracted enough to quit wailing. They'd only been gone a few hours—yet the house was transformed. Balloons and ribbons were strung room to room. A gigantic three-tiered cake stood on the kitchen table, reading EARLY HAPPY B'DAY, TESS! Gaily wrapped presents climbed halfway to the ceiling.

Every neighbor she knew—and some she didn't—were decked out in swimming suits and summer party gear. Several people in catering uniforms were sweeping through, carrying trays of drinks and food. The doors to the back deck and pool were gaping open, letting in the broiling humid air—but also revealing a set-up bar and buffet outside.

And there was Graham, bearing down on her with a smile and a small, oblong gift box.

"I think we managed to surprise her, don't you think?" he said heartily to the crowd.

"I'll say," Kasey said weakly. A sense of déjà vu hit her like a slap. She recognized part of this day in Camelot from before. She'd been at a block party with this same group of neighbors the afternoon her water broke. She'd been embarrassed to death then, wanted to crawl in a hole and disappear. The circumstances were different, but the hole wish was just as real.

"I can't believe this!" She more than couldn't believe it.

The party was not just a startling surprise—it was downright amazing. She'd told Graham the night before that she'd seen a lawyer about a divorce.

Graham pushed closer, close enough to press a kiss on her forehead. Nothing in his expression revealed to anyone that he'd ever heard the word *divorce*—or anything beyond his pleasure at springing a surprise party on her. "I know Tess's first birthday isn't for a couple weeks, but that's exactly why I wanted to do this now. It's the only way I knew you couldn't guess and would really be surprised."

"I am, God knows."

He took the baby, a little gingerly when he realized how damp-hot Tess was, and pushed the box in her hands. "Open it, Kasey."

She stared at him.

"Come on, everyone, make her open it!" The crowd responded to his call to arms by chanting a plea for her to open the box. "The other presents are for Tess, but this one's just for you. Because you've been through such a hard year and I love you so much." His voice didn't boom, but it was meant to carry—meant to invoke the expressions of isn't-he-a-darling-husband from the crowd.

Kasey felt more cornered than a mouse in a cage. She opened the gift box with wooden fingers. The necklace inside was a stunning choker of rubies, sapphires and diamonds.

When she didn't lift it for the crowd to see, Graham did, arousing a predictable response of oooh's and aaaah's. "I was thinking something for fun, for the Fourth of July. Do you like it?"

"I'm speechless."

The crowd laughed. Graham handed the baby to some-one. "Come on, I'll put it on you."

He spun her around, fastening it before she could object. The stones felt heavy and cold against her neck. Whistles of appreciation echoed through the partiers. "I'll get you a plate, darling."

She heard Tess cry out again, but couldn't see her. A plate was put in her hands, heaped with cold, raw shrimp, lobster dripping in ice, chilled sweet cherries. She heard someone saying, "God, she's so lucky. He's so in love with her" and "There's nothing he wouldn't do for her" and then "Graham said he was taking you to Paris for a second honeymoon."

"Did he," Kasey said.

Someone else patted her arm. "So Graham let Laura go to Colorado for the summer, did he? I'll bet she's having a ball."

"So she tells us," Kasey said, because by then she'd picked up the rhythm. It wasn't as if she didn't know all the words to this song. Graham himself had taught her how a master manipulator could spin anything to his advantage.

She tracked down Tess within minutes, though, because the baby's wails got more insistent when she couldn't find her mom. "I'll bet she's wet," Kasey said with a laugh, and carted her upstairs to the nursery.

If she was hoping for a moment's breathing space, it didn't happen. Neighbors traipsed upstairs with her—Dorian and Mary Ellen and Karen. Tess quieted the instant she was set free on the carpet with her wet diaper off.

"She looks so wonderful, Kasey," Karen said warmly. "Graham told us about your going to the hospital in Boston. The wonderful news that she's really going to be all right."

"We can't be positive, not for a while yet. But it looks that way." Kasey's gaze strayed to the baby, who was rolling over to reach for her red ball. It still made her breath catch. Seeing her roll over. And yeah, other babies did it months before Tess had conquered the skill...but months ago no one had believed she would ever do it.

"Graham said that the doctors had a whole list of things they thought could have been the problem," Mary Ellen added.

"Yeah, a whole range. Cerebral palsy. An underdeveloped brain. Some birth defect with a seven-syllable title. And a zillion things could have happened to her in the birth process. But what the Boston medical team could guarantee for us is that the original scary diagnosis was simply wrong."

"I don't get it, Kasey. How could that happen?"

Kasey shook her head. "Believe me, I wish we knew. The original symptoms were really terrifying. No one seems absolutely certain why they've disappeared. It's unsettling. I mean, if there was a genetic reason for sure, then we could make a choice about having more children. If a doctor was at fault, we could make a choice about suing, to make sure it didn't happen to someone else. But as it is..." She lifted her hands. "I'm just so grateful the first diagnosis was wrong."

"I'd feel the same way," Karen said warmly. "It's just so wonderfully amazing."

"And lucky," Kasey whispered. She'd never forget that night in Dr. Eames's office. Jake, holding her, right after hearing the good news. Jake, sitting on the floor with the baby, as if he were the dad...and the three of them were the family.

The three neighbors looked at each other, and then Karen

leaned forward. "Kasey, it's really bothered us, that we were so unhelpful for you. We did call. We did offer. But Graham counseled us that you needed to get away from the baby, get your mind on other things. We all thought you were in denial. God knows we weren't trying to be callous."

Mary Ellen added, "Now we realize you were really struggling alone with this. We're sorry. I swear, we wanted to help—"

"Don't, all of you. Darn it, you're going to make me cry. Don't feel badly. I didn't know what to do, either."

"Then everything's back to normal? Completely back to normal now?"

Someone called from the stairwell, and that was the end of their minigathering. The partiers stayed another two hours, and would have likely stayed forever if it weren't for the storm. Around seven, thunder suddenly drumrolled in the west. Clouds hurtled across the sky, bringing pitchforks of sterling-silver lightning. Fat raindrops brought on laughter and yelps from the women, and that started the exodus.

An hour later, the house was quiet—a disastrous mess, but quiet—when Graham tracked her down in the bedroom. Lights flickered on and off as he stood in the doorway.

Kasey saw him. She'd just changed clothes. The khaki shorts and polo shirt had been gifts from Graham. Now, from the oversize print T-shirt to her underpants, she was wearing clothes she'd had from before the marriage, although she doubted he'd know or notice that. She kept moving, searching in the back of her closet for her old Birks.

"You can't still be angry," he said.

"I'm not angry." She glanced at him. "And I wasn't angry

yesterday, when I told you I'd seen a lawyer and was filing for divorce."

"I know what you said. But I thought you'd come to your senses—especially after tonight. I gave you the necklace. Told everyone about taking you to Paris."

"Yes, you did."

"I threw the party. For you."

"For you," she corrected him, and then unclipped the heavy necklace, laid it back in its box, and set it gently down on his bureau—not hers.

"I thought the party would make you change your mind."

"No, you didn't." Again, she said it quietly. "You thought it would blackmail me into staying." She realized she was wearing a watch—not a major fancy watch, one for everyday. But still it was one he'd given her. She'd forgotten. Now she removed that, too. "You were setting me up."

"Setting you up? What do you mean?"

"You were setting me up to look like a jerk if I left you. And it'll work, Graham," she assured him. "I'll leave, and you'll look like a saint. Everyone'll say, my God, he was a prince, the most generous, loving husband a woman could possibly have. And now you won't have to worry about looking bad by divorcing a woman with a handicapped child. It's all right now. No one'll judge you. The only one they'll judge is me."

Graham fell silent. "I don't understand you," he said finally. "Is this because you want me to do something about the baby? Because I already decided I'd do that, Kasey. Hire a team of investigators. Get my full legal staff on it. If there's any conceivable way to uncover why she started out with those symptoms, I'll do it."

"I wish there were some sure answers," she admitted. "For your sake, for mine, for Tess's. But that doesn't have anything to do with our marriage, Graham."

"You can't leave." When she didn't respond, he said, "Kasey, for God's sake, everything's fine now. Everything can go back to the way it was before. You know I'll give you anything you ask for. The baby's going to be all right. You haven't got a reason in hell to leave."

"That's what you can tell everyone," she agreed, and left the room.

Damned if her hands weren't shaking. She spent ages pacing downstairs, too shook up to think coherently. She went through her kitchen desk, gathered Tess's toys and baby gear, tried to organize what she hadn't already. Yesterday, after seeing the lawyer, she'd stashed some suitcases out of sight. She hadn't known at what exact point she was going to leave, just that she wanted to be prepared to leave quickly if that became necessary.

The storm blustered and grew. As night fell, Kasey realized the obvious. She didn't have to leave quickly. But she did have to leave. She'd long, long overstayed her time with Graham.

When she hiked upstairs to get Tess, then hurried back down to store the last of their things in the Volvo, her heart was pounding like a cyclone in a tin can. Graham had closed himself in their bedroom and hadn't come out, but she was still afraid he'd try to do something to stop her, create some kind of impossible scene...but she was getting less afraid, minute by minute. Her husband was skilled at threats and intimidation, but seemed to have no skills at all at keeping people. As she snapped Tess in the car seat, the thought suddenly poked in her mind that it seemed unfair not to give him a chance to say goodbye to the baby...but then she had to roll her eyes.

What a silly thought. He'd never really said hello to his daughter, so what would the point have been in his saying goodbye?

The rain was still sloshing down, but at least most of the lightning had moved off to the east as she drove down Lakeshore. Unsaid words stuck in her throat like lumps. Maybe she should have invited a last, final yelling match with Graham, but there seemed no point. She was reminded of the old bumper sticker about parachutes and minds being alike; neither worked unless they were open.

Graham saw himself as a prince. No matter what she said, he'd manage to twist it around so he was still a prince.

She had words she wanted to say. A heart she wanted to share. But never again, to someone who didn't value her.

On the twenty-minute drive to Jake's apartment, her mind replayed the same petrifying question—how on earth had a nice woman, such as herself, gotten herself into such an unholy mess? Once upon a time, she'd never envisioned walking out on a marriage—much less with a baby and barely more than the clothes on her back. Once upon a time, she'd been a good girl, a diplomat and soother and accommodator extraordinaire. Once upon a time, she'd been a hard-core coward, and that was the toughest thing to understand—how the Sam Hill she could have turned into a woman who was suddenly leaping off emotional cliffs without a single qualm?

She pulled into a parking space near Jake's front door, cut

the engine, and promptly suffered three hiccups in a row. "Maybe we'd better not rush into bringing all the suitcases in quite yet, punkin. You think?"

Tess reached out her arms, in a universal baby gesture that meant get-me-the-hell-out-of-this-car-seat contraption.

"Look. It's crazy, not calling him first. I mean, the last I knew, he wanted us. But maybe he had second thoughts about taking on a not-yet-divorced woman and a baby. Maybe we should double check with him before just pouncing on him, you know?"

"Oogla ba! Bwna!"

"Okay, okay. I'm not going back to the woman I used to be. It was just a momentary flashback. Don't be mad at me. We've had a long day." Kasey opened the back door to swiftly unstrap her daughter. Naturally the clouds chose that instant to dump another deluge. She ran to the door with the baby tucked inside her rain jacket. It was pitch dark by then. Crystals driveled down the windows—the noticeably dark windows. She rang the bell.

And rang it again.

A light popped on inside. She held her breath, willing the panicked hiccups to stop. And then there he was, shaggy-haired as if he'd just been wakened, wearing jeans and a yawn. A big yawn—until he saw her.

In one second flat, the whole world eclipsed to his face. He looked at her the way the sun cherished light on the morning horizon...the way a man looked at the only woman who mattered to him.

"You took," he said, "one hell of a long time to get here."

There. Just like that, the hiccups were gone and her heart

seemed to soar straight out of the stratosphere. She handed him the baby. "When you left us in Boston, I just couldn't call, Jake. Not until I could come to you. And I had a really tall mountain to climb before I had that right."

"I had some mountains to climb, too. Before I really understood that it was okay to love you." He pulled her in, closed the door, locked it. And with Tess on one arm, he folded her close with the other, kissing her long and hard. He took his time, breathing in the promise of her. Breathing in the love of her. Breathing in the future.

"I need to tell you two things," she said.

"No, you don't."

"Yeah, I do. The first is…I've been going to meetings. AA meetings, so I'd have a better idea what you're up against. I'm not saying that I know what you feel or what you go through. But I love you and I care. And I'll be part of whatever happens between us, the good and the bad."

He needed it said; she could see it in his eyes. "I never thought I'd be asking another woman to take me on. Ever," he admitted. "But I also realized that we've both honestly been through a trial by fire. And the only thing I fell for was you."

He looked as if he wanted to reach for her again, but then remembered the hefty squirt in his arms. He snuzzled a sleepy kiss on Tess, but then quickly created a makeshift bed on the couch for her.

Kasey had expected to feel jubilation, and did. Really did. Yet deep on the inside, she felt assailed by an unexpected feeling of complete calm as well. She tested out the feeling of Jake, caring for the baby. Of her, being with him.

Nothing, ever, had felt this right.

"And the second thing I need to tell you…I just don't want any question in your mind. That I left a marriage to jump in your arms. I didn't fall from Graham's arms into yours, Jake. I wanted to leave him a long time ago. The only reason I stayed was because he'd made me afraid of what he would do about Tess. I didn't feel I had any other choice."

"You believed in Tess from the get-go, love. But you didn't believe in yourself. That's what had to happen. For you to trust what you felt. For you to credit your own feelings."

She nodded. "I should have known you'd understand."

Once Tess was secured in the makeshift bed, he turned to her again. This kiss had absolutely nothing separating them. Lightning streaked up her spine that had nothing to do with the night's storm, and everything to do with the power of emotion she felt for this man…this man who so knew how to love, who believed in her.

For so long, she'd misunderstood what being lucky really meant.

Now, finally, she got it. The only luck that mattered was the kind a woman reached out and claimed for herself. She reached for Jake with both hands and a heart full of hope.

Turn the page for another exciting NEXT read that will have all your friends talking.

Read on for a special preview of RIGGS PARK,
a novel by critically acclaimed author Ellyn Bache
available now from Harlequin NEXT.

Wrightsville Beach, NC
October 2000

Until Marilyn called, I had no thought of being flung back into the warm and rushing stream of my own youth. I was having enough trouble with the present. Staring out at the sea without really seeing it, I had spent the last hour mentally snatching petals from a daisy—he loves me, he loves me not. Subtract fifty years, add an actual flower, and I might have been eight. I hardly heard the phone. Two rings. Three. The answering machine could take it. Then I got curious and picked up.

"Well, it's back," Marilyn announced. Pert and casual. Not even a hello. Her same peppy self.

"What's back?" As if I didn't know. "The decent fall weather's back?" My heart always skipped a beat or two when I lied, but as much as it scared me, I fibbed on. "Washington's always pretty in the fall."

"No, no. Not the weather. The beast."

Slay the beast had been our motto.

"Oh, Marilyn, no. When did you find out?"

"They told me for sure this morning. I swear, I always get cancer on Thursday and then I have to wait the whole damn weekend for the test results."

"But *Thursday!* That was a week ago yesterday. Why didn't you call me?"

"I wanted to. I just couldn't." The cheery tone drained to a whisper. "Don't be angry, Barbara. It was such a seesaw. The doctor found the lump on Thursday, they did the mammogram Friday, all weekend I was catatonic, and on Monday they told me it looked suspicious. Tuesday they did the biopsy. I kept hoping they'd say it was a false alarm and I'd be able to call you and we'd have a good laugh about it." She ran out of air, took a long breath. "Then I got the diagnosis this morning."

I opened my mouth, but my voice had left me. I willed it back. "It must have been a nightmare," I rasped. "I hope Bernie was with you. I hope he held your hand through all this."

"You kidding? My paramour and protector? He wouldn't have missed it. My sainted husband says—" Marilyn imitated his low growl "'—You beat it before, so you'll beat it again.'"

"Well, he's right. You did and you will. I bet you already have a plan."

"I do. Listen, when can you come? You can't refuse a dying friend."

"Stop that!"

"And I have things to tell you. Things I don't want to take to my grave."

"One more morbid comment and I'm hanging up."

"I'm serious, Barbara. I don't want to discuss this on the phone."

"You think my line is tapped? You think you can't trust me unless you whisper it personally into my ear? This is Barbara Cohen you're talking to. We've known each other over fifty years."

"Good grief, we have, haven't we?"

The fact hung in the air between us, rendering us momentarily speechless. In the spring of 1946, at the age of four and a half, I'd moved to the corner of Washington called Riggs Park, two doors away from Marilyn's house, and we'd been inseparable ever since. More than half a century ago! On that first day, my mother, Ida, had scoured the neighborhood for playmates for me and my older sister so she could unpack knickknacks in peace. I vividly remembered the gray weather outside and satisfying bright colors within: the new smell of pink paint on the walls of the first bedroom I'd had all to myself, and the satisfying presence of this cheerful, ginger-haired girl who didn't mind what game we played or what we ate—peanut butter sandwiches, Oreos, warmish milk—and who from that day on would be my undisputed best friend.

"We might have known each other forever," Marilyn said now, "but that doesn't mean I've told you everything." Her voice dropped a notch. "It's about Penny."

So of course I had to go.

Here's an exciting sneak peek of OLD BOYFRIENDS,
a brand-new novel by
USA TODAY bestselling author Rexanne Becnel,
available now from Harlequin NEXT.

My friend M.J.'s husband died on a Friday, lying on the
table during a therapeutic massage. A massive heart attack,
that's how the newspaper reported it. But that's only because
his son and the PR firm for their restaurant chain made sure
that's what they reported.

The truth? Viagra and the too-capable ministrations of a
pseudowoman, pseudomasseuse wearing a black Oriental wig,
a red thong and fishnet hose are what did in Frank Hollander. The table was actually a round bed covered with
black satin sheets, with an honest-to-God mirror on the ceiling. The House of the Rising Sun serves a very good hot-and-
sour soup downstairs, but the therapy going on upstairs isn't
the sort that the chairman of this year's United Way Fund
Drive could afford to be associated with.

Needless to say, the funeral was huge. The mayor spoke,
the bishop said the mass and the choir from St. Joseph's Special School, a major beneficiary of the United Way, sang
good old Frank into the ground. As pure as those kids' souls
were, even they couldn't have sung Frank into heaven.

Afterward, M.J.'s stepchildren entertained the mourners at her home, where everyone came up to the widow and said all the things they were supposed to:

"I'm so sorry, Mrs. Hollander."

"If I can do anything, Mary Jo, just call. Promise me you'll call."

"Your husband was a great man, Mrs. Hollander. We'll all miss him."

Blah, blah, blah. It was all I could do to keep my mouth shut. But Bitsey had given me my marching orders and I knew my role. I was there to support M.J.

Thank God for Bitsey—and I'm not using the Lord's name casually when I say that. Thank you, God, for giving me Bitsey. She's like the voice of reason in my life, the perfect mother image for someone sorely deprived of that in her biological parent.

M.J., Bitsey and me. Three girls raised in the South, but trapped in California.

Well, I think that maybe I was the only one who felt trapped in the vast, arid beigeness of Southern California. But then, I felt trapped wherever I was. I was slowly figuring that out.

That Tuesday, however, we were all feeling trapped at M.J.'s palatial home with the air-conditioning running double time and Frank Jr.'s Pacific rim-fusion restaurant catering the after-funeral festivities. Sushi at a funeral is beyond unreal.

Bitsey had explained to M.J. that she had to stay downstairs until the last guests left. She was the hostess, and it was only right. But yes, she could anesthetize herself if she wanted to. Everyone else was.

So M.J., in her perfect size-six black Giselle dress and her Jimmy Choo sling backs, with her Effay makeup and Liz Taylor fragrance, sat in Frank Sr.'s favorite fake leopard-skin chair and tossed back five vodka martinis in less than two hours.

M.J. drank, Bitsey ate and I fumed and wanted to get the hell out of there. That awful, morbid couple of hours sums up pretty well how the three of us react to any stress thrown our way. And God knows there's enough of it. When Bitsey hurts, she eats. Even when she was on fen-phen, and now Meridia, if she's hurting—especially if her husband, Jack, pulls some stunt—she eats. Considering that Jack Albertson can be a coldhearted bastard, and unlike Frank, doesn't bother to hide it, it's no wonder she's packed close to two hundred pounds onto her five-foot frame. The more she eats, the fatter she gets, and the more remote and critical he gets. Which, of course, makes her eat even more.

But I digress, which I do a lot. According to my sometimes therapist, that's a typical coping mechanism: catalog everybody else's flaws and you'll be too busy to examine your own. M.J. drinks, Bitsey eats and I run. New job. New man. New apartment.

Today, however, I had vowed to hang in there, bite my tongue and generally struggle against every impulse I had.